I0581023

CAREFUL OF THY WISHES

CAREFUL OF THY WISHES

REG RAWLINS, PSYCHIC INVESTIGATOR #13

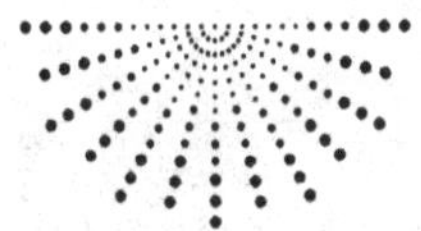

P.D. WORKMAN

Copyright © 2022 by P.D. Workman

All rights reserved.

No part of this book may be reproduced in any form or by any electronic or mechanical means, including information storage and retrieval systems, without written permission from the author, except for the use of brief quotations in a book review.

ISBN: 9781774681503 (IS Hardcover)

ISBN: 9781774681497 (IS Paperback)

ISBN: 9781774681473 (IS Large Print)

ISBN: 9781774681480 (KDP Paperback)

ISBN: 9781774681459 (Kindle)

ISBN: 9781774681466 (ePub)

pdworkman

ALSO BY P.D. WORKMAN

MYSTERY/SUSPENSE:

Reg Rawlins, Psychic Detective
What the Cat Knew
A Psychic with Catitude
A Catastrophic Theft
Night of Nine Tails
Telepathy of Gardens
Delusions of the Past
Fairy Blade Unmade
Web of Nightmares
A Whisker's Breadth
Skunk Man Swamp
Magic Ain't A Game
Without Foresight
Careful of Thy Wishes
Time to Your Elf (Coming Soon)
Undiscovered Tomb (Coming Soon)

Auntie Clem's Bakery
Gluten-Free Murder
Dairy-Free Death
Allergen-Free Assignation
Witch-Free Halloween (Halloween Short)
Dog-Free Dinner (Christmas Short)

Stirring Up Murder

Brewing Death

Coup de Glace

Sour Cherry Turnover

Apple-achian Treasure

Vegan Baked Alaska

Muffins Masks Murder

Tai Chi and Chai Tea

Santa Shortbread

Cold as Ice Cream

Changing Fortune Cookies

Hot on the Trail Mix

Fateful Plateful (Coming Soon)

Cut Out Cookie (Coming Soon)

On the Slab Pie (Coming Soon)

Recipes from Auntie Clem's Bakery

Parks Pat Mysteries

Out with the Sunset

Long Climb to the Top

Dark Water Under the Bridge

Immersed in the View (Coming Soon)

Skimming Over the Lake (Coming Soon)

Hazard of the Hills (Coming Soon)

High-Tech Crime Solvers Series

Virtually Harmless

AND MORE AT PDWORKMAN.COM

For those who have wished to help

CHAPTER ONE

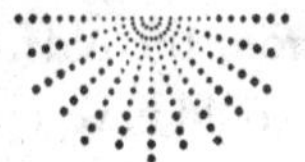

Reg had been putting it off for too long. She had been spending more, knowing that she had the gems to fall back on, so, although she had been doing okay with her psychic services business, she had been spending more than she was making, which wasn't a great way to keep her bank balance in the black.

She kept putting off cashing in a couple of the gems because of the work involved. She hadn't ever done it before, for one thing. She had used pawnshops in the past to get a bit of cash for jewelry she had acquired through one means or another, but she knew that she didn't get anywhere near what they were worth. And she couldn't take cut, unset gemstones to a pawnshop. They weren't jewelers. They wouldn't know how much they were worth or give her a fair price.

That meant that she had to figure out where to go to sell the gems. She found several gemstone buyers in nearby cities; that was an easy enough internet search. The problem was finding one that would not only give her a fair price, but would look the other way on gems that might not have come through *regular channels*.

The stores in Black Sands would be more understanding about how she had acquired the gems, but she didn't think it was a good idea for anyone in Black Sands to know about the fact that she had a small chest of cut gems in her possession. She hadn't yet rented a safe deposit box like Sarah, her landlord, had suggested, which meant that the box of gems was in Reg's closet. Or under the bed. Or whatever other place she had chosen to hide it in temporarily. She moved it around regularly because she knew it wasn't safe. There wasn't anywhere secure to hide it within the guest cottage she rented from the older woman. If word got out that she had the gems, she could have a problem.

Of course, the cottage was protected with magical wards and charms, but Reg knew that there were still ways for less-honorable thieves to find their way around the wards, or for powerful beings to break them. She knew because it had happened before. Sarah had helped her to set new wards several times. She always rolled her eyes and gave Reg a stern lecture on not allowing herself to be talked into releasing the wards, allowing a pixie into the house, or surrendering by any other means to which the wards were vulnerable.

So Reg knew that she couldn't liquidate any of the jewels in Black Sands. It was too risky. She would have to go into one of the bigger cities where she was unknown and where she would not be required to explain how the stones had come into her possession. And those kinds of places didn't advertise the fact on public websites.

But she couldn't afford to wait any longer.

There were a few interesting listings on Craigslist and eBay. Reg made screenshots of them and looked up the addresses on the maps app on her phone.

"What do you think?" she mused aloud.

Starlight looked at her, blinking first his blue eye and then his green. She didn't know how much of commerce or the internet he understood. His psychic powers might not extend that far.

"I need money if I'm going to get you food and kitty litter. So you want to help me with that, right?"

He blinked again, both eyes together this time. Reg focused

on the white mark in the third eye position on his forehead. The star that gave him his name. She squinted her eyes slightly and let them go out of focus, thinking about the listings that she had just found on her phone, trying to sort out which of them was the best bet. She brought up the first one in her mind, a David Price of Rite Price Gem Exchange and immediately felt a sense of foreboding. Her stomach tied itself in a tight, heavy knot that nearly made her physically sick.

She didn't know what the danger was in going to Price, but she knew it was not a good idea. She mentally struck that one off her list.

"Okay…"

She opened her eyes for a couple of seconds to check out the next listing. *Dreame Jewelry. Achieve your highest dreams.* That one sounded even sleazier than the first. But she focused her eyes on Starlight's white star again and thought about it.

She had never dreamed that she would come into possession of such a fortune. There had been plenty of times in the past when she had dreamed of somewhere safe and sheltered to live and a bowl of warm soup in her hands. Reg had found that and more in Black Sands, a little Florida community that had seemed ripe for all kinds of paranormal cons. But, as she had soon discovered, there was more to Black Sands than just a high percentage of practicing psychics and retirees with thick wallets that needed unburdening. Instead, she had found a community that had not only accepted her as a bona fide psychic, but had opened up to her a whole new world of paranormal practitioners and experiences that were often difficult for her to believe existed.

She still woke up some mornings wondering if the past year had all been a dream and she didn't really possess any unusual psychic or paranormal abilities. Maybe there were no witches, fairies, sirens, or immortals. Maybe it was all just a very detailed and involved hallucination.

And then she talked to her cat and pulled out the little chest of gems and looked out the window at Sarah's backyard garden, flourishing under the care of Forst, the garden gnome. And she knew that it was all real.

"Do you think they would give me what the gems are worth?"

Not what they were worth, of course, but at least enough that she wouldn't have to worry about her bank account again for a few months.

She had a good feeling about Dreame Jewelry. Maybe it was the right place to go.

There were still more places on her list, but she didn't want to go over all of them with Starlight. Using her psychic powers, even with Starlight, was tiring, and she couldn't maintain her focus for that long.

Besides, it was nearly noon, and she was ready for some breakfast.

CHAPTER TWO

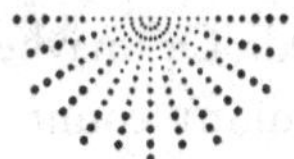

*I*t had taken Reg a couple of hours to get to the city and locate the little store front that Dreame Jewelry worked out of. When she saw the dingy front window with dusty displays of what clearly was not real jewelry, she nearly changed her mind. There were several other jewelers on her list. Dreame really did not live up to its name.

But she was there. She might as well at least check it out. She'd had a good feeling about the place initially. Maybe it was a diamond in the rough. So to speak.

Reg pushed open the door. A bell tinkled, announcing her arrival. The interior was dim after the bright Florida sunlight outside. She couldn't see much at first. She closed her eyes, then opened them again and squinted around.

There were a few display cases with much the same kind of product as she had seen in the window. Maybe a few real pieces, but even the ones that appeared to be real weren't spectacular. They needed a good cleaning, to begin with. The store smelled dusty and old and sort of oily. A jewelry store shouldn't smell oily, should it?

Reg browsed through the displays. When she looked up, she saw a man standing behind the one that had been on her right when she had pushed her way through the door. She was sure that he hadn't been there, standing in the dim recesses of the room, when she had arrived. But he had either appeared out of nowhere or had crept in from the back of the store so quietly that she had not heard him or been aware of his presence.

"Oh. Hi there. I didn't see you."

The man was dark-skinned and had a short black beard that was not properly trimmed. Or maybe it was just a few days' growth of whiskers that didn't count as a beard. His face was round and his body wide.

"Good afternoon," he greeted in a resonant, surprisingly reassuring voice. "Jean Beaugrand at your service. How can I help you today?"

"Well, I was just looking…" Reg indicated the display cases, not yet showing her hand. Maybe she was just a tourist who had wandered in off the street.

The man's eyes traveled over Reg, from the multicolored headscarf around her head, to her red box braids, to her flowing peasant shirt and skirt. Maybe she didn't look like a tourist. But Beaugrand would have no way of knowing who she was. She didn't know anyone in the area and she wouldn't tell him that she had come from Black Sands.

"Are you here to buy or to sell?" he asked, getting immediately to the crux of the matter.

Reg pursed her lips, thinking about what to say. Admit that she was there looking for a buyer? Or continue to look at his wares and feel him out before revealing the fact?

She didn't say anything at first. She ignored his question as if she hadn't heard or understood it and browsed through the display case that he was standing behind, getting closer to him, reaching out with all of her senses to examine him, to read and classify him. She was good at cold-reading people. Or what she had always thought of as cold reading but might actually have been using her psychic powers before she knew she had them.

"Like what you see?" the man inquired mildly.

There was more to Beaugrand than met the eye. Few people showed their true selves to the world, but she sensed that he was hiding more than most. While his face and voice suggested that he was open and honest, there was a cloak of mystery and secrecy around him. Something stopped her from being able to probe him further.

"Well, there are a couple of pieces," Reg said, turning her attention back to the jewelry and pretending that was what he had been asking. She indicated a necklace that was almost directly in front of him. The ruby in the pendant was real. She could feel that. After having handled her own gems regularly, she could sense the power of a real stone. "This one…"

The man smiled, showing two rows of white, even teeth. "That is a very nice piece," he agreed. "Are you interested in buying?"

There was no price tag on it. Reg studied his face. He did not appear to be sarcastic or judging her as being too poor to afford it. It was a simple question about her interest in it.

"No," Reg admitted. She pulled a small velvet pouch out of her pocket. "I saw on Craigslist that you purchase gemstones. I don't see any out, so I was just wondering…"

"I do not display them," Beaugrand agreed. "I sell them privately to silver- and goldsmiths. People don't generally walk in off the street looking for unset stones."

Reg hesitated for another instant, reaching out to assess his feelings and intentions again. Either he was very good at blocking her, or he was an honest man. She loosened the strings on the pouch and spilled the gems she had brought with her onto her palm. She didn't know if he would be interested in everything, or whether he only bought certain gems. Or perhaps only what he knew his smiths were currently looking for.

The man leaned forward to look at them. He opened a drawer and put a shallow tray on top of the display case. "You can put them in there, and I will have a look."

He pulled a loupe from a pocket and picked up a ruby. He looked at it for a few moments, then put it back and picked up a blue gem, a sapphire, Reg assumed. He studied it for only an instant before putting it back.

He shook his head slowly. The opening move of his negotiation. Reg was familiar with negotiation, and he wasn't going to scare her away by declaring that her gems were worth very little or nothing. She could be hard-nosed and get a fair price. She'd had a lot of practice when she had been a lot more desperate than she was now.

"They are real," Reg asserted, looking him in the eye.

Beaugrand nodded. "Oh, yes. They are real. And good quality."

She was surprised to hear him concede that. But maybe it was part of his strategy. A little carrot to tempt her.

"Then what is the problem? They're good stones, you purchase stones for your smithies. Why wouldn't you be interested?"

"Do you know anything about the provenance of these stones?"

She had sold enough family heirlooms to know that provenance referred to being able to prove where the goods had come from and what hands they had passed through. She hadn't bothered to doctor any papers to give the gems fake histories.

"I understood from what I read that you… will purchase gems without provenance," Reg said delicately. She didn't want to imply that he was doing something against the law, or even unethical. But she'd done her research. She knew that Dreame dealt in… shadier areas.

"This is true," he tilted his head in a slight nod. "However, I wondered if you know *anything* about these gems. How did they come into your hands?"

"They are not stolen."

"That is good, but does not answer the question." The man pulled a stool over and sat down, resting his meaty forearms on the top of the case.

"They were given to me as a gift."

She doubted he would believe that, but he didn't give any sign of disbelief. "And did you accept them? Or did you say that you would check them out first?" He looked down at the gems in the tray.

"They are mine. I can sell them or do whatever I like with them."

"So, you accepted the gift."

Reg nodded impatiently. "Yes. Of course. Who wouldn't?"

Beaugrand smiled, showing his teeth again. "Perhaps someone who is not as rash as you."

Reg's stomach knotted. This did not sound good. Why should it be a problem that she had accepted the stones that were given to her as a gift? Unless they were stolen property, she couldn't see what was wrong with her owning them. The police couldn't do anything about that.

"Why? What do you mean?"

"I cannot buy these stones from you. You will need to find another avenue to rid yourself of them."

Reg stared at him, frowning.

CHAPTER THREE

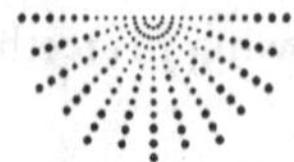

*R*eg left the man in Dreame and returned to her car with the gems back safely in the pouch in her pocket. She sat in the driver's seat and considered the situation.

The man had not given her any further information on why he would not or could not take the gems, or why Reg should not have accepted the gift from the fairies. She thought about all the rest of the gemstones in the small chest under her bed at the cottage. If she would be in trouble for accepting the small sampling of gems that she had shown to the man in the store, then how serious of a position was she in for having accepted hundreds more?

She rubbed her temples, trying to think. She'd been having a lot of issues since her encounter in the graveyard. Apparently, being possessed for more than a few minutes could do that to a person. She had holes in her memory, problems with concentration, and a certain level of decision paralysis in going ahead with anything. She didn't know whether the paralysis was the result of the other issues or a separate issue all on its own. It was hard to make a decision or be motivated to proceed with a plan of action when she wasn't sure that she had considered all the important points.

She thought back to the arrival of the gems, trying to remember every detail. She'd thought at first that it was a package from Amazon, but hadn't been able to remember anything she'd had on order. Sarah had brought it in to her, so Sarah was the one person who knew that she had them. Reg was sure that she would have been very careful not to mention them to anyone else. She didn't want the cottage to be broken into.

The gems had come in a small wooden chest, which they were currently stored in. There had been no explanatory note, just a small announcement card that said they were from the Papillon family. It had made perfect sense at the time. Reg had helped save their daughter Calliopia, who had been suffering from a nearly-fatal knife wound. No one else had given adolescent Callie any hope of survival, and Ruan, her mate, had even been willing to dispatch her himself rather than to let her continue to suffer.

But Reg had done it. She had been able to save Calliopia when no one else could, and Callie's parents had rewarded Reg with the gift of the gemstones. While it was a very lavish gift for a human, Reg had assumed that the fairies had far more access to jewels and that it was probably just a trifle to them. A small thank you for what Reg had done for their daughter.

She couldn't think of any reason she should not have accepted the jewels. Sarah had not said that she shouldn't, and Sarah was the one Reg relied on to tell her about things in the magical world. Reg had not been raised in a magical household, so she had no idea about many of the things that other practitioners thought normal or that anyone would know.

If there were something wrong with accepting the gift, then Sarah should have told her.

But there was something niggling at the back of Reg's mind, and she couldn't put her finger on what it was.

Maybe if she just relaxed and didn't try to think about it, it would come to her later.

* * *

But Dreame Jewelry was not the only purchaser on her list. Just because he had refused to buy the gems, that didn't mean that she couldn't sell them. There were plenty of others who were, she was sure, less scrupulous than Mr. Beaugrand.

She hadn't told him her name, so he wouldn't be able to report her to the authorities if there were something wrong with the gems. He had asked her about their provenance, so she had to assume there was something wrong with the chain of ownership of the gems. Had the Papillons reported them stolen after giving them to Reg? Though she knew that the fairies did not have the same ethics as humans, she couldn't see Mr. and Mrs. Papillon doing something to harm her after what she had done for them.

Reg clicked on her phone and looked at the various listings she had captured earlier. The next closest one was The Sapphire Exchange. The listing said that they dealt in all kinds of precious and semi-precious stones, and they were only a few minutes away, so they seemed like a good bet.

The contrast between the two stores was startling. The Sapphire Exchange was brightly lit, with lots of lights and white counters and reflective surfaces. Reg couldn't imagine working there and having to deal with the bright lights all day long. It was enough to give her a headache just walking into the store.

It had a spacious, open plan that made Reg think of a spa or an exclusive perfume store. Very high-end furnishings. There was a uniformed guard at the door who looked at Reg with suspicion but did not challenge her. A willowy young woman stepped forward to meet her, taking Reg's hand in her slim one.

"Welcome to The Sapphire Exchange," she said in a musical voice. "We're so delighted to have you here. Would you like to speak with one of our consultants?" She motioned to a counter where a man sat waiting, a tray like the one Beaugrand had used in front of him awaiting the next customer.

He gave her a pinched smile and tilted his head back so that he was looking down his nose at her even though she was standing and he was sitting on a stool.

"Come," the woman encouraged, touching Reg on the arm to encourage her forward.

Reg resisted, not liking the looks of the man.

"Ignore the sourpuss," the woman whispered in Reg's ear. "Mr. Cuttleby will be happy to serve you."

Reg let herself be urged forward to the counter. Unlike at Dreame Jewelry, there were trays full of row upon row of cut gemstones for buyers to see. But Reg didn't get much of a feeling from them. There was a certain feeling that they were genuine stones, but no power, as she got from Sarah's emerald, or her own gems, or the ruby necklace at Dreame Jewelry. They felt… common and… Reg couldn't think of the right word for them. *Farmed? Cultivated? Domesticated?*

Mr. Cuttleby continued to smile in his narrow, pinched way at Reg. His eyes went briefly to the young woman who had escorted her over.

"And what do we have here?"

Reg hadn't told her escort anything about who she was or what she wanted, so she didn't expect her to be able to tell the man anything. The young lady grabbed one of the tall stools ranged throughout the store and placed it in front of Reg.

"A seller," she told Cuttleby. "I'm sorry, I didn't catch your name, Miss…?"

Reg was so startled by the woman knowing that she had something to sell that she didn't have the sense to make up a name.

"Rawlins."

"Miss Rawlins is here looking for a buyer," she told Cuttleby with a nod. She put a hand on Reg's shoulder as she slid onto the stool. "Mr. Cuttleby here will be happy to help."

She nodded and drifted away from the two of them. Reg swiveled to watch her go. She turned back to Cuttleby. "How did…?"

"She is very… intuitive," Cuttleby explained carefully. "So, what are you trying to sell today?"

The woman was clearly a psychic, and yet Reg hadn't felt

anything from her. No probe into her mind and consciousness. If the woman had read her, she had a very light touch.

Reg tried to force her attention from the woman to Mr. Cuttleby, but found it difficult. While she was talking to him, her mind was still whirring away in the background, trying to analyze the woman and to keep track of her behind Reg, supervising, welcoming other customers, and keeping everything running smoothly.

Mr. Cuttleby waited. Reg pulled out the little pouch of gems.

Did she still want to sell them to The Sapphire Exchange? It felt dangerous that the woman had read her so easily. But there were only two reasons for someone to go into the store. She was either buying or selling, so the woman automatically had a fifty percent chance of getting it right. She only had to read a few indicators to guess which Reg was doing. She wasn't wealthy; the clinking bracelets and other bits of jewelry she was wearing were all just costume stuff. Nothing of any value. Perhaps she looked more desperate than she had realized.

She loosened the strings of the pouch and emptied it into the waiting tray. She was reassured that they were all there. Nothing had disappeared into Mr. Beaugrand's palm or been lifted by the woman as she helped Reg across the store.

"Ahh." Cuttleby leaned forward and looked at the stones. "Some very handsome specimens."

Reg couldn't help leaning forward to look at them as well, feeling warm and validated by Cuttleby's manner.

Cuttleby examined each stone one at a time with a loupe and the aid of glasses with a complex eyepiece. Reg had performed her own examination of the stones and had not been able to identify any flaws or identifying marks. They were, as far as she could tell, perfectly cut to show off their color and clarity and should be the envy of any collector or jeweler.

Eventually, Cuttleby laid his loupe aside and folded his hands. He looked at Reg.

"We cannot buy these."

CHAPTER FOUR

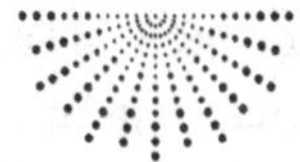

Reg stared at him. "What are you talking about? What do you mean, you can't buy them?"

He raised one eyebrow, looking at her. As if she were trying to scam him and already knew the answer to that question herself. "I'm sure you must understand that we cannot buy every stone that comes into the store…"

"No, I guess not, but these are really good quality. They are genuine. There must be a good market for them."

"You have proof of the provenance of the gems?"

"No… but I understood that…" Reg shifted uncomfortably on the stool. "I thought that there were ways *around* that."

"We understand, of course, that sometimes stones have been in the family for a long time. They are not new imports and are therefore not etched with an identification number."

Reg nodded her agreement. He was feeding her everything she needed to say. Providing a pathway through all the red tape for her. "Yes. They've been in the family for decades. Centuries. Before they started tracking gems like that."

She wondered if she had gone too far. Centuries? Would he believe that?

"And documents are sometimes lost during wartime or other unrest," Cuttleby provided.

"Yes. Exactly. When you are fleeing for your life, you're lucky to be able to hold on to the gems themselves."

"But these gems," Cuttleby indicated the stones in the tray. "These were clearly not in your family originally."

"Originally?" Reg echoed.

Of course they had not been in her family originally. Gems passed through many different hands. Her family had clearly not mined them personally. They had to have come from somewhere.

"These stones will need to be… *cleansed* before you can get anything for them."

Cleansed?

Reg slowly started to pick up the gems and return them to her bag. Was that some sort of certification process they needed to go through? Was it like laundering money? Using them for some kind of legitimate purpose before they could be sold? But that didn't make any sense.

"Do you know of *anyone* who would be willing to buy these?" she asked Cuttleby, desperate for more information. If she couldn't liquidate some of the gems, she would be in a very tight position. She wouldn't be out on the street, because Sarah would be willing to let her rent slide if she weren't able to raise it. But Reg had been feeling very proud of herself for being able to have a house of her own and be able to afford not only enough food, but the clothing and other little luxuries that she'd never been able to afford before, taking care of a cat and running her own business. She was acting like an adult, a respectable adult, for once.

If she couldn't sell the gems, all of that could come to an end.

What was the good of a chest of jewels if she couldn't do anything with them?

CHAPTER FIVE

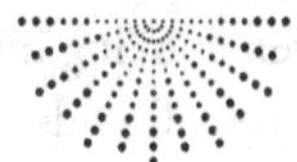

$\mathcal{A}$t Cuttleby's grave head shake, Reg slid the bag of gems back into her pocket and stood up from the stool. She was shaken by the experience. Both of the places she had picked out so far had been a complete bust. Neither one even considered buying the gems. Neither was even willing to negotiate. Reg had expected some haggling, but she hadn't even considered that they wouldn't want to buy the gems at all.

She headed for the door. The young greeter turned and met her eyes, smiling. As Reg got closer to her, the smile faded.

"No luck?" she asked, brows drawn down in puzzlement.

"No," Reg agreed. She didn't want to talk about it. She didn't know how to deal with it. She had to rethink her entire life in Black Sands. She'd been letting her psychic business slide a little since people had found out that her mother was a siren. With the amount of hate and prejudice aimed at her, she hadn't been advertising, worried that it would draw more people out against her who would damage her property or cast spells or even to take it a step further and commit direct physical violence against her.

It was beginning to look as though she might have to leave town. Try again another place. She had thought that she had found her niche in Black Sands, but with each revelation about her past and her own nature, it was getting harder and harder to stay there and pretend that she was just a regular psychic like all the others who were already practicing there. It was bizarre that having additional powers would make her as much of a pariah as being poor and homeless had been before arriving in Florida.

The woman took Reg's hands in her own as if they were old friends greeting one another at a funeral. Her eyes were clear and focused on Reg, as if she were looking into her soul.

"You have friends. Ask your friends."

"Um…" Reg wasn't sure how to respond to this. "Okay. Thanks."

She pulled her hands out of the woman's grip and walked away.

* * *

She could have tried a couple more places, but Reg could already see the pattern. And if she continued to go to other jewelers and exchanges, she would become known, and people would refuse to deal with her. She had to go home, reevaluate, and figure out what she needed to do to cleanse the gems so that they could be sold. Once they were clean, then she would be able to go to other dealers and see about selling them. Quietly and without attracting attention to herself. If she went to every shady dealer in the city with what she had now, it would be just like shining a spotlight on her gems. Which clearly was not a good idea.

So she turned her car around and started driving toward home.

The weather was idyllic. She had the windows down and she could smell the salty tang of the sea on the breeze. It made her want to drop all responsibilities and just go to the ocean. She could walk along the beach with her feet in the water.

She could go for a swim. For a boat ride. She could go *hunting*.

Reg immediately pushed these thoughts away and walled them

off. She was not a predator. She was not going hunting. She was going home to figure out how to deal with the gemstones so that she would be able to sell them. Either that, or to figure out how to get her business off the ground again and start making some money the old-fashioned way.

The trip home seemed to take much longer than the journey out had. When she had left, she had been anticipating a big payday. She didn't know how much the gems were worth, and she knew that it would be work to get them liquidated, but she had figured that she would be going home with a stack of cash.

Not with the gems still in her pocket.

She swore to herself several times.

How could she have screwed it up? She had looked at the gems with an eyepiece that would magnify them enough to see any identification numbers etched into them. She knew that there were no markings on them. So what had Beaugrand and Cuttleby seen when they had looked at them? What had told them that there was something wrong with the provenance of the gems and that they couldn't purchase them?

It didn't make any sense.

* * *

Reg stalked from her car toward the back yard where her cottage was located behind Sarah's big house. Her thoughts were confused and angry and she wasn't paying much attention to anything around her.

She didn't see or sense Corvin until he stepped out from behind a bush right in front of her. She was moving so quickly, her anger burning so hot, that he was lucky she didn't mow him right down. As it was, Reg gasped and brought her hands up to protect herself against him.

When she saw Corvin's incredibly handsome face, the clear bright eyes and neatly-trimmed beard that she had come to know so well, her anger flared even more. Corvin raised his hands defensively.

"Reg—it's me."

"I know it's you," Reg snapped. "I don't know what you're doing here, but I cannot deal with this right now. Get out of my way."

He raised one eyebrow, surprised. He poured on the charm, so that Reg could feel the heat emanating from him and smell the scent of roses. Her anger dampened, her body betraying her, heart beating faster in anticipation and endorphins flooding her brain. Reg tried to steel herself. She could resist him. She'd done so countless times since she'd come to Black Sands. But her unchecked anger had apparently opened the emotional connection between them, and she felt the attraction even more strongly than usual.

"Stop that," she told him. They were standing too close together. She wanted to step right into his arms. She had been through a big disappointment. Anyone would want the comfort of a friend. To be swallowed up in his arms and to give herself to him. "Stop," she repeated in a quieter, more subdued voice.

"I'm not doing anything." His voice was rich and soothing. It always sent a wave of warmth over her, as if she were being wrapped in a warm blanket on a chilly day. Or slipping into a warm bath.

The thought of sliding into warm water helped clarify her thoughts. She needed to fight back against him. He was dangerous, but so was she, if she called on her powers to fight back against him. Or to entrap him, as he was trying to entrap her.

"You are too. Turn it off."

"I can't help my natural reactions," he reminded her. An excuse he had given repeatedly in the past for stepping over the line. "When you come storming over here, act like you're going to attack, my natural defenses…" He held his hands palms-up in mute appeal. "Would you blame your cat for raising its hackles at a threat?"

"I didn't threaten you. I just told you to get out of my way. So that I can get home and relax. You know that I wasn't attacking you."

"What the brain knows and what the body perceives are very different. I'm not trying to do anything to harm you." He leaned forward despite his words, the heady scent of roses swirling around her. Reg could almost see the pheromones, like in a cartoon where a stream of perfume snakes through the air and beckons to the target, physically lifting him off of his feet and transporting him. She drew the warm air into her lungs and savored it like a smoker.

"Stop." Her protest was faint.

"Why don't we go to your house, and you can tell me what's got you so riled up today."

He backed up so that she could continue down the pathway toward the cottage. Reg didn't hesitate to close the distance between her and her house, though her strides did seem more difficult than usual. Swimming through setting concrete might have been faster. She knew that if she got through the gate, she would enter the space that was protected by Sarah's charms and wards, and Corvin would not be able to follow her. No one who intended her harm would be able to get into the yard. A necessary protection after everything that had happened recently.

But as she reached the gate, Corvin was right behind her, and he put his hand on her arm as if to escort her to her cottage in safety. Reg passed through the portal and, with his hand on her, Corvin was able to enter with her. Reg turned her head toward him.

"You can't do that! You're not welcome here!"

"And yet, here I am." He smiled, his eyes dancing. His amused, little-boy smirk just pulled her in harder. Was there no end to the wiles he could use on her?

"And you can go right back out." Reg gave him a shove with one hand. Even with a layer of cloth between them, she could still feel the buzz of electricity that always sparked between them. He resisted, his muscles contracting under his cloak and shirt. Reg wanted to explore all his muscles. Very slowly. She pushed harder. She marshaled all of her willpower to push back against him mentally. She could protect herself. She could make an envelope of power around herself that would prevent her from falling victim to his entrancing scent and magical charms.

It was difficult. After her fruitless errand to the city, Reg was tired and frustrated and didn't have the patience to deal with the unbelievably gorgeous warlock. She knew that she was only seeing and feeling what he wanted her to. It wasn't real. Her perceptions were magically enhanced. She was already partially under his spell.

But she worked hard to reflect back the heat he was generating and the rest of the charms, to force them back upon him like a weapon. Corvin stepped back slightly. It was barely perceptible, but she felt his muscles slacken under her hand as he tried to defend himself against her considerable skills.

"There's no need…" he purred in protest.

"Get back from me. Get out of my yard. And don't try to use your charms on me!"

"Regina." He said it in that alluring way he had, reaching into her soul, looking for another way in. "I'm just here to talk. I'm your friend."

"You're not being my friend. You're trying to ensorcel me. Again."

"As I said, it's just my body's natural defense. We both know what I am…"

"You have plenty of other defenses. Aren't you claiming to be one of the most powerful beings in the world, with all the power you absorbed from the Witch Doctor, and his horde, and everything else you have consumed? From me when you took my power in the mountain?"

"That was at your request. I took nothing more than I was allowed."

"Huh. We both know that's not true. And even if it was, that's not what I asked. If you're so all powerful, then why do you have to use your charms against me? If you really needed to defend yourself, you have plenty of ways to do that."

He shrugged and smirked.

"I don't need your help," Reg asserted.

"Another thing we both know—that it isn't true. You do need my help. You are still weak from being possessed by another. Your mind is damaged. There are holes in your memories and knowledge…"

The wizard had taken more from Reg than she was willing to admit. But Corvin wasn't there to help her. He was there to take advantage of her in her weakened state.

"You can't help me. And I don't want your help even if you could. I want you to stay away from me and my house. What are you even doing here?"

Reg would admit that she had called Corvin in the past when she needed company, usually late at night when she didn't know who else would be up, or to ask him a question that he, as a professor and a scholar of magical history, might have the answer for. She could see him in her mind when she wanted to, to know whether he was up and what he was doing. But she called him on the phone, so it was safe. She didn't ask him to come over in person.

Usually.

Almost never.

"Like I said," he leaned against a tree, "I came to see whether I could help you. I know how much trouble you have been having lately. I can feel…" He trailed off, and she could feel him poking at her consciousness, prodding and trying to find his way in that way since his pheromones had failed. "I can feel how much difficulty you are having, how many roadblocks you are running into. I can help."

It was tempting, but she knew that his "help" would only lead to further harm. Yes, he had helped her in the past, but she had needed others there to help her, or else she had unleashed the siren powers inherited from her mother, which she did not want to do.

If she used them, there was no guarantee that she would be able to stop herself, either. She might go too far, and although she feared what Corvin could do to her, she worried more about what she could do to him.

She would never forgive herself if she let those instincts take over and irreparable harm were done.

Reg forced these thoughts from her mind and pushed Corvin's consciousness as far from her as she could too. "Stay out of my brain. Go home. Or to look for other prey. You can't have my powers. That will never happen again."

He slunk back from her, still eyeing her as if wondering what other strategy he could use to get what he wanted. He wouldn't give up. However close they became as friends or however distant due to both of their natures, they would always be inseparably connected by the powers they had shared in the past.

No one could undo that.

CHAPTER SIX

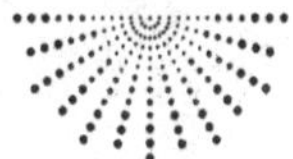

Eventually, Corvin left the yard and Reg was able to relax. She was pretty sure that she understood the wards that Sarah had set well enough to know that even though Corvin had entered the yard once on her arm, they would not allow him in again alone. She was pretty sure of that.

Mostly.

She monitored Corvin's position as he headed back to his car, making sure that he actually left and didn't stick around, waiting for round two. Once she was sure he was gone, she headed to the cottage. But upon reaching her doorstep, Reg changed her mind. She needed to learn more about the gems and what she would have to do to be able to sell them, and she would not get that from an internet search.

Sarah had a very powerful emerald that helped to keep her young and vibrant. Sarah knew about stones of power, and she would be able to help Reg. She would know what to do about it.

Reg went to the back door of the big house, knocked, and entered. "Sarah? Are you home?"

Reg could feel her presence in the house, so she didn't really need to ask. She was just being polite and announcing herself.

"Reg? I'm just getting dressed, come on up."

Having seen Sarah's rooms full of clothes, Reg knew that getting dressed was something that might take Sarah a few seconds or a few hours, depending on where she were going. If it were out on a date with one of her younger men or to a community dance or event, she might go through a dozen different outfits before settling on one.

Reg climbed the stairs and followed the sound of hangers sliding and clicking along rods, to find Sarah going through a rack of formal wear.

"Hi. Going out?"

"Well, I'm not decluttering, I'll tell you that!" Sarah laughed merrily.

Reg laughed. Sarah's house was packed to the gills with her possessions. She wasn't a hoarder exactly, everything was neat and clean and properly stored, but if a hoarder could be neat, then maybe she was.

"You could probably get rid of a *few* things," she ventured.

"Reg, dear, once you have lived out of a tent, you learn the value of having everything you need right at hand. If I got rid of all the 'extras' around here, you can bet I would end up needing it again the next week."

Reg nodded. She hadn't lived out of a tent, but she had lived rough on the street. And it hadn't been easy. She could relate to Sarah's desire to hold on to as many possessions as she could. Reg too had a difficult time letting things go, even when they were old and worn and no longer useful. She would have a very difficult time packing up and leaving Black Sands if she had to. She had gotten used to having *things*.

"So, what's up with you?" Sarah asked.

"Just ran into Corvin in the yard," Reg said with a grimace.

"What's he doing down there? Get me my broom and I'll send him packing!"

Reg laughed. She remembered the way Sarah had wielded her broom when chasing a stray cat out of her garden. The devastation had been significant. But she also remembered how Corvin had helped Sarah out when she had been sick, and that despite her warnings for Reg to stay away from him, Sarah still seemed to have quite an affection for him.

"He's gone now. He said he wanted to 'help' me."

"Help himself *to* you, more like." Sarah pulled a dress off the rack and held it up to her shoulders. It was black with sequins and Reg thought maybe a bit young for a woman of Sarah's age. Or a woman who looked Sarah's age. Reg had no idea how old she really was. From the picture of Sarah that she had seen in a history book about the settlement of Black Sands, she was very old. But she only looked about sixty. She was a little overweight, with gray hair, and looked very grandmotherly. She treated Reg like a daughter, but at other times her behavior was not quite so age-appropriate.

Sarah put the dress back.

"Good for you. We don't want his kind hanging around here. We have quite enough troubles without him adding to it."

Reg bit her lip and was quiet. She was the one who was causing Sarah most of those problems. It was because of Reg that Sarah had to deal with vandals and witches trying to vanquish Reg from the community.

Sarah looked at her. "Nothing to do with you, Reg. Now, what can I help you with? Are you looking for a dress?"

"No. Thank you. You sure have some nice ones, though."

"You should feel free to borrow anytime. I may be quite a bit thicker than you, but it is easy to alter the size of a dress, if you know how." Reg suspected she was talking about witchcraft rather than sewing alterations. "You know I have more here than I can ever use and I won't miss anything you borrow."

"Yes. I will, sometime." If she stayed in Black Sands. "Actually… I wondered how much you know about gems."

"Not my area of expertise. The emerald is one of the only stones of power that I have. Lesser stones look nice in jewelry. Some can be used in meditations or magnifying spells. Why?"

"I was trying to liquidate a few of the gems that I got from the Papillons. The fairies."

"Oh."

Sarah turned away from Reg to look at the dresses she was going through. She didn't offer any immediate advice. So maybe she didn't know that Reg would have problems selling them. Maybe Sarah had never had a stone she wanted to sell, only ones she intended to keep.

"I went into the city today, hoping to find a buyer."

Sarah said nothing.

"I went to a couple of places, but they both said that they wouldn't buy them," Reg went on. "I guess they saw something that they didn't like. I knew there might be problems with not being able to prove their provenance, but that's why I picked the buyers I did. They were places that were supposed to be more accepting of... unpapered stones."

"Yes. Very interesting."

Reg was getting frustrated. Sarah was usually very helpful, offering more suggestions than Reg needed. Her stubborn silence grated on Reg's nerves.

"Do you know of anyone who would buy them? Or can you explain to me what the problem might be?"

"I don't have any suggestions for buyers, I'm sorry. That's not something I do."

"Okay... I was hoping you would at least have some suggestions. I thought you must have heard about someone, after all the years you've lived in this community..."

"No."

Reg blew out her breath and shook her head. "Well, maybe you could help me to understand why they would not want to buy them. I mean, I've done my homework. I know that they take older gemstones that don't have any provenance. It's only the new gems that need ID numbers etched onto them."

"Not really my area..."

"You don't know anything about it?" Reg challenged, getting

the feeling that Sarah was intentionally blocking her. It wasn't that she didn't know what Reg was talking about. It was that she didn't want to talk about it. Maybe didn't even want Reg to talk about it.

"No."

"You don't know why no one would buy my gems."

Sarah finally turned her face toward Reg. She blinked several times, focusing on her accuser. Her face was devoid of expression, as if she were wearing a mask.

"Because they are cursed."

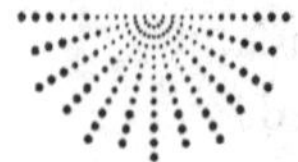

CHAPTER SEVEN

*I*f Reg had been chewing gum, she would have spat it out. Or swallowed it. She stared at Sarah, who did not change her expression, but went back to examining the clothing on the rack.

"They are *cursed?*" Reg repeated.

Sarah nodded. "Yes."

"How do you know that?"

"They have a certain… feeling. Once you have held a cursed gem in your hands, you will know it again."

Reg thought about the way she felt when she handled the gems. She had been able to feel their power, just like with Sarah's emerald, but she hadn't felt anything bad.

"Are you sure? Maybe they're just… they have power."

"I can tell the difference between a powerful gem and a cursed one. Not that the two are exclusive. They are not."

"Can you look at me, Sarah? Can you explain it to me?"

There was silence as Sarah continued to look through the clothing, ignoring Reg's question. Reg said nothing, standing there waiting. Finally, Sarah turned her face toward Reg, though she didn't move her body, so she was just looking back over her shoulder at Reg.

"We don't talk about such things."

Her words lay heavily in the air for a long time as Reg tried to decide what to do about them.

"We don't talk about them. Why not?"

"There are some things that are just not… discussed in polite company."

Reg remembered another such comment. "Some things," she repeated, "like about people like Corvin? The way you don't discuss what his abilities are, what his 'curse' is, not warning the innocent people who could become his prey?"

Sarah nodded. "Certainly not. It would be extremely gauche to bring up such a thing. It's like…" Sarah shook her head as she tried to think of a comparison that Reg would understand. "It would be like discussing sex at the dinner table. It simply is not done. There are some things that are… simply too delicate."

"So it's more important to avoid making people uncomfortable than it is to prevent them from being hurt."

"I did warn you," Sarah reminded Reg. "I told you more than once that he was dangerous and that you should not go out with him or be left alone with him. You cannot deny that."

"No. But you didn't tell me why. I thought you were just saying that… he might take advantage of me. But I'm a big girl and I can take care of myself. I didn't understand his… gift, or curse, or whatever you call it. Because people thought it would be impolite to tell me."

Sarah shrugged. "We can only do what we can. If you do not want to listen or do not understand, then that isn't on us. That's on you."

"How could I understand if no one would tell me?" Reg demanded, the frustration that she had previously put aside on the topic coming to the surface again. "Explain that to me."

"By listening to what you are told. I told you enough for you to understand that he was a danger to you. You are the one who chose not to listen, to go out with him and then to bring him back here, by yourself, and to break the wards that I had set to protect you."

"I didn't bring him back here, I…" Reg faltered under Sarah's glare. "Well, I did, but that wasn't because I wanted to, he had control over me."

Sarah's eyebrows lifted in disbelief.

"You know what effect he has on people. How was I supposed to resist that?"

Sarah said nothing, but Reg heard again her accusation, that Reg should have listened to what she was told. That if she didn't, then she was the one who was at fault. Not the people who didn't explain it to her in detail. The people who should have known that she didn't understand and that she was treading on thin ice.

"You're blaming the victim," Reg pointed out.

"Yes." Sarah agreed.

"I didn't ask for him to take my powers."

"Well, that is debatable."

They were at a stalemate. Reg knew that she wouldn't convince Sarah of anything. She had already made up her mind.

"Fine, then. But I need you to explain to me about the gems being cursed."

Sarah took a couple of dresses off the rack without even looking at them, much less holding them up to herself. She sighed and walked out of the room. Reg assumed she was to follow, and did so.

"As I said, it really is not seemly for me to be discussing it with you."

"Then how am I supposed to know that the gems are cursed or what I can do about it?"

"You should be able to sense it yourself. You have psychic powers. Are you telling me that you feel nothing when you hold the gems?"

"Well… no. I can feel that they are powerful, like you said. But that doesn't mean that they feel… dangerous. Or cursed or whatever."

"What did these buyers tell you?"

"Nothing. One said…" Reg tried to remember the words that had been used. "That I should not have accepted a gift. And that I would have to show their history. The other one said that they had to be cleansed."

Sarah nodded and shrugged as if that explained everything.

"That doesn't help me!" Reg snapped. "I have no idea where they came from, other than from Calliopia's family, and I don't have the first clue how to cleanse gems. They're *cursed*? How do gems get cursed?"

"You would have to look at their history to find that out."

Reg shook her head. "How do I do that?"

"I have never accepted a gift of cursed gems," Sarah said, raising her brows. "So I'm afraid I cannot help you with that."

Reg folded her arms across her chest. "So once again, it is my fault. Because no one will talk to me. You are the one person who knew about me getting the gems. You couldn't have given me a heads-up? You couldn't tell me that you thought they were cursed and maybe I shouldn't accept them, or I would have to *cleanse* them before I could use them for anything?"

"I fail to see, Reg, how it is my fault that you did something rash."

Reg tried to figure out a way to explain to Sarah that it was clearly her fault, and not Reg's own, if no one had taught her about cursed gems and what to do about them. But she couldn't find any argument that Sarah wouldn't just throw back in her face. Why hadn't Reg educated herself? Why had she just assumed that it was okay to accept such an elaborate gift? Hadn't she seen that there was something wrong with it? Didn't she sense that the gems were cursed, with all that psychic power she was supposed to possess?

One of her foster mothers had once told her "If it sounds too good to be true, then it probably is."

It was advice that Reg had used, not necessarily in her own purchases and ventures, but as a guide to conning other people out of their money. Make something sound *too* good, and people wouldn't do it. They would pull back, suspecting that something was wrong. Make it just a little better than they could get anywhere else, with a good sob story as to why you were willing to give them what they wanted at such a low price, and they were far more likely to buy into it. Give them just the barest hint that the reason the goods or services were lower was that they *might* have fallen off the back of a truck or because Reg was in desperate need to pay her rent the next day, and they would willingly accept it. Make it too low and they would know they were being conned.

And the fairies giving Reg a chest full of jewels? Reg hadn't thought that was too good to be true?

In fact, the thought had crossed her mind. But she knew that the fairies were fabulously wealthy compared to her and that she had nearly killed herself trying to bring the Papillon's daughter back from the brink of death, and it didn't seem to be that much out of proportion. She definitely deserved more than a simple thank you. She had put herself in considerable danger more than once to save Calliopia.

She deserved a reward. And maybe the Papillons had meant her to split the treasure between all the people in her company, everyone who had helped to save Calliopia. There hadn't been any instructions, and Reg hadn't distributed the gems, even though she had thought more than once that she probably should. It was hard for her, after being so poor her whole life. She was used to taking care of herself, to considering her own need for safety and stability, not anyone else's.

"You're not going to help me?" she asked Sarah.

"I'm afraid I can't, Reg."

Reg was pretty sure that she could. If she wanted to.

CHAPTER EIGHT

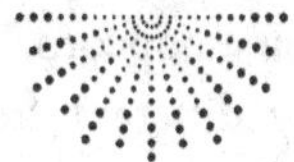

*I*f Sarah wouldn't talk to her about the gems, then there was another party that already knew about the jewels that Reg could talk to. She didn't look forward to going back to the Papillon mansion to try to get some information on the history of the gems, but she didn't want to reveal the fact that she possessed the gems to anyone else. If she went to Davyn or Corvin or someone else who might be able to help her to cleanse them, then more people would know about her treasure. With every person who knew about the gemstones, the odds of their getting stolen skyrocketed. She might trust Davyn, but she didn't trust that he wouldn't just happen to say something to his new friend Julian or to someone else who would spread the word around.

So, it was time to see the fairies and ask them about it.

Mrs. Papillon had told her that she was welcome at the mansion anytime. Reg had, of course, never taken her up on it, and Mrs. Papillon had undoubtedly expected that she never would. Reg really didn't have any reason to go to the mansion. Except now she did. She would have to put that invitation to the test.

Reg first returned to her cottage to pet Starlight and make sure that his dishes were freshly filled with adequate nourishment. She had only been gone for a few hours, but these things were important to a cat. Reg didn't tell him what she had discovered so far. It was one thing when Sarah looked at her with that expression of disdain when she had done something stupid or not known the most basic of magical traditions and practice. It was quite another when her cat did it.

"I'll be back later," she told Starlight breezily. "Maybe we'll put on a movie tonight. Pop some popcorn."

Not that that was any different from any other night they spent together. Sometimes Reg invited a few of her friends over to watch the movie with her. And on occasion, she had gone to a community event. She was supposed to be meeting new people, expanding her business base, but Reg was currently trying to stay low until people forgot about her mother being a siren and started treating her like a normal person again. The same person she had been when she had first arrived in Black Sands.

The trees and vegetation growing beside the road were green. Everything in Florida was green. It was one of the few places Reg had ever been where they didn't have to worry about what to do if there were a drought.

Her surroundings grew wilder, but she could also tell that she was getting close to the mansion. They were wild in a perfect way, as if they had been grown and trimmed to the exact shape they were in order to look wild. Window dressing or camouflage? Did the fairies want to be seen or to be hidden? Reg couldn't figure out which it was.

She watched carefully for the turnoff, and then took the pathway that went deeper and deeper into the forest. It wound around, and the foliage around her grew even more gorgeous. It was really stunning, comparable to the garden Forst had created at Sarah's house. Though Reg would never tell him that. Or the fairies. They would probably both take it as an insult.

She didn't know how fairies and gnomes got along together, but she knew that fairies and pixies didn't get along. Or fairies and cats. Fairies and humans weren't the best of friends, for that matter. So it was entirely feasible that fairies didn't get along with gnomes or any of the other races in the area either.

Reg pulled into a clearing in the forest to see the Papillon mansion towering above her, looking just like the castle out of a fairy tale. The lawn and trees and gardens around the mansion were all groomed and manicured and trimmed to look absolutely perfect. She was almost afraid to get out of the car, for fear that the illusion would break and she would find herself looking at a normal yard and house.

She sat there for a moment and then forced herself to get out.

She rang the doorbell and knocked for good measure. Sometimes the butler was inclined to be condescending and pretended he didn't hear her or said that she would have to come back another time, when she had actually been invited. But she hadn't been back since Mrs. Papillon had told her that she was welcome there anytime, so maybe things had changed.

The tall, pale-faced butler swung open the door and looked down his nose at Reg.

"Is Mrs. Papillon in?" Reg inquired. "I'd like to speak with her for a few minutes."

He appeared to be considering the question, and Reg didn't want him to come to the wrong answer. "She said I could visit anytime."

His lips puckered sourly and his nostrils flared. He still said nothing, but eventually opened the door the rest of the way and stepped back to allow her to enter.

Reg stepped into the mansion and looked around. It was a big house and she wasn't sure where the proprietors would be. The greenhouse where she had watched them pot plants? One of the arboretums she had previously visited Calliopia or her parents in? She would not be going to Calliopia's bedroom this time. Callie was no longer there. She had broken away from the community, committing an unpardonable offense.

"This way," the butler told Reg haughtily, as if he'd been trying to get her attention earlier and she hadn't been paying attention.

In all honestly, she hadn't been, but neither had he said anything to her aloud. If he expected her to read his mind or some nonverbal signal he had given her, he would have to be more clear. She had been taught that it was rude to read people's minds without their express permission. And usually she didn't. If she could help it.

Reg swiveled and followed the tall fairy, feeling like a child being left behind by his long strides.

He waited at the entrance of one of the rooms. Reg caught up with him and tried to slow her breathing. She didn't want to run into the room out of breath, scaring people into thinking there was something wrong or that she was being disrespectful by running in their house.

She walked into the room at what she hoped was a stately speed, and found Mr. and Mrs. Papillon sitting among the indoor trees, deep in discussion.

They stopped speaking when they saw Reg. Mrs. Papillon rose swiftly to her feet and extended a hand to Reg.

"Welcome, Reg Rawlins. You honor us with your presence."

Reg wasn't sure whether Mrs. Papillon was expecting her to shake hands, or to kiss her fingers, or if it were just a grand gesture. She bent her knees in a small curtsy and hoped that would be enough to show her hosts respect.

"I'm sorry to come here without an invitation. I hope I didn't interrupt anything."

"Of course not. You are always welcome here."

Mrs. Papillon motioned to another seat, a white wicker chair that was nestled under a tree with long, broad leaves. Reg sat perched on the edge of it. She didn't intend to get comfortable. It wasn't exactly a comfortable topic that she had come to speak to them about. They might just throw her out the moment she opened her mouth about the gemstones.

Reg looked around, wondering if she needed to start with some small talk. She didn't know if that were customary with fairies, or just a human thing. When she had talked with fairies before, it seemed that there had always been some special reason to meet and they had gotten directly to the topic. When Calliopia had been on her deathbed—well, they didn't begin with discussing the weather.

"How is Calliopia?" Reg tried. "Have you talked to her at all?"

"She is not in contact with the kin," Mr. Papillon said archly. "She has chosen to live outside our community."

Because she had chosen a pixie for a partner. Something that was taboo in both communities. By choosing each other as mates, Calliopia and Ruan had been expelled from both of their families. Reg wondered how many other fairy and pixie couples there were out there, on the outskirts of society, choosing to live in exile rather than complying with the expectations of their magical races. She was sure that Calliopia and Ruan could not be the only ones. But such things were not discussed. Yet another topic that was forbidden in polite company. Like the one that Reg was planning to bring up.

"Yes, I just wondered whether… word had gotten to you. Sometimes children still write letters home… or get a message to you through another source. Or maybe you just hear rumors through a messenger. Someone who has happened to see her."

Mr. Papillon looked at his wife and did not say anything. She gave Reg a bland, beatific smile, and did not fill her in on any knowledge of Calliopia's life.

"Is that all that Reg Rawlins came to inquire about today?"

"No," Reg admitted. "That's not why I am here."

They looked at her, faces blank, waiting for her to tell them her reason for the visit.

"I neglected to thank you for the gift that you sent me after Calliopia's recovery," Reg said slowly. Since there had been no accompanying note with the gems, she was feeling her way through the subject, and thought it best not to say that it was compensation for her healing Calliopia or anything that they might take umbrage with. "That was a very generous gift."

Mrs. Papillon inclined her head in a brief nod of acknowledgment but didn't say anything else about their gratitude for what Reg had done or that she deserved the rich reward they had given her. Reg rubbed her sweating palms along her thighs, drying them on her skirt. Her palms were wet and her mouth dry, and she desperately wished that she had brought a water bottle or that they had offered her some refreshment.

"It was really too generous," Reg suggested. "I should probably have returned them to you right away. I should not have accepted them."

Mrs. Papillon glanced at her husband.

"Why should you return what was freely given?" Mr. Papillon asked. "The stones now belong to you."

Reg felt as if a weight had been added to her shoulders. If the gems were cursed, it was clear that the Papillons wanted nothing to do with them any longer. They were happy to have transferred ownership to another being. She had been a dupe. They had known or hoped that she wouldn't recognize that they were transferring a curse to her, so that they could be rid of it.

Reg hadn't asked Sarah what kind of a curse it was. Something that would make her sick or cause her early death? A bad luck curse? She hadn't exactly had an easy life since she had acquired the gems but, on the other hand, she hadn't contracted some rare disease that was rapidly subtracting years from her life.

At least, not as far as she knew.

Maybe the recipient of the curse had to know about it for it to be effective. Maybe there was a psychological aspect to it. A person was only cursed if they believed in the curse. Maybe by being unaware, she had avoided any negative effects up until then.

"I was hoping to be able to sell some of the stones. I'm short on cash, and humans need a certain amount to be able to pay the bills. House rental, utilities, internet…" Reg trailed off, knowing that the fairies would know next to nothing about these human concepts. "So anyway. I took them to a couple of places in the city to see if I could get some money to pay the bills."

They both just looked at her, not filling in the empty

space, not acknowledging that they knew where she was going with this. Maybe they thought that humans could sell anything, that the curse wouldn't have any effect on commerce.

"But I was told by the jewelers I talked to today that they could not buy the stones, because of the curse on them."

Mr. Papillon nodded slowly. Not a surprise, then.

"I need to be able to sell them," Reg pointed out. "They are useless to me otherwise. Just having them doesn't do me any good."

"They do have power," Mr. Papillon pointed out. He shook his head slightly. "Humans are so avaricious… they see only the opportunity for profit. But the stones have value in themselves. Power and beauty. You do not need to sell them to profit from them."

"But I do. And I need to understand what this curse is. I don't get it. I didn't even know that they were cursed until today. Can you tell me what it is? Where it came from? What does it mean to me?"

He was silent, gazing at her.

"Please," Reg tacked on. "This is very important to me."

"We… cannot help you," Mrs. Papillon said.

"You must know something about this curse."

A shrug.

"Did you know that they were cursed?" Reg tried. "Or is that just a human thing?"

"The stones belong to you now."

"Yes, okay. But I need to know something about their history. The jewelers said that I needed to understand the history of the gems and where they came from. But the only thing I know about is that they came from you. I don't know where they came from before that."

She was met with blank faces and stares. No sign that they understood her need to know this information or that they intended to help her.

"Have they been in your family for long? They are quite old, right?"

"All gems spring from ancient lineage," Mr. Papillon said logically. Of course they hadn't just been created recently. They had been formed in the earth thousands of years before and had waited there for someone to dig them up. They were all old.

Reg thought that he knew what she meant, though. Fairies and some of the other races were very pedantic and expected everyone to follow their rules and conventions, and anything that fell outside those parameters was wrong and needed to be corrected, until the person could say or do things the way that the kin did. They weren't willing to bend to human conventions, but expected other races to conform to theirs.

"Right. And they've been in your family for...?" Not a flicker on Mr. Papillon's face to indicate that he intended to fill in the blank. "For how long?" Reg prompted, hoping that he was just waiting for her to finish the question properly.

"They are yours now," he repeated firmly. "They are your responsibility and we have nothing more to do with them."

"I could really use your help, though."

No answer.

"Your advice." Reg hoped that if she didn't imply that he still had some responsibility for the gems that he would soften. "Your race is so wise in these matters. If you could help someone who has not grown up in the magical community..."

"We keep to ourselves. We do not wish to be involved in this matter."

"You didn't keep to yourselves when you needed help finding Calliopia. And you were happy for my help when I came to see her, when she was hurt. I've given you a lot of help and advice. I would think that you could reciprocate."

"We have paid you handsomely for your services," Mr. Papillon disagreed. "A king's ransom. We do not owe you anything further."

A king's ransom? Was it just a figure of speech, or was it literal? Was it a clue?

"If there is anything you could tell me about the gems or about their origin or this curse, I would be really grateful," Reg said earnestly, putting as much emotion and sincerity into her words as she could. "It would be really helpful for me."

"I am sorry," Mr. Papillon said again. "I cannot help you."

He stood up. An unmistakable signal that it was time for Reg to leave. Reg stayed where she was, resisting.

"Maybe Callie would be able to help me," she suggested. "I could find her and see if she knows anything about the provenance of the jewels."

Mr. Papillon's expression was thunderous. "Our daughter knows nothing about these stones. You will leave her out of it."

Reg didn't really intend to track Calliopia down and find out if she knew anything about the gems, but it was interesting to observe Mr. Papillon's reaction to the suggestion. Was he angry just because she had mentioned Calliopia? Because she was no longer part of their household? Because he saw it as a threat? Or was there any possibility that Calliopia really did know the secret the gems held and might be able to tell Reg what she needed to know?

"She is no longer part of your household. I didn't think you considered her part of your family anymore."

Mrs. Papillon looked at her husband, weighing her words against his reaction. "Calliopia will always be a part of this family. No matter how far away she is."

"No matter what she does? No matter what your community thinks of her?" Reg knew that the Papillons were concerned with how they looked in their community. It had been obvious to her in her previous interactions with them that they had been unwilling to go against any of the conventions of their race.

"She is our daughter. No matter what the kin say," Calliopia's mother said firmly.

Mr. Papillon's eyes flashed to his wife, but he did not dispute what she said. There might be a discussion about this matter after Reg had left, but he would not call her out in front of Reg.

"There are only so many places I can go to find out what the problem is with these gems, what the curse on them is all about. So if you don't want me to make any inquiries, then you should tell me yourself. That would be the logical thing to do."

"We cannot help you with this."

Reg finally rose to her feet as well. She didn't even come close to matching Mr. Papillon's height. He towered above her. She felt like a child standing next to him. And he had always treated her like a child; all the fairies did. Reg's limited human years meant that she would always be a naive young child compared to the longer-lived races. Sarah, with her centuries, might be someone worth speaking to. But not Reg.

The butler appeared in the doorway, stiffening and waiting for Reg to follow him. Reg looked at the Papillons, hoping against hope that they would throw her a bone. Just one little tidbit that would get her started in the right direction.

But there was nothing. They both watched her impassively, waiting for her to leave. Mrs. Papillon did not bother to tell Reg this time that she would always be welcome.

Reg followed the butler to the front door.

CHAPTER NINE

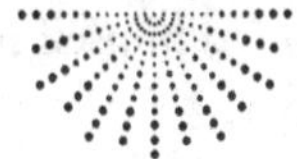

Reg bought a big, greasy burger on the way home, and when she arrived at the cottage, plopped herself down in front of the TV and didn't move for a couple of hours. She was discouraged about the whole gem thing and determined to put it out of her mind and not think about it anymore.

But her brain was not cooperating. Reg sat with Starlight in her lap, petting him and trying to remain focused on the miniseries she had turned on. But she still had the little bag of gems in her pocket, and it was like they were burning a hole there. She couldn't think of anything else.

Eventually, she got up to have a drink, then sat again, flipping through channels to try to come up with something better. Anything that would keep her attention. But all the shows she turned on just seemed to remind her of her own troubles and she couldn't get into anything else. She could have a warm bath and head to bed, seeing if sleep would erase the subject from her mind, but of course she knew that would not work. She would just toss and turn, thinking about the gems and how she would rid herself of them. It would keep her from being able to get to sleep, until she was too exhausted to stay awake anymore.

She turned the TV off, grumpy and dissatisfied. Starlight put his ears back, listening to her. He didn't turn to look at her, but his ears gave him away. He wasn't used to her turning off the TV in the evening unless she were getting ready for bed or a visitor.

"What do you think I should do?" Reg asked him, although she hadn't explained the problem to him at all. Exactly how did she expect him to give her advice on a human problem when she hadn't told him anything about it?

Sunlight purred and curled himself into a ball, showing her his white tuxedo chin and throat.

"Yes, you're cute." She rubbed his jaw and chin. "But that doesn't really help me."

He purred more loudly.

"Cute kitty isn't solving any of my problems."

Although stroking his silky soft fur didn't make things any worse, either. What was it like to be a cat? Nice not to have all of the human worries? Or harder because they were not in control of anything and had to get humans to do everything for them?

Starlight twisted to look at her with one slitted eye. She bent down and kissed him on the nose, which caused him to snort and shake his head, flapping his ears.

Reg got out her phone and thumbed through her mail and her social networks. Nothing important going on there. Nothing that interested her, even when she went to YouTube to check on her favorite channels.

The phone rang.

Reg didn't need to look at the picture on the screen to know who it would be. Only one person could read her mind well enough to know that she was restless and out of sorts. Only one person would intentionally call her when she was in that kind of a mood and risk how she might react.

"Corvin."

"Regina," he purred. "How are you this beautiful evening?"

"Ugh. Angry. Irritated. Depressed. What makes you think it is such a beautiful evening?"

"The sky is clear; the moon is out. Jupiter is rising. Why would I not be in a good mood?"

His cheer just put her into a worse mood. And he probably knew that. He liked to poke at her, irritate her.

"Why don't you go jump in a lake?" Reg suggested.

"Is that an invitation? Do you have any particular lake in mind?"

Reg wondered fleetingly if a freshwater lake would set off her siren instincts like the saltwater of the ocean. Probably. Did Florida even have freshwater lakes?

"Did you call me because you wanted something?"

"No. Just thought you might enjoy a chat."

"Well, I'm in a pretty bad mood right now, so it probably isn't a good idea."

"You were upset earlier today too. What's going on?"

"You ambushed me earlier."

"Well, it wasn't meant that way. I was just staying out of Sarah's way until you got home. I didn't mean to be… lurking."

"You're lucky she didn't see you. She was talking about going after you with the broom when I mentioned you were around."

"I've seen that witch wield a broom. I wouldn't want to be on the other end of it."

"Me neither," Reg agreed, allowing a small laugh.

"She should be out enjoying the night life by now. I could come over and try to cheer you up."

"No, you couldn't. I wouldn't let you in."

"We could sit outside in the garden and enjoy the night air."

"Not even that." She knew only too well that he could charm her almost as easily outside as in.

"What is on my sweet Regina's mind?"

"Your sweet Regina?" Reg snorted. Had he been drinking? "I don't think you've ever tried that one before. I'm anything but sweet. Especially today."

"Then tell me about it, sourpuss."

Reg thought about it. Corvin had been more forthcoming in

the past than some of the other witches and warlocks she was acquainted with. Being somewhat a pariah anyway, he was more likely to flaunt the rules of the society and step out of bounds. Maybe that meant that he would be more willing to discuss gems and curses with her too. Reg got comfortable and started scratching Starlight's ears again.

"Well… let's say I have a friend who has a problem."

"A friend. All right. You have a friend with a problem. What sort of problem is this?"

"He has come into possession of some… *artifacts*."

"Yes? What sort of artifacts?"

"Well, these artifacts are valuable. But where they came from and how they ended up in his possession is not very clear."

Corvin chuckled.

"And your friend is looking for a way to *rehome* these artifacts? Or does he want to keep them?"

"Well, he needs to liquidate some of them, at least."

"There are places one can go. Certain dealers who are willing to overlook a less well-known history."

"But let's say that one or two of those places say that… there are issues that they can't overlook."

"Hmm. That could be troublesome."

Reg waited for further information, but it did not appear to be forthcoming.

"So… what could he do?"

"What kind of problem is he having?"

"Well…" Reg hesitated. Corvin knew, of course, that she was talking about herself. Even if her explanation hadn't been transparent, he could access her thoughts and feelings only too easily.

"What kind of artifacts are we talking about?" Corvin tried.

"Some… gemstones."

"Oh." Corvin sounded surprised and interested. "And where did your friend get these gemstones?"

"They were… a gift."

"From a friend or an enemy?"

"Hmm." Reg stroked Starlight's first slowly. "Someone… he thought was friendly."

"That's not quite the same thing as a friend."

"No. I wouldn't say… a friend."

"Your friend should beware of taking gifts from people who are not exactly friends."

"So I gather. My friend didn't know she—he—had to be careful."

"Regina. Have you learned so little in the time you have been here?"

"Don't blame me," Reg snapped. "It's not my fault. It isn't as if anyone told me!"

"Some things you would be expected to understand."

"But if you haven't grown up in a community like this, in a household where that kind of thing was taught, then how are you supposed to know? Is that something that's just built into your DNA?"

"Most practitioners have grown up in practicing households," Corvin admitted. "It can be hard to understand what someone who was raised in a conventional home would know or not know."

"How about you assume that I don't know anything? Because I don't. I wasn't taught any of this stuff. And if my friends aren't up to telling me, then how am I supposed to figure it out on my own?"

"You *are* a psychic." He sounded amused. Just the attitude Reg didn't need from him.

"But apparently, reading people's minds without their permission, delving down into their psyches and all their life experiences, is frowned upon."

"Yes," he agreed, more soberly. "I can see how that would not be an option. It was just a joke."

Reg sighed. "So you can't help me."

"I didn't say that. We haven't really even gotten to the problem yet. Where did the jewels come from?"

"I'm not going to tell you that."

"Then how do you expect me to offer you any advice?"

"I already went to the person who gave them to me, and they were not helpful. They wouldn't tell me anything about their history or what to do about them being… a problem."

Corvin sighed. "I don't suppose you've ever heard of blood diamonds."

"Of course I've heard of blood diamonds. Everybody has."

"Oh. Well, as you know, I'm not a good judge of what you might know or not know about the magical world."

"The magical world?" Reg repeated. "Blood diamonds don't have anything to do with the magical world."

There was only silence in response.

Reg pounded her fist against her forehead. Was she ever going to understand the ins and outs of the community she was a part of?

"Okay, explain to me how blood diamonds are a part of the magical world."

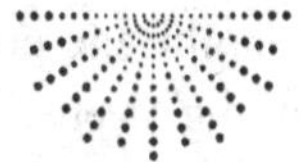

CHAPTER TEN

"What do you know about blood diamonds?" Corvin asked. "Maybe we should start there."

"I know that… you're not allowed to buy diamonds from certain countries, because of the way they are used to fund wars. Because of the way the people who mine them are taken advantage of. So there's a certification system to make sure that all newly imported diamonds are etched with a serial number. Then they can be traced so you can be sure you are getting stones that haven't been used to fund war. Where people haven't been treated badly to get them."

"That's a reasonable description," Corvin agreed. "As far as the non-magical world understands it."

"But there's something missing from it."

"Yes." Reg pictured Corvin in her mind's eye. Stroking his neatly-trimmed beard while he thought about what she knew and what he needed to explain to her. "What is missing is that many of these wars are funded by practicing warlords. That stones are mined not just for their monetary value as trinkets for men and women in the western world, but also for their magical properties. Their innate power. Those who are obsessed with gaining power —" It was almost funny that he would refer to other people as being obsessed, when Reg didn't know anyone who was more focused on the acquisition of power than Corvin himself. "—they will go to great lengths to mine and buy these gems."

"So… what kind of power? You mean like Sarah's emerald? The one that keeps her from getting older?"

"There are as many different powers as there are gems. But as the gems are added to existing hoards, there are fewer and fewer in circulation that have any significant power. This forces warlords and other practitioners to dig deeper and deeper to find new ones."

"And since they are scarce, the price goes up," Reg suggested.

"Basic economics. And the more valuable they are, the more warlords are willing to risk to find them. The dirtier the game gets. The more desperate the miners' circumstances become."

Reg didn't like to think of the trouble that the gems she had in her pocket might have caused. She had been thinking of them only as a means to plump up her bank balance. Not as artifacts with a history. Not of the blood that might have been shed to obtain them.

"But not all gems are blood diamonds, right? There are plenty that have been in families for generations. Just because a gem isn't etched, that doesn't mean that it came from one of these countries. That there was any blood shed over them."

"No," Corvin agreed. "There are certainly gems that were obtained without being part of one of these conflicts. But many of them, even ones that have been passed down through the generations, have long histories of bloodshed. Look up any of the larger gems currently on display in museums, and you will see long lists of battles fought over them and kings and queens and royal progeny who were killed for them."

"But these gems that I have—that my friend has—"

"Really, Reg, you can drop the subterfuge. You aren't actually very subtle."

"Well, okay. These gems that I have, there is no way to know what their history is. Whether they were part of any conflict. Right?"

"There are several ways that their pasts, or parts of their pasts, can be revealed."

"How?"

"The battles that have been fought, the owners that the gems have been torn away from, they leave a…" Corvin hunted for the words. "They leave a sort of a psychic imprint on the gems. They are not unaffected."

"And how would anyone know that they had a psychic imprint?"

"Well, someone like you, who has psychic powers, and has been trained in reading gems. They would be employed by any of the practicing jewelers so that they could analyze the gems brought in for trade."

"So when they were looking at the gems, they weren't just checking color and clarity."

"No. The people that you consulted with were psychic themselves, and recognizing the history of these gems, they would have… *scruples* about buying them."

"But there have to be people who were still willing to buy them. Right?"

"I wish that I could just say yes. There may be. But it will depend on the level of damage to the stones."

"They are damaged?"

"This psychic imprint is not just a mark on the surface of the gem. It affects the power of the gem. And the effect of that power on the possessor. A gem that has a long history of violence becomes—"

"Cursed?"

There was a long pause.

"Cursed," Corvin said finally. "If that's what you want to call it."

"Would you call it something different?"

"No. I don't suppose so. Mostly… we avoid saying anything at all. It isn't something that is discussed."

"So I've found out." Reg sighed. "You know, all these things that are not discussed in polite company in the magical community…? It would be nice to have a list of them. And maybe some kind of primer about not getting involved with warlocks of a particular ilk. Or giving anyone your keys. Or accepting gifts from fairies."

"You got these gems from fairies?"

CHAPTER ELEVEN

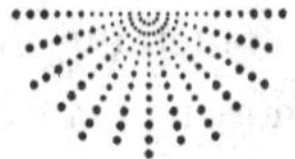

*W*ell..." Reg didn't want to give him any details.

"I'm sure we've talked before about gifts from fairies," Corvin said. "Haven't you ever read a fairy tale?"

"I know fairy tales," Reg retorted. She might not have read any herself, but she'd heard fairy tales. She'd watched the Disney movies. She knew as much as the next person did about them.

But maybe not as much as a magical practitioner.

"I'm not talking about the pap on TV and at the movie theater," Corvin said, sensing the direction of her thoughts. "I mean real fairy tales, in their original form, or at least before they were watered down for modern children."

Reg shook her head and didn't say anything. She had not grown up in a magical home. She had not gone to university or studied literature. Corvin knew all those things. If he expected her to know what he was talking about, he would have to explain it clearly.

"The older versions of the fairy tales are closer to the truth," Corvin said. "Fairies don't grant wishes. And when they give gifts or perform magic, there is always a catch. Always. They are not humans. They don't give gifts out of tender feelings. They do it because there is something in it for them. They give with one hand and take away with the other. Bartering with a fairy is never a good idea. They will always end up with the better end of the bargain, even if you think you have thought everything through and that you are getting the better deal. It isn't going to happen. You will always lose."

"But it wasn't just a gift. And it wasn't something that I asked for or bartered for."

"You think it was just something they gave you because they thought you deserved it? Showing gratitude or helping you out?"

"Well, yes. And what about Lord Bernier? He helped me and testified against you at the tribunal. Why did he do that? What did he get out of that?"

"I don't know, Reg. But you can bet that he got something out of it. Maybe just the opportunity to stick it to someone like me. Whether you can see his reason or not, you can bet that he had one. He had an ulterior motive. Fairies don't do anything for anyone other than the kin out of the goodness of their hearts. You can bank on that. They come from a different culture."

Reg wiped her hand across her face, mentally pushing the topic away and trying to reset. They weren't talking about fairies and the consequences of taking gifts from them. Reg had already made that mistake, so there was nothing she could do to change the past. And she already knew that even if she tried to gift the gems back to the Papillons, they would not take them. They had passed the responsibility for the gems on to Reg, and they didn't want them back.

"But that doesn't answer my question. What can I do about the gems? How can I cleanse them so that I can cash them in? I don't want to hang on to them. They don't do me any good just sitting there. I need to be able to liquidate them. And if they are cursed—what does that mean? Am I going to die? Have a run of bad luck? What?"

"Much like people who have been traumatized, gems that have violent histories can be very unpredictable. You don't know what consequences might result from owning cursed gems until you do…"

"Are you telling me that these gems have PTSD?" Reg barked out a laugh.

Corvin chuckled. "More or less, yes."

"The jeweler I talked to said that they can be cleansed."

Corvin pondered this. "I am not an expert in gems and curses," he said finally. "I might be able to offer some suggestions if I saw them, but you understand that it is not my area of expertise. I can go back over some of the stories and legends about fairy gifts and cursed gems and see whether I can find anything in the historical records I have gathered, but…"

"That sounds like something that will take a lot of time."

"It sounds as if you've got nothing but time."

"I need to sell them to pay my way," Reg said. "I can't live on nothing."

"Sarah would let you ride for a while. I don't think she needs the money at all, she just wants to have someone close, and not leave the cottage standing empty. What I'm saying is, if you can't sell them, then what's the difference between sitting on them and not doing anything, and sitting on them while you wait for me to do some research?"

"I guess if you're doing the research, at least I have a better chance," Reg admitted. "But I was hoping that you—or someone else—might have the answer more quickly."

"I wish I could offer a name. This is an area that most practitioners that I know of stay well away from."

Reg sighed heavily. "Why do things have to be so complicated? I thought that fairy tales were simple. They're for children. They can't be that complex."

"But the reality behind the fairy tales can be very complex. Fairy tales are just a window for us into the magical or paranormal worlds. You wouldn't expect a painting of a house to show you everything in the world. Just the house."

"You need to see the gems to figure it out?"

"I can't really read them from here, can I? I won't be able to read them as clearly as your jewelers, but I should be able to sense something. Maybe what effect they are having on you. Maybe what happened to them or how to cleanse them."

"Can't you just take the power out of them?" Reg asked, and then regretted it. She didn't want to give Corvin any more power than he already had. He was too strong as it was.

"I expect I could," Corvin said slowly, "although the power of a cursed gem might be locked up tight inside, like a turtle in a shell. A self-defense mechanism."

"You make them sound as if they are alive. Being traumatized. Hiding inside themselves. They're rocks, not people."

"I'm sure they're just as alive to a practitioner who understands them as Forst's plants are to him. You told me that Forst said that his plants have feelings and preferences."

Reg nodded in response, thinking about it. Just because she couldn't hear or feel the feelings of an inanimate object like a gem, that didn't mean that it didn't have any. Sarah could not hear the thoughts of her garden gnome, and so she thought that he chose not to speak to humans any more than necessary. She hadn't known that the gnomes spoke to each other with telepathy, or their "inside words," and just were not very adept at speaking in their "outside words." The fact that Corvin didn't know anything about what Starlight was thinking or feeling didn't mean that her cat didn't have any thoughts or feelings, just that Corvin didn't have the skill or power to feel them.

"You still there, Reg?"

"Yeah. Maybe… I could bring them to you tomorrow. Would that be good? We could meet at The Crystal Bowl."

Then Reg remembered.

"Oh, maybe somewhere else, since The Crystal Bowl has decided that they don't serve my kind."

"Dinner tomorrow somewhere more accommodating?" Corvin asked.

"Do we have to wait until evening? We lose another whole

day. I know Sarah won't push it, but I'd like to move these gems as quickly as I can. I don't like not having anything to fall back on. I thought that I had enough that I didn't have to worry. No one said that I would have any trouble liquidating these stones."

"How many people know that you have them?"

Reg bit her lip. "No one."

"No one? I know now. And the fairies. And someone else must know, or you wouldn't have said that someone should have told you about them."

"Sarah," Reg admitted finally.

"Sarah and who else?"

"No one else. I haven't told anyone. I didn't want to have them stolen."

"No. That's a good point. Although, at least that's one way to rid yourself of a cursed treasure."

"I don't want to just get rid of it. I want to be able to use it. I haven't been making very much as a psychic lately. Not with people deciding that I'm too dangerous. Word spreads, so that even the non-practitioners think that I can't be trusted, even if they don't exactly know why."

"Maybe phone or computer consultations would be a good idea. If you don't have to meet with them face-to-face, then they don't have to worry about… other things."

Reg wrinkled her nose, considering it. She'd always hated phone line psychics. She liked the personal touch, being able to see people face-to-face. The psychic hotlines had always seemed like too obvious a scam. It was a lot harder to read someone over the phone. But it might be the only option she had. At least a video chat would give her a little bit more information and a better chance of reading the person. With Starlight's power and her crystal ball, maybe it would be enough to remotely read someone.

"I guess. I'll have to look into it."

"Make it about them," Corvin suggested. "Market it as a new service that serves their needs. Readings from the comfort of their own homes. No need to drive anywhere. No matter how remote or hermit-like they are, they can still access your services."

"Thanks. Yeah."

"So if you don't want to wait until tomorrow night, then why don't we meet tonight? It isn't that late. I know you stay up until the small hours of the morning anyway, whether you have clients or not. I won't be disrupting any planned seances. So how about it?"

"Where? Your club?"

Corvin considered this. Reg pushed harder to sense his feelings. Did he want to take her home? To somewhere more private than his club, where Reg always insisted on using the main dining room where there were other people around to act as witnesses or to help her if Corvin decided to take advantage of her proximity?

"The club would work," Corvin decided. Maybe best not to try to introduce her to somewhere new or to invite her to his house. She wouldn't accept. And she wouldn't invite him to the cottage, which was where he would really have liked to be. "Shall we say an hour? I need time to get ready. I'm not exactly prepared to entertain at the moment."

Reg sensed the humor in his voice and wondered briefly why he wasn't prepared to entertain. He was deep in some experiment or spell, with ingredients spread out around him? He was in his jammies, a housecoat, or sky clad, reading a book in his library? She withdrew her psychic connection with him as much as possible rather than using her vision to see him. She really didn't want to know.

Corvin chuckled. "No need to get shy now, Regina."

"An hour is fine," Reg agreed. "I need to get ready too."

"I'll pick you up."

"No. I'll meet you there. I don't want you driving me home."

That always seemed to end up being a problem. The enclosed space of his car, the proximity of her cottage while she grew intoxicated with his charms—not a good idea.

CHAPTER TWELVE

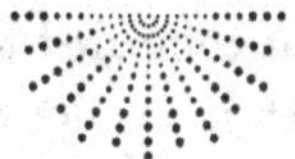

After Reg hung up the phone, she tried to shift Starlight from her lap. The cat clearly did not want to move, comfortable where he was.

"Come on," Reg groaned, sliding her hands underneath him and trying to avoid his kicking feet with their razor-sharp claws. "I need to get up. You can curl up and go to sleep here. Or on the bed. But I need to go out tonight."

She put him down on the couch beside her. Starlight sneezed, snorted, and jumped to the floor, stalking off grumpily into the kitchen.

"I'm sorry. But you know I have to figure out what to do with these gems."

Or maybe he didn't. That was a pretty complex thing for a cat brain to understand, even if Starlight had been a more complex being in previous lives. Commerce didn't mean much to cats. They understood whether there was any fish in their food bowls, but not the fact that she needed money to buy the fish, that she hadn't gone to the ocean to catch it herself.

Reg's mouth watered at the thought, and she tried to put all thoughts of the ocean and hunting and fishing out of her brain.

She wasn't going to the ocean any time soon. Not until she could be sure that she wouldn't do something she would later regret.

She ignored Starlight's snit and went to her closet to find something suitable.

Maybe it was having seen Sarah's rooms full of clothing earlier in the day, but the little collection of dresses and skirts in her closet looked very small and pitiful. It was probably more than she had ever owned before, but compared to even some of the single moms who had fostered her, it was not a very grand offering. And Corvin had probably seen each piece she owned.

Not that it should matter. She wasn't going on a date with him. She was consulting with him on a financial matter, that was all. Men wore the same suit to all kinds of meetings, Corvin usually wore the same cloak with the same or similar clothing beneath it. If men could wear the same outfit on multiple dates —*business meetings*—then why couldn't women?

Still, she tried to pair a dress with a headscarf and wrap that she hadn't worn on any previous occasion with him, doing her best to make it look fresh and new. He probably wouldn't even notice. All he would care about was her warm body close to his and her powers just tantalizingly out of his reach.

* * *

One of the gorgeous, sexily-clad hostesses at the club met Reg at the door and knew immediately to escort her to the dining room. Either Corvin had called ahead to let them know that they would be there, or Reg had been there enough times with him that they knew Reg's preference for a public meeting. She didn't like the possibility that she was meeting with Corvin often enough for people to remember her from one time to the next. She told herself that she only saw him once in a blue moon, when it was really necessary for the two of them to meet. And it was only because it wasn't safe for her to meet him at her home or his that they always ended up going out for dinner together at his club.

She missed The Crystal Bowl. At least that had been a casual, pub-like atmosphere where she felt comfortable. She hated the feeling that she was on display and being evaluated when she was at Corvin's private club.

Corvin was there ahead of Reg, even though it had not yet been the hour that he had suggested. He stood immediately when Reg entered the dining room and pulled a chair out for her. Reg let him push it in as she sat down, ignoring his body heat next to her and the scent of roses that already infused the air.

"Thank you." Reg looked at the waitress who approached the table. "Can I get a glass of wine? Actually…" Reg checked herself. She should know by now that alcohol went to her head much too quickly when she was around Corvin. "Just, uh, water. With a twist of lemon."

The waitress nodded, smiling.

"No wine?" Corvin demanded, looking at Reg with his brows drawn down. "How about a little scotch in that water?"

"No. Not today."

She didn't tell him that she wanted to keep a clear head. He would just argue with her. Corvin stood there next to her, waiting for an explanation. Reg smiled and nodded at the waitress, waiting for her to take Corvin's order. The woman looked at Corvin expectantly.

"Well, I'm not teetotaling," Corvin said. "Single malt on the rocks."

She nodded and fluttered her lashes at him. "Right away, Mr. Hunter."

Corvin sat down next to Reg, already looking disgruntled. Reg reminded herself that he was there to help her. She should at least try to make it a pleasant evening. She blew her breath out and tried not to breathe in any more of his enchanting pheromones than she absolutely had to.

"Do you think you could turn down the charm?" she suggested. "You've already got the waitress swooning."

"She wasn't…" Corvin looked in the direction the waitress had gone. "Well, she might have been a little smitten. But that could just be my ruggedly handsome good looks."

Reg had to admit that he was among the most attractive men she had ever known. Maybe the most handsome she had ever known in person, rather than just worshiping from afar.

"I'm sure that doesn't help," she agreed as coolly as possible. "But seriously. We're not going to be able to get anything productive done here if I'm all fuzzy-headed."

He smiled, eyeing her. Enjoying the fact that she was as much as admitting her attraction toward him. It made sense to build up his ego. He was far more likely to help her if he felt flattered and appreciated.

Reg could feel him dialing back the charm a little, though she still felt an intense attraction toward him, which she strove to ignore.

The waitress returned promptly with their drinks. She stood a little too close to Corvin, bent down just a little too far, and held on to his glass for just an instant too long. She met his eyes and smiled, then reluctantly straightened.

"Did you want dinner?" she breathed.

"No. Just the drinks."

The waitress gave a small pout and withdrew.

Reg watched the waitress go. She reached into her purse and took out the little bag containing the gemstones.

"Really," Corvin said, putting his hand over hers before she could open the bag to show him the gems. "You don't want to be flashing those around here. Not if you're hoping to keep them a secret."

"Well, we can't exactly do this in private." It was too dangerous for her to be alone with him. She was strong enough to fight back against his charms. Most of the time. If she were focused. But she wasn't confident that she would always win. The more he grew into his powers, the more reason she had to be concerned.

Corvin's hand slid under hers, so that the bag was under his hand, Reg's hand resting over his. As usual, the touch of his skin to hers was like an intense electrical shock. It was difficult not to react to it by jerking her hand back away. Corvin smiled, enjoying her discomfort.

He closed his eyes like a purring cat, focusing on the gems in the bag.

"Nice," he breathed, "very nice."

She wasn't one hundred percent sure that he was talking about the gems. She tried to withdraw her hand, but he put his other hand over it, sandwiching her hand between both of his.

"Stay. I want to feel the effect of the stones on you."

That made some sense, so Reg left her hand where it was, although she was very self-conscious with both of his hands touching hers. She felt the eyes of the others in the dining room upon her. As if she had been caught in a compromising position.

Did everybody else there know what kind of a warlock he was? Did he bring other women there other days and then take them home with him and steal their powers? Were they used to seeing him there with vulnerable women, knowing what would happen next?

She hated the idea of their watching and being complicit in his predatory behavior.

There should be rules against it. But as she had discovered in the past, the rules that governed Corvin were too lax to provide anyone any real protection.

CHAPTER THIRTEEN

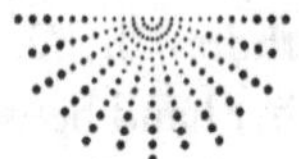

$\mathcal{R}$eg waited, watching Corvin's face, trying to shut out everything else in the dining room to feel what he was feeling and learn more about the gems. That was what she was there for.

"They do have… a history," Corvin confirmed.

"Well, we knew that. How could they not have a history?"

He removed the hand that was on top of hers, but left the other in place. "A violent history, I mean."

Reg nodded. They had already guessed as much. Maybe the confirmation was important. He had said that the gems were affected by the violence. She tried to think of it in a scientific way. They absorbed the negative energy or were imprinted with the violence that went on around them. But the picture that came into her mind was not of rocks absorbing the heat of a fire or mirrors reflecting their surroundings, but that of a child, knees drawn to chest, hiding her eyes, as the world exploded around her.

Corvin looked at her curiously. "You can feel it too."

"I can? I can feel that they have power, but that they are cursed?" Reg shook her head. "I don't think so. They don't feel… evil."

"No," he agreed.

Reg looked down at her hand, warm beneath his. "Can you do something about it? Can you cleanse them?"

Corvin's eyes were focused somewhere else. No longer on Reg's face. He turned his hand over, palm up, with the bag in it. He squeezed Reg's hand with the bag of gems sandwiched between them. Reg tried to focus her attention on the stones. She could help with whatever it was Corvin was doing.

Eventually, Corvin shook his head. "It will take someone with more skill than I." Removing his hand from hers, he picked up his glass and took a drink. "But then, you knew it was a long shot. I told you that I am not experienced in this sort of work."

"So I have to find someone who can do… a special kind of magic on gemstones?"

"It isn't the magic that is special… just the expertise. I wouldn't want to experiment, get it wrong, maybe devalue the gems." He had another drink of his scotch. Reg picked up her own glass and had a sip of the cold water. It tasted horrible; she regretted not ordering a real drink.

"If you had more, I might suggest some experiments," Corvin said. "But as you have only a few gems to start with, I wouldn't recommend it. If you take a misstep, you could lose a large portion of your fortune." He said fortune with an ironic twist of his mouth that told her that the money she got from the gems would not be very much. But it didn't really matter how much one gem was worth. Not when she had as many as she did.

"What would you suggest?"

"There are more, then?" His tone of voice told her that he had already guessed that. Maybe from the gems themselves. Maybe Reg had given it away herself, not guarding her thoughts and feelings carefully enough. But it was impossible to shut Corvin out completely and she had stopped trying.

She shrugged. Let him think what he liked. She wasn't going to quantify it for him. He didn't need any more explanation.

"If it was me… I would try a few different… exercises. Try giving one away as a gift. Try giving one as payment for services, without cashing it in first. Maybe Sarah would take one by way of payment for your rent."

Reg shook her head. "How would that help anything?"

If it worked, it might relieve some of the financial pressure that she was under, but she couldn't pay for everything using gemstones. She would still have to be able to get cash for some of them. She couldn't use a diamond to pay for her groceries.

"I told you that the magic, the *curse* on these stones could be unpredictable. I can't tell, just holding them, what effect they might have on the owner," he gave a nod to Reg herself. "Or to your ability to traffic them. You may be able to give them away, so that the curse does not fall on the person you give it to. And if that works, then maybe they could gift a portion back to you, now cleansed, and keep a portion as payment for laundering the gems for you. If you are able to use them as payment, even better. You don't need to worry about getting money back for them, or getting the gems themselves back, because you are able to get something else of value."

Reg nodded. "I guess."

"It's an experiment. I don't know how these gems are going to behave."

Reg laughed. "You make them sound human."

"I have possessed many different gems and have found that their properties are extremely varied. They each seem to have their own... personality. A temperament that I can't really explain any other way. The races that traffic in gemstones regularly treat them as their children. As if they are sentient."

"Okay. So you don't know how they will behave." Reg shook her head in amusement. "Should I... give one to you? As the first experiment?"

His eyes glittered. "Are you giving it freely as a gift? Or are you expecting something in return?"

"Maybe as payment for you examining them for me," Reg suggested. "Services performed."

Corvin shook his head. "That was done as a friend. If you

muddy the waters, that will mess with the experiment. If you pay for something that I was not expecting payment for, then what is it?"

"Okay." Reg shrugged. She didn't care or see what difference it could make. "Then how about… as a gift. Can I give you one of them?"

He considered for a moment. Reg had expected him to jump at the chance to get one of them for himself. Corvin was nothing if not greedy. But maybe receiving the gift of a cursed gem was different. If Reg should not have accepted them from the fairies, then maybe Corvin should not accept them from her either. Even if she was giving them freely, not expecting anything from the transaction.

"All right," Corvin said eventually. "How about the sapphire?"

Reg tried not to show her surprise. "How did you know there was a sapphire?" He had never opened the bag and set eyes on them.

Corvin smiled. "I could tell."

Reg shook her head. She glanced around to see whether anyone was watching them or if the waitress was headed back over to refill their drinks. Reg had barely touched hers. She wished she had gone with her first impulse and ordered a glass of wine. She could have kept it to one glass. That wouldn't have been a problem, even dealing with Corvin's proximity.

No one appeared to be watching them. Reg loosened the strings of the bag and tipped it so that the gems fell close enough to the mouth to see which was which. She pressed her finger into the blue sapphire, and the moisture of her skin provided enough adhesion for her to lift her finger and turn it over, the sapphire sticking to it. She offered it to Corvin.

He put out his hand, palm up, to receive it. Reg transferred the gem to him, dropping the stone into his outstretched hand. He jumped and quickly tipped his hand to roll the sapphire off of it and onto the table. Reg looked at his face.

"What is it?"

"It's hot."

Reg did what any self-respecting child would do when told something was hot and reached out her finger to touch it herself. It was still cool to her touch.

She looked at Corvin, raising an eyebrow. "Seems fine to me."

Corvin put his hand over it for a moment, then touched it again, with just the tip of his finger. As before, he jerked back.

"Nope."

Reg studied it. So her first little gem had a hot temper. "We should try another one," she suggested.

Corvin shrugged and didn't agree or disagree. Reg picked the sapphire up and put it back into her bag. She gave the bag a little shake and the ruby came up close to the mouth. She picked it out, pinched between two fingers, and offered it to Corvin. He touched it, but this one did not seem to be too hot for him to handle. He put out his palm, and she again deposited a gem into it. Corvin held on to the ruby for a moment, as if waiting for it to do something. They both watched it carefully.

Reg felt a little silly. What were they waiting for? Did she think it was going to jump from his hand back into the bag? She'd accepted Corvin's description of their having feelings and desires a little too quickly. As a scholar and a professor, he should have been more objective about it. And she shouldn't have been so quick to buy into his description.

"There. That's better. So… how do we tell whether it is still C-U-R-E-D?"

"Cured?" Corvin said with a smile.

"No." Reg scowled, trying to picture the word in her mind to figure out how she'd screwed it up. Spelling—anything to do with reading and writing—was not her strong point. And spelling out loud required her full concentration as she tried to picture the word and sound it out at the same time as keeping track of which letter she had said and which came next. "*Cursed.* You know what I meant."

"Do yourself a favor and don't bother trying to spell in front of the stones. It isn't as if they understand what you are saying."

"How do you know? If they understand that they were stolen, or whatever it was that happened in the past, then how do we know they don't understand what we are saying? They could!"

Corvin shrugged. He studied the ruby, tilting his hand back and forth, catching it in the light. "It is a very pretty little jewel."

"Do you want a loupe?" Reg patted her pockets, then went to her purse. "I think I put it…" It took her a minute rummaging through the clutch purse she had brought with her, small though it was, to find the jeweler's loupe. She didn't like to think of how long it would have taken if she had her main shoulder bag with her. It was so full of stuff that she was afraid to dump it out and start inventorying it. Who knew what had been left there over the past months? It would be like an archaeological dig.

Corvin took the loupe from her, looking amused. Reg realized he wasn't trained in what to look for in a gem. Was there actually something she knew more about than he did?

"You're looking at the color, cut, and clarity," she told him. "Looking for any visible flaws, how rich and even the color is, how it catches the light."

Corvin adjusted the focal distance, squinting slightly, eventually settling on the best distance for him to examine the stone. He shrugged and handed back the loupe.

"That's really good ruby," Reg told him. "It should bring in a lot of money. If I can find someone to buy it. If we can cleanse it."

"I understand what you're trying to do."

"Okay, well… so what can you tell? Do we have to wait for something? Can you tell whether it is still cursed or not?"

He closed his eyes for a moment, then opened them and nodded. "Yes. Still is."

Reg swore. "I guess it couldn't be that easy, could it? What if you keep it for a while? Maybe you haven't really accepted it yet, because you are thinking of giving it back. How does the ruby know if you've accepted my gift or not?"

"I don't know if there are any particular rules or guidelines, why it works one time but not another. It isn't like a computer program or code. You can't be sure what will happen."

"Maybe you could talk to it."

"Talk to it?"

Reg nodded. "Tell it… that you like it. Take it home with you and find a special place for it and tell it that you're keeping it." Reg tried to think of what else might make the gem feel like it had been accepted by a new owner. What things had made her feel better about a family when she was in foster care? What things had made her feel more at home? "Tell it that you'll take care of it and protect it so that nothing bad happens to it again."

Corvin's eyes rested on Reg's face. She looked away, embarrassed, her face warming. Probably blushing brilliantly.

"I'm just trying to think of what might work," she said, trying to brush it off. "I've never had any gems before. I don't know how it all works."

"I think we're going to need to find an expert. I'll do like you said, and you can try some more experiments, but I think that you need someone who really knows what they are talking about."

CHAPTER FOURTEEN

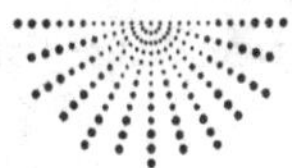

Reg was glad that she had brought her own car and that she hadn't had any wine, even though the water had been awful. She was still clear-headed at the end of her consultation with Corvin. It was not a date. She wasn't going anywhere with him afterward, regardless of the sad eyes he made at her when she refused. She was just going home. She could smell the roses as he attempted to talk her into it, and stood up.

"I've got to go home. Let me know if you make any progress with that ruby or find someone I can talk to about the gems."

"What's the hurry, Regina? You don't have anywhere to be tonight."

"It's been a long day,"

"Don't try that 'I'm tired and I'm going to bed as soon as I get home' crap with me."

Reg shrugged. "Would you rather hear the truth?"

He glared at her. Of course he knew why she wouldn't get into the car with him, wouldn't let him into the cottage, or go anywhere they were alone and he could try to overcome her resistance and steal her powers. Was it better to say that than that she wanted to go home because it had been a long day and they hadn't succeeded in figuring out how to cleanse the gems?

"You are strong enough to resist me," he pointed out. "You've done it enough times. So why do we have to keep up this charade of the helpless female? If you want your sex to be equal and respected, then why don't you drop the victim role?"

Reg's anger flared. Despite his challenge, Corvin leaned away from her, his eyes sharp and calculating. Things happened around Reg when she got really angry.

"Staying out of the tiger cage isn't playing a role," Reg snapped. "It's being smart."

He chuckled, a low, warm sound. "Comparing me with a cat? Not the most appropriate metaphor. Besides, don't you like to play with furry kitties? Come play in the tiger cage, Reg..." he wheedled.

Reg laughed and shook her head. "Not a chance."

She turned and walked away from him.

The air outside the dining room was more breathable. When Reg got into her car, she cranked the windows down and let the breeze blow in her face, even though it was a little chilly. When she got home, she was feeling awake and alert, and knew it would be a long time before she could get to sleep.

* * *

When she eventually went to bed, the sun was up over the horizon. She still didn't feel particularly tired, and tossed and turned trying to find a comfortable position and to get settled in for sleep. Starlight sat on the windowsill and watched her, meowing a couple of times that it was time for her to get out of bed and to feed him, even though it was much earlier than she ever got up. Cats really did seem to think that humans only existed to feed them and change their kitty litter. And maybe to play with them and groom them when they were in the mood.

Starlight watched her, ears pricked forward, knowing that she was thinking about cats. But when it didn't lead to her getting up to feed him, he eventually jumped down from the window and walked his rounds of the rest of the house.

She wished that Starlight could talk, and then immediately rescinded the wish. It would be much worse if he could order her around and tell her all his opinions of her. A person had to be careful what she wished for.

That was when she remembered.

It hadn't been that along ago, just at winter solstice. But so much had happened since then and Reg's brain *had* been inhabited by an evil entity during part of that time, which had made it almost impossible to access the memories she wanted when she wanted them. It was as if he had taken all the filing boxes that held her memories in neat, orderly sections and had dumped them all out on the floor and stirred them around. She didn't know how many memories might be gone forever, and how many of them she would be able to recover and eventually put back in order again. But until she could, she would have to put up with not being able to access them when she wanted to and having them surface at unexpected times.

But she had just remembered that Harrison had put in an appearance during their Yuletide celebration. Even though she had invited him, she hadn't expected her immortal godfather to show up, not being limited to a linear timeline like Reg.

And he had asked her what her wish was.

"My wish?"

"Is there not…" he made a twirling motion with his finger to indicate the Yule decorations and guests, "…a wish made for this observance?"

"Well… I don't know if there usually is or not." No one had mentioned making a wish, but Reg wasn't about to turn it down. "I wish… for safety for Starlight. And wealth. I could use a little extra money, just to make sure I have something to fall back on."

Fir had been kneeling down to talk to Starlight. He rose to his feet. "Be careful of thy wishes. You never know which ones will be granted."

Reg sat up in bed and stared at the closet. Not a very inspiring sight. But that wasn't really what she was looking at. She replayed the memory several times. She had wished for wealth. And it was after that she had received the gift of gems from the fairies. She hadn't connected the two incidents. There was nothing about the fairy gift that had made her think back to the spur-of-the-moment wish she had made at Yule.

"Harrison!"

She said his name out loud. Not really calling him or reprimanding him for what he had done, if he had been complicit somehow in the gems coming to her. But at the same time, she did want him to come to her and to reassure her that he'd had nothing to do with the gift.

If fairy gifts were dangerous, immortal wishes could be even more devastating. She had learned that from the experience of Vivian, a client she had tried to help.

Reg swung her feet over the side of the bed and got up. When Harrison came, he didn't always show up in the room that she expected him to. In fact, she should probably not even bother to call him from any room other than the kitchen, with his being so enamored with mortal food.

She didn't find him in the kitchen eating a chocolate cake or pizza that he had produced out of thin air. Reg breathed out slowly, not sure whether to be irritated or relieved. She wanted to talk to him, but she didn't want to at the same time. She didn't want to have to deal with the problem or to find out that again, it had been her own doing. Or that it had been partially her own fault for making a wish that had kicked off a series of events that ended up with her being burdened by a chest of cursed gems that she couldn't do anything with.

"If you do not want them, then do not wish them," Harrison said logically.

Reg turned toward the living room, where Harrison was sitting on the couch with his long legs stretched out on top of the coffee table. Starlight was in his lap. Of course.

Harrison's long, spindly legs were encased in black and white horizontally striped tights. On top, we wore a long-sleeved yellow shirt and a black vest bedazzled with jewels. He twirled the ends of his long thin mustache, smiling at her.

"Uncle Harrison!"

"You called?"

"No. Yes. I guess maybe I did."

"You did," he confirmed.

"Okay, well, I just didn't know whether I really wanted you to come or not."

He shook his head. "You should only ask for that which you really want."

"Probably. I'm worried that's what got me into the middle of this mess in the first place."

"Mess?" Harrison looked around the tidy room.

"Not that kind of mess. The kind of mess where I have a hoard of cursed gems."

"Ahh." Harrison nodded sagely. "That mess."

"Is this because… did I get those gems because I wished for wealth? Is that the way that you granted my wish?"

He considered this thoughtfully. And Reg really knew better than to ask him questions, because he never gave her a straight answer when she did, and she always ended up more confused than she was when she started.

"Perhaps," Harrison said eventually. Which was more definitive than many of his answers.

"But I wanted wealth that I could use. So that I could pay my expenses. There is no point in having a bunch of jewels that I can't do anything with."

He nodded. "That is a problem."

"Then why did you do that? Why not give me money that I can use? Just drop it into my bank account or give me gold. Or jewels that I can actually use."

He waved his hand as if it were of no consequence. "That is not what happened."

"No, it isn't," Reg agreed dryly. "But that's what I want."

"Perhaps when you make your next wish. Is it your birthday?"

"No, it's not my birthday or any other wishing day. And I don't think I'll be making any other wishes, because who knows how they might be fulfilled."

"Yes."

"If you knew what I wanted, then why couldn't you give it to me? Is there some rule in the universe that you can never give me what I really want?"

Harrison petted Starlight with long, slow strokes. "Why do you not wish for what you really need?"

"I did! But you didn't give me what I needed. You gave me cursed gemstones."

"No, I did not. The fairy folk did."

"I know that's who they came from, but it was because of you. Because of the wish that I made. Isn't it?"

He twirled his mustache. "The universe," he said thoughtfully.

"What about the universe?"

"Are there rules? In your universe?"

"Well… yes. *You* have rules you have to follow, don't you?"

She knew that there were rules governing some of the immortals' behavior. A rule that they weren't supposed to do anything to harm another of their kind, which seemed to Reg to be ignored more often than it was followed. And a rule that they were not supposed to procreate with mortals. Ditto. They clearly didn't obey that one either. Were there rules about what wishes they could grant? Or how they were allowed to grant them?

"There are rules among my kind," Harrison confirmed.

"Rules about granting wishes?"

"Oh, yes."

"Like that I can't ever get what I wished for?"

He blinked at her. For a moment, he looked away from her, lavishing attention on Starlight, scratching his ears and jaw.

"You did get what you wished for."

"No, I didn't."

He shook his head.

"Maybe you should try again," Reg suggested. "You can take the gems back and give me cash instead. Cash that isn't cursed. I don't care if it's in my bank account or in hard currency. Just as long as I can spend it."

"Humans are very short-sighted."

Reg closed her mouth and considered that for a moment. Harrison was not constrained by the same natural laws as she was. He could travel back to the past, and she assumed to the future too. He could go anywhere and make things happen as he pleased. Was he saying that humans were short-sighted in general, or was he referring specifically to her insistence that she needed cold, hard cash? Was something going to happen in the future that would render the money useless, and there would be something else she wished she had asked for instead?

"What do you mean by that?"

Harrison raised one eyebrow. "They cannot see very far. Only what is in front of their own faces."

"I know what short-sighted means."

He shrugged. If she knew, then why had she asked?

"I mean... why did you say it now? Is there something that I'm being short-sighted about?"

"Yes."

"About the money?"

His head tilted to the side. *Maybe yes, maybe no.*

"Why am I being short-sighted?" Reg tried.

"It is only human. You can't help it."

"Can you tell me what's going to happen? What it is you think I am being short-sighted about right now?"

But she should have known that there was no way to pin an immortal down and get a straight answer. Even when it was a clear answer, it wasn't the one she wanted.

"Yes."

Reg waited. Harrison shifted Starlight from his lap to the couch beside him. And then he vanished.

CHAPTER FIFTEEN

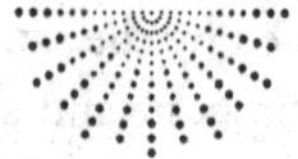

"Argh!"

Reg looked around for something to throw. She was still standing near the kitchen island, and she grabbed a spoon and fired it across the room in the direction of the couch. Starlight jumped down from the couch and crouched down, looking at her with his ears back.

"I unwish it!" Reg shouted. "Do you hear me, Harrison? I take it back; I don't want the gems anymore. You can take them away and give them to someone else!"

But she knew what he had said in the past. There was no unwishing. She couldn't change what she had wished for, get him to change things back to the way they had been. Even though he had returned to the past before and changed this around. If he could do that for his own reasons, why couldn't he do it for her? Just run back in time, and when she was about to voice her wish about wealth, warn her that she didn't want to make a wish like that and get her to wish for something less controversial. A wish that an immortal couldn't screw up.

If there was such a thing.

"Stupid immortals!" Reg growled. She knew she wouldn't be

able to get to sleep, so she started tidying up the kitchen to burn off her angry energy. Maybe it was time for her to start behaving like an adult with adult responsibilities instead of sitting around feeling sorry for herself because a box full of gems weren't going to change her life. Why would they? How often had she heard that money wasn't the solution to life's problems?

She had never believed it, but she'd heard it enough times.

When a person was barely scraping by, having trouble just getting enough food to subsist on, there was no point in saying that money wouldn't solve her problems. When eating was the problem, money was definitely a solution.

But she wasn't in that situation. Not again. Not yet. She had a place to live that was warm and safe and there was a friend nearby to keep an eye on things and to give her advice or other help when she needed it. She had all the food she really needed, between the little that she had stocked herself and the various leftovers and other bits that Sarah brought over from time to time. Really, despite her low bank account, it was the wealthiest she had ever been, even without the jewels.

By the time she burned out her anger, the kitchen was spick-and-span. Sarah would be impressed.

* * *

It was a while before Starlight was on speaking terms with Reg again. He didn't like her shouting and throwing things around. And she could understand that. She had never liked it when she had lived in homes where people shouted and threw things either. She knew better and shouldn't have let her anger and frustration get the better of her.

But eventually, with Reg sitting sideways on the couch with her feet up, browsing through funny YouTube clips on her phone, Starlight decided to forgive her. He jumped up onto the couch and curled up in her lap, purring away as if he were perfectly contented. Reg vowed to herself that she would never throw something in his direction again. He hadn't done anything wrong. And even if he had, that wouldn't excuse throwing cutlery at him.

There was a knock on the door.

Reg sat up, surprised. Starlight looked toward the door, his ears pointing directly at it, listening intently. Was it a client? Reg looked down at herself. She was still dressed in her pajamas. It wasn't as if they were indecent or even revealing, but it was obvious from the style and fabric and the muted colors that it was her pajamas. She had been up for several hours; why hadn't she bothered to change?

She hadn't been expecting company.

There was another knock followed by the chime of the doorbell. Reg put Starlight gently to the side and got up. She left the chain on and opened the door a crack to see who it was. Best not to open it all the way in case it was a witch who intended her harm, or Corvin, or someone else she didn't want to let into the house. They shouldn't be able to get into the yard if they had evil intentions toward her, but Reg had seen too many magical loopholes to trust that the wards set to protect her would do it flawlessly and continue to work forever. Mortals made mistakes. All mortals, including Sarah.

She peeked through the narrow opening at a woman with long, spiraling blond hair and an all-black cat in her arms.

"Oh! Francesca!" Reg shut the door to slide the chain and opened it up to allow Francesca and Nicole in. Nicole pronounced in Francesca's beautiful Haitian accent, of course, as NEE-cole. "Was that today? I totally lost track of time!"

"Yes, today," Francesca agreed in a clipped voice. "You put it in your phone. You said you would put it on your client calendar so that you would not forget." She nodded to the date book that lived on Reg's kitchen island, where she and Sarah both wrote down any client appointments they made for psychic services. Of course, it had been completely blank lately and Reg hadn't opened it, even if she had written it down.

Francesca bent over as she let go of Nicole, so that Nicole and Starlight could play together. The two cats touched noses and rubbed against each other, purring and chirping greetings. Reg couldn't help laughing at their joy over seeing each other. It had been a long time since their last play date.

"Come on in, have a seat," Reg invited, motioning to the couch. "I'll put on the kettle."

Francesca obeyed, alighting gracefully on the couch and watching the two cats until they retreated to the back rooms of the house for some privacy.

"Nicole is very happy to see Starlight," she observed.

"Yes. I forgot how much fun it is to get the two of them together. After all the hassle with the kittens, it's nice to have just the two of them again."

Francesca nodded.

"How is Nicole doing? Does she miss them?"

"She does sometimes, I think… but she is also happy to be on her own again. It is not easy suddenly being the mama of nine kattakyns!"

The kittens were not actually Nicole's. Rather than being normal kittens, they were draugar—a sort of a zombie creature— that had transformed into cats and had been charmed and locked into that form by Francesca as part of their efforts to defeat Samyr Destine, one of the immortals, also known as The Witch Doctor. After binding his essence to the kattakyns, Francesca had found new homes for the kittens around the world, distributing them as far apart as possible, to prevent the immortal from re-forming. As long as Destine was bound, the world was safe from his evil.

"I'm sure she's probably happy to be able to get a good sleep," Reg agreed. "It must be murder trying to get enough rest with nine kittens to look after. Especially when one of them is Nico."

Reg had a special place in her heart for Nico, who had been very difficult to manage. Reg could relate to the poor guy and had fostered him for a short time when he became too much for Francesca. Reg was happy that she had found a place for him in the dwarf mountain, where he was revered as a warrior cat instead of constantly being yelled at for climbing the curtains and knocking over vases.

"That little fellow was a challenge," Francesca agreed, rolling her eyes.

Reg busied herself with getting the tea tray together while she waited for the kettle to whistle. "Any preferences for your tea today?"

"Maybe something citrus?" Francesca suggested.

Reg nodded and got out a couple of lemon or orange teas to add to the tray. Though Francesca was a charmer rather than a psychic and could not read tea leaves, she still preferred the loose-leaf tea. Reg made sure that there was plenty of honey for her own tea. While she regularly drank tea with Francesca or her clients, Reg had a sweet tooth and found the teas more palatable with a significant amount of sugar.

The kettle whistled. Reg poured the hot water into the teapot and took the tray over to the coffee table, where she set it down. She sat on one of the wicker chairs and, after preparing her cup of tea, tucked her feet up on the seat beside her to get comfortable.

"You know, I really appreciate that you still bring Nicole here to visit with Starlight. After... everything that has happened... there are a lot of practitioners who won't have anything to do with me anymore."

If she were perfectly honest, Reg would have to admit that she was fishing for reassurance. She wanted to hear Francesca say that Reg was the same person she had always been, and Francesca trusted her completely. That her possible parentage did not make a bit of difference.

Francesca stirred her tea thoughtfully for a few moments, appearing to give it all of her attention. But Reg could tell that she wasn't thinking about tea. Or about the cats.

"Life... is very complicated," Francesca said finally. "As much as you would like everything to be black and white, it is not." Her lilting accent took a bit of the sting out of the fact that she had not said that she liked or trusted Reg and would never let anyone sway her opinion of her friend. "You are a friend. You have done nothing to harm me. I have not seen any of this... worrisome behavior. If ever I do... I will judge by what I see."

"You know what kind of a person I am," Reg asserted, hoping for a stronger message of support.

"I think I know."

Francesca wasn't going to go any further than that. And if Reg kept pressing her, she would probably be disappointed when Francesca was forced to admit that no, she didn't trust Reg and could no longer be so sure that she was a friend or would remain one. And Reg didn't want to hear that.

"So... have you heard from any of the kattakyns' owners? How they are settling in?"

Francesca nodded and took a sip of her tea. "Yes, I occasionally hear from them. The ones who don't call me, I like to reach out to now and then just to make sure that everything is going well and that... they haven't decided to give the kittens away to someone else. That could be disastrous."

Reg nodded. While the kattakyns could not exercise all the magic that the Witch Doctor had once held, much of which had now been transferred to Corvin, they each did have a part of him. And if that power ended up in the wrong hands...

Reg didn't like to think about what could happen. That was why they had been so careful to hand pick the kattakyns' human companions.

"But they haven't, right? The kittens are still in the homes we placed them in?"

It had really been Francesca's project, but Reg had helped out a bit. As much as she was able. And she was the one who had found Nico a home. Nico had been the most difficult.

"So far, they are all where they should be." Francesca took another drink and licked her lips. "I am concerned, though..."

"Not about Nico…?"

"Not Nico in particular." Francesca pressed her lips together, trying to decide what to tell Reg and what to hold back. "It is… the immortal that is of concern."

CHAPTER SIXTEEN

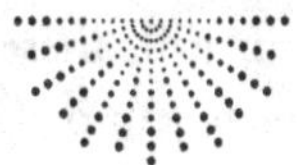

"The immortal?" Reg asked, a sinking feeling in her stomach. "Which one?"

She hoped that it was someone other than Harrison or Weston. An immortal she had never heard of before. Someone less closely connected with her. She didn't like the idea of there being even more immortals around poking their noses into human business, she really didn't want to deal with the news that Harrison or Weston were, once again, causing chaos.

"You know which one," Francesca said darkly. "Your Harrison."

"Harrison?" Reg grimaced. She held herself back from protesting that he wasn't *her* Harrison. She didn't have any control over him. She didn't own him. She barely had any influence over him. But he was her Uncle Harrison. Her immortal godfather. She couldn't completely disclaim any relationship with him. "What has he done now?"

Francesca shook her head grimly. "He has been to visit several of the kittens."

"Several of them?" Reg echoed in dismay. She searched for a reasonable explanation. "But just visiting… that's not dangerous, is it? He couldn't do anything…"

"You do not know the power these immortals have. *I* do not know the power the immortals have, and I have been close to them. Too close to them. It is not good. I fear for what he could do."

"He doesn't want The Witch Doctor to re-form," Reg pointed out. "He knows that evil, the problems that were caused by Destine trying to gather so much power to him."

"They do not believe in evil, these immortals. They do not understand it the same way as you or I. To them… these are just games they are playing. Poking a stick into an anthill and watching all the little creatures scurrying around in panic. Is someone who pokes an anthill evil?"

"Well… to the ants, I guess."

Francesca nodded. "To the ants. But not to themselves. They see no harm in it. Humans to them are just pests. Little, scurrying pests that have overpopulated the world that the immortals once claimed as their own. They do not care whether the Witch Doctor remains bound. Harrison is probably bored. Looking for a new playmate."

Reg shook her head slowly. "I'll talk to him. I'll tell him that he can't do anything to free Destine. He'll listen to me."

"Will he?" Francesca raised one brow skeptically. "This… I do not know."

"But he can't. I'll talk to him. I'll explain it. He'll listen."

Francesca shrugged. She sipped her tea. "If you would do that, perhaps there is a chance. Otherwise… there is nothing we can do. We cannot hide the kattakyns from him. We cannot stop him from gathering them and allowing the Witch Doctor his freedom. It is very bad."

Reg did not like hearing "very bad" from Francesca. The battle against the Witch Doctor had been hard won. Francesca had assured them that there would be no way for Destine to form again for another thousand years. But if another immortal aided him, bringing the kattakyns back together and releasing him from his prison…

They had enough to worry about with Weston being free. And Harrison, for that matter. Even when he was trying to help Reg, he was just as likely to screw it up and make things worse for her or her friends. Even when he granted Reg's wish, it ended up coming back to bite her in the butt. Suddenly, instead of being wealthy, she had a bunch of cursed gems she couldn't get rid of or cash in on. A responsibility that she had never wanted.

"Hey, I have something for you," she told Francesca, thinking about the gems.

"Something for me?" Francesca gave a little smile, surprised by the segue, curious as to what it was. Reg had never given her a gift before. They didn't normally have that kind of a friendship. They talked on the phone. Rehomed kittens. Brought the adult cats on play dates.

"Yes. Just wait here for a minute."

Reg went to her bedroom, where she found the two cats together on the bed, cuddled up and grooming each other.

"Don't do anything I wouldn't do!" Reg told them with a laugh.

She found the skirt she had worn the previous day on the floor and searched through the folds for a few minutes before finding the little bag of gems in one of the pockets. Had she become so careless about the gems that she would just leave them in a pile of clothes on the floor?

She remembered that she had, in fact, nearly forgotten them under the bed when she had left Black Sands in a hurry to avoid trouble. How could someone forget something so priceless? She hadn't even known back then about their being cursed. She had thought they would be easy to sell, that she would be able to live off of them for the rest of her life.

Reg opened the bag and shook it until one of the gems tumbled into her waiting palm. An emerald. A beautifully cut teardrop shape. It would look lovely in a pendant on a necklace. It was nothing like Sarah's emerald, of course, but it was still beautiful and would bring in a good amount of money if it weren't cursed.

She took it back out to the living room, and handed it to Francesca, keeping her movements as casual as possible. As if she gave her friends expensive gemstones all the time.

Francesca looked down at the stone in her hand. "Why, this is lovely, Regina. Where did you get it?"

Reg didn't tell her where. "I wanted you to have it," she said. "You've been such a good friend to me. I came into... I inherited... received several stones, and I thought you would like that one."

"Oh, I could not accept it," Francesca said, trying to hand it back. "This is yours. If it is real, it must be very valuable. I couldn't take something like that from you."

"I want you to have it."

"Really... I have nothing to give you in return."

"I don't expect anything in return. I just want to share with my friends."

"I don't know..."

"I was thinking it would look nice on a necklace. Don't you think so?"

Francesca played with it in her hand. "Well, yes. It is very pretty."

"I think it would look really good on you," Reg said. "It complements your eyes." She was using all the con skills that she had learned over the years. Putting it into Francesca's hand. Making her imagine how she would use it, how it would make her look and feel beautiful. Few people could turn you down once they had held the product in their hands and imagined how they would use it.

But she saw Francesca's shoulders square and heard her take a deep, bracing breath. She held it out to give it back to Reg. "No. I cannot accept this."

Reg didn't put her hand out to take it back. They looked at each other. Eventually, Francesca placed the emerald on the tea tray in front of her. She would not accept it. Somehow, she had known or felt what Reg had not, that accepting the gem as a gift would not be a good idea. It would not end well.

Reg shook her head. She was the psychic. Shouldn't she have had a feeling about the gems? If it was unwise to accept gifts from fairies or to make wishes, then why hadn't she sensed that? When she held the gems in her hand, why didn't she feel a sense of foreboding, a knowledge that they were cursed and that they would not bring her the wealth and security that she desired?

It had been the same with the key that had released Weston from his self-imposed prison. Even though Forst had warned her that it was a dark key, she had felt attracted to it. She had known that she wanted to possess it, even when it had been dirty and corroded. She should have felt something from it other than attraction. The knowledge that it didn't open the door to a great treasure, but to an immortal who could affect the course of her life if she released him.

But when she'd held the key, she had known that she was destined to use it, to match the key to the lock that it would eventually open.

And when she held the gems in her hand, she felt their power and potential, not an evil force or the dark cloud of a curse over her life.

What did that say about her nature?

"What is it?" Francesca asked, drawing Reg away from her contemplation. "I am sorry if I have insulted you. But it is not wise to accept such things."

"To accept what things?" Reg probed. Gems? Cursed objects? What did Francesca sense when she held the emerald in her hand?

"To accept gifts of such value without having earned them." Francesca shook her head. "It is not wise," she repeated.

If it sounds too good to be true, it probably is. Reg heard her foster mother's words in her head once more. Words that she should have heard when the gift from the fairies had first arrived. She had known that it was too much, even for having saved

Calliopia's life. It was a king's ransom, and Calliopia was only an adolescent fairy from a household that, as far as Reg knew, was not of royal lineage. Reg had explained it away to herself. She'd told herself that it had not been worth that much to the Papillons. Fairies owned a lot of jewels, and as a product that was not scarce to them, it was of less value. It was valuable to her as a human because humans did not have such hoards.

Reg sighed again.

It wouldn't be as easy to give the jewels to others as gifts as she had hoped. Not if everyone were as savvy as Francesca.

CHAPTER SEVENTEEN

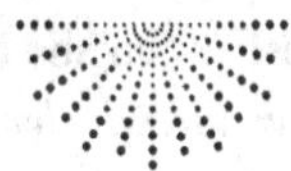

After Francesca and Nicole had gone home, Reg went for a walk in the garden. It was an enchanted place, the plants practically vibrating with magic and vitality. Sarah had been right when she had said that a garden gnome would be able to do a much better job with the garden than any human could. Forst had turned a broken, desolate wreck into a paradise.

She stooped to smell a flower, then continued to walk, keeping an eye out for the little red-capped old man who seemed to be able to blend in with the plants and the dirt in a way that should have been impossible. She wondered sometimes if he could actually enter into the plants or the soil he tended and become part of their structure. There was definitely magic at work there that she couldn't fathom.

Reg sat down on the stone bench that was surrounded by heady blooms in a riot of colors, buzzing bees, and fluttering butterflies. She closed her eyes and breathed in the sweetly scented breeze. She could smell not just the flowers, but the green of the leaves and the moist soil they sprang from. She felt as if she could almost drink the smells, they were so rich.

Reg Rawlins is welcome here.

Reg opened her eyes and smiled at the little gnome in front of her. While his words might have startled her if they were said out loud, she was not surprised at hearing them inside her head.

Good morning, Forst.

It is early for Reg Rawlins to be enjoying the garden.

It is, Reg acknowledged. Forst, like many others, probably thought her a slob for sleeping so late most days. But that was just the schedule that her body preferred, and a schedule that allowed her to do late-night seances. When she actually had clients calling her. *Would you believe I've already had company today? I don't think I actually got to sleep last night.*

Take care of thyself, he warned solemnly, pulling out his curved pipe and filling it with tobacco. *You have but one lifetime in this body.*

I know. It wasn't on purpose, believe me.

Something is on your mind?

Reg nodded. *Lots of somethings. I wish that I understood the magical world better. It seems like I am always getting myself into trouble one way or another.*

You cannot fight your nature. He lit the pipe and took a few puffs. The comforting smell of the tobacco merged with the other smells in the air. *The many great things you have done would not be without the choices you have made.*

Reg laughed. *The many great things?*

He looked at her, gaze unwavering. Reg was the first to look away. She knew that Forst and others believed she had greater powers than she did. She had skated through some of her more difficult adventures, surviving just by the skin of her teeth and a few happy coincidences or a bit of quick-thinking and deception on her part. She was not nearly as powerful or smart as he thought. But as she had once helped Forst's twin, Fir, when he had been in police custody, he revered her. It was something that any other human could have done just as easily, not actually requiring any magic, only a familiarity with the legal system and human nature, but she was the one who had stepped forward to help, so she had earned Forst's loyalty.

Reg put her hands down beside her on the bench as she leaned back, turning her face up toward the sun. As a redhead, she couldn't spend much time worshiping the sun, but the warmth on her skin did lift her mood.

There was a sharp bit of gravel on the bench under one hand, and Reg drew up her hand to brush it away. She frowned, looking down at the red stone that had embedded itself into her palm. A ruby.

Where did this come from? Reg demanded.

Forst chuckled as he drew on his pipe. *I found it as I was working this morning, dropped on the pathway. I knew it must be thine, so I left it here for you to find it. Or for it to find you.* His eyes twinkled.

How did you know it was mine? Reg asked, staring at the ruby. It was, she was sure, the same one she had given Corvin the night before. How had it found its way back into her yard?

Forst shrugged. *Sarah would not have dropped it back here. She uses the front sidewalk to get to her car and would not bring an unset gem into the back yard.*

Well, she could, Reg countered.

Is it not thy stone?

Yes. I mean. It was. I gave it away, which is why I don't understand how it could be here. What's going on?

I know not, it has not told me its story. He smiled and blew a couple of smoke rings. Reg watched them drift up into the sky, expanding and breaking apart.

I gave it to Corvin. Reg looked around, as if he might be hiding in some shadow of the garden. But she knew he couldn't get into the yard and, if he were there, she would be able to feel his presence. He couldn't get close to her without her knowing it. *It doesn't make any sense.*

You give gifts to the power drinker? Forst's bushy brows drew down and he shook his head. *You should not have anything to do with that one.*

I am careful. We were not alone. Reg paused, thinking about it. *Is there a reason I should not give him something? I don't understand all the magical rules. It doesn't… I haven't entered into some kind of contract by giving him a gift?*

Accepting the gift of the fairies had been a mistake; was the same true of giving a gift? Especially to someone like Corvin? He had argued in the past that she had given her permission for the liberties he had taken, and she didn't want to think that her gift to him might mean that they were now engaged or had made some other kind of agreement.

They are cunning, his kind. You don't want to get too comfortable around him, thinking that he is just another human, another warlock. Forst shook his head. *Encouraging his interest in you is very unwise. You have shown him too much courtesy in the past.*

But you don't think that I did something wrong. That I contracted with him for my firstborn child or anything.

Forst stroked his beard and shook his head. *No, no. He is not a fairy.*

Having had some dealing with the fairies about changelings before, Reg had an idea of what Forst was talking about. The fairies did not reproduce quickly enough to support their population, and so they found ways to get the babies of other species and turn them into fairies through their magic. Calliopia had been one such child.

How did the ruby get back here? Corvin couldn't get into the yard. The wards keep him out. Reg looked around her, reaching out all of her senses to make sure the barriers were still there and had not been broken. Everything seemed warm and safe and protected.

Perhaps he sent another. Or perhaps it was taken from him without his knowledge. Or he lost it somewhere else, and it made its way back here.

Reg laughed. *It doesn't have legs,* she pointed out. *Or movement or will of its own. So how would it get back here by itself?*

Not by itself. But make no mistake, such a stone can have a will. Forst gazed at the stone, nodding sagely. *Many humans believe only what their eyes can see and ears can hear, but you are not one of those people, Reg Rawlins. Use your other senses and do not be deceived.*

Reg wasn't sure she would ever get used to the magical world. Gems that could make up their minds and transport themselves from one place to another? It didn't make any sense. Not logically.

But the magical world frequently defied her logic.

CHAPTER EIGHTEEN

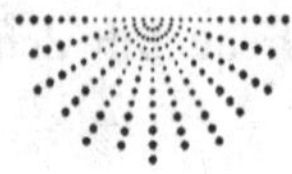

*R*eg had another cup of coffee before calling Corvin. She wasn't sure how to begin a conversation with him about the delinquent ruby. It seemed silly to be calling him to ask whether he had the ruby. If it was the same ruby, how it had ended up in her possession again?

By the time she reached the bottom of her coffee mug, her phone was ringing, and Corvin's face was on the screen. Reg put her empty cup on the coffee table, pulled her feet up on the couch, and answered the call.

"Corvin."

"Regina. I trust you slept well."

"No. I don't think I got a wink of sleep. What about you? Were you up wandering all night?"

Corvin cleared his throat and Reg waited for his explanation. "No… I was not wandering. I returned home."

"Really? You went directly home? And didn't go anywhere else?"

Corvin was slow to answer. They shared enough that he probably knew that lying to her wasn't going to work. "No. Not directly home. Why?"

"Because strange things are happening, and I don't know how

you are involved."

"Strange things? Do tell. What sort of strange things?"

"Have you had any luck with that ruby? Figuring out how to remove the curse?"

"No. I haven't spent any time on it yet. These things take time, and I will need to do a considerable amount of research to come up with some ideas."

"And you will need the ruby."

He was silent for a few beats, then cleared his throat. "Yes, of course."

"And you don't, do you?"

"I don't what?"

"You're as good as Harrison at not answering questions properly. You don't have the ruby anymore."

"What makes you think that?"

"Because I do."

"How did you get the ruby back?" His tone was sharp, as if she had done something wrong. All Reg had done was go out to her garden for a stroll and found the ruby there.

"It was in my yard. Were you here? Before you went home last night? Did you come by to make sure that I was safe and settled for the night?" She offered a reason for him to have been by, the type of excuse that he often gave her.

"No. I wasn't in your yard."

"Not in the back yard, no. But I wonder if you were in the front. Or maybe stopped to visit Sarah. Or just pulled over for a few minutes to… check your email."

"I wasn't there," Corvin growled. "Not at all!"

"Where did you go, then? Because despite appearances, I'm sure this ruby couldn't get all the way back to me all on its own."

"Cursed gems," Corvin muttered. "You never know what they will do. I warned you about that. Don't know what I was doing, taking it from you in the first place."

"How did you lose it, then?"

"I don't know. A pickpocket?" He considered. Reg could feel

his seething beneath the surface. "I stopped for a drink. Talked to… a couple of people. Maybe somebody managed to take it off me. Or it fell out of my pocket." As if anticipating her skepticism, he repeated, "You don't know what a cursed gem will do. You may think you've got deep pockets, or it is locked away safely, but if it has other ideas…"

"I don't quite buy the idea that a stone could have a mind of its own."

"When you've lived a few centuries, maybe you won't be so naive. I would think that from what you have seen of the paranormal world so far that you wouldn't be quite so quick to declare what is possible and what is not."

"So someone just happened to guess that you had a ruby in your pocket and lifted it. Or you dropped it. And then what? It sprouted legs and walked to my house? Jumped out of the next person's pocket all on its own? What?"

"I don't know how, and I wouldn't want to say. Somehow… maybe it fell on the ground and a bird picked it up. Or another creature that likes sparkly things or was attracted to its power. I told you that cursed gems are unpredictable. And they are not quite as easy to rid yourself of as you would like to think."

Reg thought about it. It wasn't exactly as though she was worried about having the gems in her possession. It was irritating and inconvenient if she couldn't liquidate them somehow, but she didn't see the harm in simply possessing them. Despite everything that Harrison and Sarah had said so far, nothing really bad had happened to her. She hadn't had the best of luck recently, but when had she? After the life she had led so far, Reg didn't expect things to be easy.

"Okay," she sighed. "I guess that experiment is finished, then. I can't give the jewels away. But that was never really what I wanted to do anyway. I was hoping that after I gave them away, they would be clean, and I could work out some kind of deal to still make money off of them. But if that doesn't work… then it doesn't work."

"I think… you're taking the matter all too lightly," Corvin warned. "You seem to think that you can keep holding on to the gems forever. That you won't suffer any harm or setbacks because of them."

"Well, I've been okay so far. Nothing *terrible* has happened."

Just minor things. Like being poisoned by a serial killer. Being kidnapped by a swamp goblin. Being investigated by the magical equivalent of the FBI. Fighting sirens. Being made an outcast. And being possessed by an evil wizard. Minor stuff.

Reg sat there thinking about it. Of course, she couldn't attribute any of those things to owning the gems. It had all seemed like a natural progression from the things that had happened to her before she had been given the gems. It wasn't as if she'd been living a charmed life before that.

"Reg, just because nothing terrible has happened, that doesn't mean that it won't. Have you read any of the accounts of what has happened to people who have possessed cursed stones in the past?"

"Well, no." Reading wasn't Reg's thing, and even if it had been, what reason would she have to study up on cursed gems?

"We're not talking about minor inconveniences," Corvin explained. "The owner or their families getting killed, the gems stolen in bloody wars, plagues and sicknesses. Financial ruin."

"I don't have any family, money, or a kingdom," Reg pointed out. "I could get sick or die, but… what are the chances of that?"

"Pretty good, I'm thinking. These gems you are in possession of are a pretty powerful source. You may only have a small number, but it isn't really the quantity that makes the difference." It was probably a good thing he didn't know that she had a whole chest of them. "But think about the fairies you got them from. I assume it was Calliopia's family?"

Reg made a noncommittal noise.

"What happened to them? Their daughter was kidnapped. When she was returned, she ran away. And then she was mortally wounded. If it weren't for you, she would have died. It was a near thing."

"Then why did they give them to me? I was the one who saved their daughter. Why would they reward me by dumping a cursed treasure on me?"

"You're thinking in human terms. I told you before, the fairies don't think that way. They think about themselves. How they can get the best deal out of every transaction. If they could get rid of cursed gems by giving them to you, why wouldn't they? Humans like gems, you clearly don't know a lot about their world, hopefully you would take them."

Reg rested her forehead on her knees. "So I can't use the gems. I can't give them away. And I can't keep them. Does that about sum it up?"

CHAPTER NINETEEN

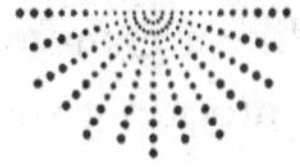

Reg worked out a new plan.

She went to a thrift store she had previously been to in Black Sands. There were not many places that sold clothing and accessories at reasonable prices, and she didn't have much capital. She would use the last of her cash, and then she would have to rely on her credit cards. She knew from experience they wouldn't last long and the fees would add up quickly.

But if she couldn't use the gems, and the curse on them had resulted in the loss of her clientele, then she wouldn't be able to raise any new capital without first ridding herself of them. So she had to spend money to make money, eventually.

The woman at the register looked at the pile of wallets and purses that Reg had placed there, bemused.

"Are you… having some kind of theme party?" she guessed.

Reg nodded, smiling pleasantly. "Yes, exactly, how did you guess?"

The cashier wanted to ask her more questions about it, but since she was the one who had suggested it was a theme party, she couldn't then claim that she didn't know what someone would do at such a party.

"Oh, that sounds like a lot of fun!"

"If it all works out, it will put a smile on my face," Reg confirmed.

The woman began to scan the items through. Reg watched the numbers carefully, pointing out if one of them was supposed to be reduced or had a broken clasp or some other reason she could ask for it at a lower price. Eventually, they were all tallied up, and Reg counted out every penny like a grandma on a fixed income. The cashier put all the purses into a big shopping bag and Reg took them home.

There, Reg went to work filling the purses with bits of paper and items from the junk drawer, as well as a small handful of gems in each. With a determined smile on her face, she drove around town, stopping every few minutes to leave a purse or wallet in a strategic area, somewhere it would look natural, as if someone had dropped it or left it behind by accident. Places that were sheltered enough that whoever found it could be assured they could walk away without anyone observing them.

The whole process from start to finish took most of the day. Or at least, until she was ready for supper. The whole venture had given her an appetite, and she was smiling as she sat down for a fish fillet Sarah had left her.

Starlight meowed around her feet, begging for his portion, and Reg put a piece of the fish patty in his bowl for him. With a sigh of satisfaction at having rid herself of the jewels, Reg checking her social networks on her phone.

She had barely started to scroll down when she saw a couple of FOUND notices, with pictures of the purses she had left behind. She shook her head in disbelief and kept scrolling. The good Samaritans could look for her all they liked, and then they could keep the cursed gems. What else could they do?

Hopefully, most of them did not have the special powers they needed to recognize the gems as cursed and would just be thanking their lucky stars that they had made such a find. Or maybe they would think that the gems were fake, because no one would leave such a precious possession on the ground like that. They would end up in the garbage, glued to a child's paper craft, sewn into a glamorous outfit, or glued into a cheap jewelry setting for dress-up. Reg took great satisfaction in the thought.

She was most of the way through the fish when she started getting instant messages and emails. Surveillance camera pictures of her dropping the wallets, or photos of the receipts and bits of paper that she had left in the wallets, with questions like "Is this you?" and "Is this your wallet?"

Reg didn't answer them, but the pictures and inquiries tumbled through her head. How had people identified her so fast? Had all the wallets been found by private investigators? People who somehow managed to trace them back to her name or social media? It was unbelievable that they could identify her so quickly from a grainy photo or faded receipt from three months before. It shouldn't be possible. She had assumed when she had been dropping them that it would not be possible.

She shook her head. Let people pursue her. They couldn't force her to take the wallets back. And if she didn't take them back, they would bear the responsibility of ownership of the gems or would have to find another way to get rid of them. It was out of her hands.

* * *

A couple of hours passed before her phone started ringing. Reg looked at the phone number. A number that she didn't know. And then another. Then a blocked number. Reg rolled her eyes. Too bad. She wouldn't answer the calls. There was no way she was taking those gems back.

Half an hour passed without the phone ringing, and Reg just started to settle into a show on the TV. Her phone buzzed again, and she looked at it reluctantly. Marta Jessup.

That would be Detective Marta Jessup.

Reg wasn't sure whether to answer it at all. Jessup might just be calling to see whether they could get together sometime. They had enjoyed a few girls' nights out, but Reg was rather irritated with having been hauled in for questioning on a murder recently. Jessup hadn't exactly extended her any courtesies for being her friend.

But if she ignored Jessup's call, then likely the next step would be finding the woman on her doorstep, inquiring to see whether she was okay.

And she did not want that. The only way to get rid of her was probably to talk to her, tell her that she was too busy to get together, and set up something indefinite in the future. If Jessup insisted on a date, then Reg would call back and break it in a day or two.

Reg swiped the screen. "Hello?"

"Reg! Good to hear your voice!"

"Yeah. You too. Are you off tonight?"

"Actually…. no. I'm on duty."

"Oh, we'd better make it quick, then." Reg couldn't exactly say "I've kept you long enough" and hang up when it was Jessup who had called her, and she hadn't said what she wanted yet. But Reg wanted to signal her that she wanted to get off the phone quickly.

"What's going on tonight, Reg?"

"Uh… I don't know. Just watching a new series."

"I'm not talking about what you're doing right now, I'm talking about this growing pile of wallets at the precinct."

Reg gulped. "What?"

"Have you been dropping purses all over Black Sands?"

"I don't know what you're talking about. Why would I do something like that?"

Jessup snorted. "That's a really good question. I have a couple of theories, but it is pretty bizarre behavior, even for you."

"Even for me?"

"Well, you have to admit, some pretty strange things have happened to you since you moved here."

Reg couldn't exactly argue with that. "Well, I'm not sure what's going on with these purses. Sorry."

"Reg, we've got surveillance pictures of you."

"It's not me. Must be someone who looks like me."

"There really aren't that many people around who could pass for a redhead in box braids wearing a flowing yellow and orange skirt."

Reg looked down at her knees, tucked up under the skirt. At least Jessup wasn't at the cottage. Reg could still deny it.

Jessup wouldn't believe her of course, but she could try to bluff her way through.

"Maybe someone is impersonating me. Trying to set me up. Or it is a doppelgänger. Do doppelgängers really exist? Maybe we should call Corvin in for a consult. He could tell us the entire history of doppelgängers since the beginning of time."

"I'm sure he could," Jessup agreed. "But on the other hand, it's not a doppelgänger. It's you. And I want to know the meaning of this."

"I don't know. The meaning of what?"

"Of the purses that you bought from Sandy Claws Thrift Shop today. It didn't exactly go unnoticed."

"Uh…"

Caught. But Reg hadn't done anything wrong. If anything, she had done something nice, spreading her wealth around the community, sharing it with people who might have less than she. Surely people weren't complaining about it.

"So, what's the deal?" Jessup demanded. "Is this some kind of joke? A social media game? Some weird new form of geocaching? What?"

"No. I just… felt like doing something nice."

"By leaving wallets all over town."

"Yeah. I figured people would be excited to find them. That

maybe they would get into the hands of the people who needed them the most. Like social programs never do."

Jessup sighed heavily. "Yeah. Sure. Well, you're going to have to come to the police station to claim them."

"I'm not claiming anything."

"You need to. We can't just keep them here. Come and pick them up and we'll forget about this."

"Forget about what?" Reg asked sweetly.

"Forget about any charges of... I don't know. Littering. Wasting police time and resources. Interfering with a police investigation."

"Interfering with what police investigation?"

"I don't know, maybe the sudden appearance of dozens of abandoned wallets?"

"No way that ever gets to the court system."

"Maybe not. But I know where you live."

Reg choked. "What?"

"If you won't come here to get them, I'll bring them to you. They can't just stay here. And you've been identified as the rightful owner, so you need to be responsible for them."

"But I don't want them."

"Then throw them in the garbage."

"Like that's gonna work," Reg muttered.

"What?"

"You go ahead and throw them in the garbage there. I don't want or need them. If you don't want them around there, then throw it in the police department bin. Why bother loading them into the car and driving them here?"

"Reg!" Jessup said firmly.

"What? I don't want them. Just throw them out. I guess my little game didn't pan out. You go ahead and just dump them."

"I'm not authorized to do something like that. It's destruction of evidence. Or of personal property. You need to take possession of this pile and throw them out yourself."

"I'm not going to."

"You have until the end of the day. If they're still here at the end of my shift…"

"Then you have my authorization to throw them out. And to go home and get a good sleep."

Reg could see that the conversation wasn't going anywhere. She hung up the phone. Jessup tried to call her back twice, but Reg didn't answer it.

She wasn't an idiot.

CHAPTER TWENTY

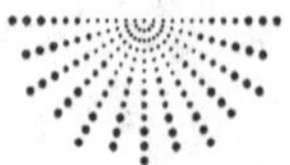

Reg kept an eye on her phone around the time she knew Jessup would be getting off of her shift, but there was no further call from her. Maybe she had accepted Reg's instructions and would just discard the wallets at the end of her shift. Then Reg would be done with them forever. She could start taking clients again and everything would go back to normal.

Or paranormal.

The way they had been before Reg accepted the gems from the fairies.

She started getting ready for bed. She had not slept well that last couple of nights and was looking forward to climbing into bed and falling asleep. Her body and her brain needed a good rest.

Starlight joined her on the bed and cuddled up with her, purring with contentment as she scratched his ears and chin. Just a regular night, like any other. Everything back to the way it should be.

* * *

When she got up in the morning, Reg felt as if she had been sleeping for days. She stretched, petted Starlight when he jumped down from the window to see her, and lazed in bed for a while longer before her body forced her to get up to use the john and scavenge in the kitchen for something suitable for breakfast. Since she didn't usually wake up hungry, she thought this was a good sign that she had caught up on the sleep she needed, and her body was ready to put energy into other things.

She found some leftover fish sticks, which she fed to Starlight, and started the coffee brewing. There wasn't anything that looked even remotely like breakfast in the fridge, so she settled for a bowl of cold spaghetti takeout from a few days earlier.

There was a knock at the door and the sound of Sarah's key in the lock.

"Just a minute!" Reg called, and hurried over to unlock the bolt, which could only be locked and unlocked from the inside.

She opened the door to Sarah, but her landlord didn't immediately step in as she usually did. Instead she looked down, frowning.

Reg followed her gaze and saw the pile of purses and wallets on the doorstep.

"Oh."

"What is all this?" Sarah asked. "What's going on?"

"Well… just a sort of a… social experiment," Reg explained. She supposed she couldn't just leave them all on the doorstep. Sarah would have something to say about that. She bent down and gathered them up in her arms, bringing them back into the cottage.

"What kind of a social experiment?" Sarah persisted.

"Seeing whether people would return lost wallets."

"I would say it was successful."

"Yeah." Reg dumped them all in the middle of the kitchen table. She would sort through them later, after Sarah was gone, and figure out what to do with them. After she emptied them, maybe she could return them to the thrift store. She didn't have any further use for them. And then she would have to figure out what to do with whatever gems had been returned.

"Any appointments today?" Sarah asked, moving over to the date book on the island to flip to the current day. Reg wasn't sure when she had last looked at it. She had broken the habit when her business had dropped off. If she wanted to get it back again, she would have to get out there and hustle. She couldn't just rely on past clients or word of mouth to do her marketing. She'd always had to hustle business before; there was no reason it should be any different now. That was why her business had dropped off. Nothing to do with cursed gems.

"I don't think so," Reg told Sarah, as they both looked at the blank page. "Why, did you have someone to schedule in?"

"No… but I think it is time to get the word out that you are accepting new clients. No need to say that the old ones have all disappeared. But I do think that we've both fallen behind on drumming up appointments."

"It isn't your responsibility," Reg protested, embarrassed that Sarah had to point this out. "You're my landlady, not my employee. I should be doing that myself."

"You know I don't mind. I like being involved in something. A person can get bored just sitting around the house all day. I'd like to know that you're going to stay around. If there's no business, I suppose you'll want to move on to somewhere there is."

"I'm not going to abandon you…" But Reg knew that Sarah was right. If they couldn't drum up any new business, she would have to consider other possibilities. One of which was leaving the cottage and Black Sands behind and finding a new center of operations where people didn't know so much about her and her family background.

"You don't owe anything to me, either," Sarah said with a sad smile. "If things aren't working out here, you aren't obligated to stay for an old woman like me. You'll need to move on."

"Well, let's not talk about that right now. I'm going to start putting up new posters and talking to people. Maybe some internet advertising too. I'll get more clients. And like Corvin said,

I can do work as a phone hotline psychic. No one will care about my parentage if they're just calling in on a hotline."

"That doesn't sound very fulfilling. I suppose young people don't mind being on the phone all day, but I would want face-to-face meetings at least some of the time. It would be very isolating to only talk to people on the phone."

Reg shrugged. She would have to do what she had to do. She'd been on the streets before. She didn't want to return to that kind of life. She would definitely choose being a hotline psychic over that kind of life.

Starlight was meowing at Sarah, rubbing against her ankles and winding around her legs as he told her all his woes.

"He's been fed," Reg said, giving Starlight a glare. "Don't let him tell you that he's hungry and I never feed him properly."

"He's just saying hello," Sarah said, and bent over to give Starlight a scratch behind the ears. She didn't like cats as a rule, but she had always behaved kindly toward Starlight, spoiling him by giving him treats that he didn't need.

Starlight glared at them both and stalked off, in a huff that he wasn't getting extra food.

Reg laughed and poured herself a cup of the freshly-brewed coffee. "Would you like a cup?"

"No, no. I just came over to see how you were and to check the calendar." Sarah looked over at the pile of wallets on the table. And to find out why there was a bunch of wallets and purses on Reg's doorstep, of course. Who wouldn't be curious about that?

Sarah checked the fridge. "I left some cabbage salad in here the other day. It really needs to be eaten in the next day or two or it will be too late."

"Okay. I'll have some," Reg agreed. "Thank you."

"Of course, dear. Always happy to help out." Sarah nodded and took her leave. She was always happy to help with everything, except for helping Reg to cleanse the gems or even to find an expert who could. Reg appreciated everything that Sarah did for her, but was frustrated with the way Sarah refused her in other areas. It wasn't the first time that Reg thought Sarah was able to help, yet wasn't willing.

People had to have boundaries, though. Sarah couldn't let Reg walk all over her. She had her health and her own responsibilities to consider. It just seemed like she was willing to offer help in everything except for when Reg really needed it.

Sipping her coffee and taking a bite of spaghetti every few minutes, Reg went through the wallets and purses, making piles for the jewels and for the junk that she had stuffed into the wallets. Who would have thought that the random bits of paper and objects would be enough for people to trace the gems back to her?

When she was finished, she put all the wallets back into the shopping bag for later and retrieved the wooden box that the jewels had been previously housed in and filled it with the jewels. Starlight jumped up on the table to look at them. He didn't normally jump onto the table; but then, Reg didn't normally use it and he was probably curious.

"Nothing to eat here," she told him.

Starlight poked his nose into the box, then looked at her. Reg looked at the little wooden chest.

"I think there are more gems in there now than when I started."

Was it possible that she had actually gotten more jewels back than she'd had to start with? Had people added their own cursed gems to the wallets? She had assumed, even when Jessup had said that she'd received all of those wallets, that she wouldn't get them all back. People would keep at least some of the wallets and gems. But her hoard of cursed gems didn't appear to have diminished.

Reg rubbed her forehead, trying to figure out what to do.

Where was a pixie when you needed one? The pixies thought they had the right to claim anything that was buried in the earth, which was their domain. And that included gemstones that had originally come out of the ground. Maybe instead of leaving wallets around town, she should have left the chest of gems in the pixie territory. It had been a while since she had been to their burrows, but she still remembered the general area, and she knew that there were plenty of pixies around guarding them and keeping a lookout on everything that was going on in the neighborhood. She didn't imagine it would take very long for them to snatch up a box of gems.

Although maybe they wouldn't if the gems were cursed. They would surely be able to sense the curse on the stones, perhaps even faster than the experts who had looked at them so far.

But maybe they would have the means to remove the curse as well, so they wouldn't care.

An idea started to form in Reg's brain. Pixies. Maybe she already knew someone who was an expert on gems and could tell her what to do about her little problem.

Ruan, Calliopia's mate, had come to Reg when she had been injured, looking for her help. And she had saved Calliopia and gotten her back on the road to recovery when everyone else had said that it was impossible. Ruan himself had been ready to end her suffering. So he owed Reg. And Ruan was a pixie.

CHAPTER TWENTY-ONE

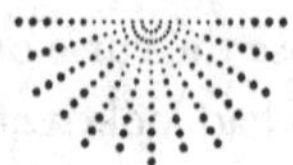

Reg had no idea where Ruan might be. They had left town once Calliopia was well enough to travel, and they had not, as far as Reg knew, told anyone where they were going. They were outcasts in both the fairy and the pixie communities, so there was no point in telling anyone where they planned to go, if they planned for their nomadic lifestyle to carry them anywhere in particular. Reg suspected that they simply went whatever direction the wind blew them.

Which meant they could be practically anywhere. Or at least, anywhere Ruan's rickety old car would take them.

Reg went to her living room and took the crystal ball off its shelf. She had been able to see Calliopia and Ruan in the crystal more than once before. She had a connection with Calliopia that they couldn't seem to break, and that would be enough for Reg to trace her, no matter how far away she was. And Ruan should be with his mate. Divorce was not a thing in the pixie and fairy worlds. Once the two were mated, that was that.

Reg got comfortable and focused her eyes in the depths of the crystal.

Where is Calliopia?

The scar on Reg's hand where she had been cut with Calliopia's fairy blade had faded until it was barely visible after the blade had been destroyed, but as she focused on the crystal and Calliopia's name, her hand began to throb. She tried to use the pain to sharpen her focus. Calliopia was out there somewhere, and the pain and the connection they had previously shared on more than one occasion should lead Reg directly to her.

She started to see images in the crystal. The pain in her hand grew hot, getting sharper and sharper until it felt as it had when she first was cut. She didn't look at her hand, afraid that if she did, she would find it once more open and bleeding.

Starlight walked over and, after standing up on his hind legs to look into the crystal, he jumped up beside her and snuggled close while she tried to focus the images. Finally, Calliopia came into focus. The pretty girl with light brown hair smiled and said something to the figure beside her. Ruan, of course, with messy brown curls and a cherubic, apple-cheeked face that made him look like a little boy, though he was undoubtedly older than Reg, probably by decades, and had a mouthful of sharp predatory teeth.

I need to speak with Ruan. Reg focused on him, trying to project her thoughts to him. She knew that he had some capacity for telepathy, but didn't know how clear it would be over the miles.

He could see Calliopia and Ruan exchanging a few words, but then the vision started to fade. Reg tried to hold on to it.

Ruan!

But it had faded into mist, and then she was just looking at the reflection on the shiny surface of the crystal ball. Reg swore. She shook her hand, trying to relieve the pain. It would fade, since she was no longer trying to reach Calliopia. She rubbed her palm with the thumb of the other hand.

Her phone started to buzz. Reg sighed and flopped her head back, tired and frustrated. She didn't want to talk to anyone on the phone. She didn't want to deal with an inquiry from Jessup or someone else who had found one of the wallets and wanted to return it to. Or talk to Corvin or anyone else. Not even a client.

But thinking about a client made her galvanize herself, and Reg reached for her phone to see who was calling.

It was a Skype call, with Ruan's dirty, laughing face on the screen. Reg stared at it for a moment, then finally moved in order to catch the call before it failed. She swiped the call and held the phone up in front of her. Ruan's picture was blurred to start with, then came into focus. He leaned toward the camera on his own phone.

"The great sorceress Reg Rawlins calls," he observed.

"I was trying to reach you!" Reg agreed. She felt a little silly for not trying to reach out to him using technology. But she didn't have his phone number and hadn't realized that he would have a phone. The pixies she had met in the underground burrows where Calliopia had been held lived without any kind of technology. She hadn't seen as much as a hand-cranked wheat grinder. The pixies were omnivorous, eating things like bugs and grubs, and she didn't know whether they ate grains, or just tuberose things that grew under the ground. Ruan had been familiar with fruit juice, but that was probably from his time living aboveground with Calliopia.

"Phones are easier," Ruan said. "And with Skype, no roaming fees, even if we are outside of human-erica."

"You're out of the country?"

"We come; we go." He made a careless gesture with his hand. "It makes no difference to our sources."

"No... I guess not. It's nice to see your face. How are you? And how is Calliopia doing? Has she completely recovered?" Fairies were quick healers, but the wound she had sustained had been very serious.

"She fares well." Ruan considered, obviously holding back. "The wound heals. It no longer pains her, except at night."

That might a psychological rather than physical pain, if it was only at night. Or maybe she only noticed it when she was not distracted by her daily activities.

"Is she sleeping better?"

Ruan shook his head. "Demons yet plague her sleep. But I do not let her sleep alone and she does not sleep with a weapon."

Callie had by now, presumably, replaced the dagger that Reg had destroyed. But they had learned the hard way that she could not be trusted with the weapon while she slept. Reg wondered how they had sorted out the sleeping arrangements, with Calliopia unable to abide the night shadows and Ruan, a creature who would normally have spent most of his time in underground burrows, needing somewhere dark and close to rest and regenerate. Maybe he built himself a little blanket fort in Calliopia's bedroom. Or slept with an eye mask on to block out the never-ending light.

"I wish there was something I could do to help," Reg said. "She really should be seeing a therapist. Someone to help her with all of this stuff."

Reg's amateur armchair diagnosis was that Calliopia suffered from some fairy form of PTSD since her kidnapping. She had found that fairies responded well to human medicine, and wondered whether antidepressants and a sleep aid might help her. Or seeing a therapist.

"Fairies do not do such things," Ruan disagreed, shaking his head.

"I know. But I think it might help."

He shrugged his thin, waifish shoulders. "But that is not why you reached out to Ruan…?"

"No." Reg squared her own shoulders, remembering the task at hand. "I don't know whether you will be able to help, but…"

"Of course I will help all I can," Ruan said, giving a small, formal bow.

Reg was glad that he was on her side. When she had been looking for Calliopia and the pixies had been holding her, he had been on the opposite side, and she had found the pixies to be an angry, bloodthirsty group. But since she had healed Calliopia, Ruan no longer considered Reg an enemy. At least, she hoped that if she were ever to meet him face-to-face again, he would still be friendly and on her side. But she would always have to be careful, because as Corvin had pointed out repeatedly, non-human creatures did not have the same morals and rules as humans did. Perhaps someone who was a friend one day would be dinner the next.

"Okay. You are a pixie, and pixies are experts of things under the earth."

He nodded his agreement. No false modesty. The underground was his domain.

"And… gems. You're familiar with precious stones and their powers and… natures."

Ruan raised an eyebrow, looking comical to Reg rather than wise. "Piskies know gems."

"I have… come into possession of some gems and I don't know if you can help and give me some advice, but…"

"What is the problem?"

"They are apparently cursed."

His previously pleasant and interested expression grew dark. He turned away from the phone camera and said something in a low voice to Calliopia, who was off-camera somewhere. Reg couldn't tell what he had said. Perhaps something in a pixie or fairy language. She realized suddenly that maybe Ruan and Calliopia were not the best ones to be talking to about the issue, when the gems had been given to her by Calliopia's family. Who knew what kind of complications might arise if Calliopia knew what her parents had done, or if they knew that Reg was consulting with a pixie about how best to remove the curse.

"Cursed gems," Ruan said darkly, shaking his head. "You should not accept them. Give them back."

"I've tried. I didn't know they were cursed until now, I accepted them as a gift a while back." She shrugged and shook her head, trying to look casual about it. "I just didn't know. I don't have a magical background. I didn't know about cursed gems."

"Didn't know about them?" Ruan's tone was scathing. "Even humans know of cursed stones."

"Well, some humans do. I didn't really know they were a thing. I mean, I knew about blood diamonds, and I knew there are stories about treasures being cursed when someone steals them from a tomb. But I didn't know… I thought that was rare, and that it didn't happen anymore, I guess."

"Reg Rawlins should not accept such gifts."

Reg nodded. "You mean something that seems so extravagant? I guess I should have realized. But I didn't stop to think about it. I was just glad… I thought it was a nice gift, that's all. I knew it was expensive, but I thought that they just weren't that valuable to… the person who gave them to me."

He shook his head. "You are like a child. Even a pixie child of a few years would know better than that."

"Okay." Reg was getting impatient with his criticism. "I realize now that I did something stupid. But we can't change that. I want to know what I can do now. To cleanse the stones."

"This is not done. Humans cannot do such a thing."

"You said I couldn't cure Calliopia, either. That I couldn't unmake the blade. But I did."

Ruan pondered this. Calliopia said something to him, but he looked lost in thought. He answered her faintly. It was some time before he focused on Reg's face on his phone screen again.

"Reg Rawlins *is* a great sorceress," he admitted. "Perhaps it is something that a great sorceress can do, even if a normal human could not."

"Right! How are we going to know if I don't try?" But she was a little worried about what he would tell her to do. Was it complex magic? Something dangerous? She didn't want to risk her life on cleansing the gems, however much she would like to be comfortably well-off and not to have to worry about raising money again.

CHAPTER TWENTY-TWO

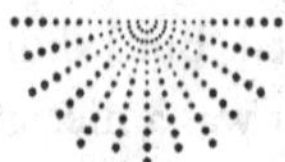

"Reg Rawlings should give the stones to the piskies," Ruan suggested. "They will take care of them."

"By take care of them, you mean that they'll take them and not give them back, right? I won't ever see them again? That's not cleansing them, that's just taking them."

If there were any chance that Reg could still get something for the stones, she didn't want to overlook it. If Ruan could tell her how to cleanse them properly...

"By giving away, they can be cleansed," Ruan asserted.

"Yeah, Corvin thought that might work too, but it doesn't. Every time I give them away, they come back."

Ruan snickered. "Cursed stones can be very stubborn."

"Well, I guess I got some really stubborn ones, because I've tried all different ways of giving them away or having someone take them, and it doesn't work. In fact, I think I ended up with more than I started with."

"Reg Rawlins must have a very inviting home."

"Well, great. I have a good home for cursed stones. I'm not sure I'd tell that to the real estate agent."

Ruan considered, rubbing his hairless chin. "Reg Rawlins has great powers. Perhaps you can use the elements."

"What elements? How would I do that?"

"You can perhaps fire them, as you did Calliopia's blade. Burn away the impurities. This is often done with precious stones and metals."

"I'm not planning on a trip back to the dwarf mountain to use their forge. How hot do I have to burn them?"

"Very hot. Reg Rawlins can do this."

"Yes," Reg had power as a firecaster, so this was right up her alley. "I can try that for sure. And that's all there is to it? I don't have to say a spell or make a potion?"

"No." Ruan rolled his eyes at her naiveté. "Just fire. If that works not… best to throw them into the sea."

"I don't want to do that. I still want to be able to use them."

"Use them?"

"For money. To pay for things."

"Ah." Ruan nodded his understanding. "Not if you throw them into the sea."

"Yeah. So is that it? If firing them doesn't remove the curse, then my only option is to throw them into the sea, to get rid of the curse? So that I don't have a bunch of bad luck?"

Ruan hesitated, looking off-camera, then nodded.

"That's it?" Reg demanded. "There's nothing else I can do to remove this curse?"

Ruan shook his head slightly, but Reg thought he was shaking his head in answer to a question Calliopia had answered, not her. She waited for him to turn his attention back to the small screen.

"Ruan."

He looked at her. "Humans do not cleanse gems," Ruan asserted again. "It is not done."

"But I can try if I want to. And I'm not exactly human. Or all human. So maybe I can."

"From whence came the stones?"

"I don't know, exactly. I mean, I know who had them last, before they were given to me, but I don't know their history."

"They have been stolen? How were they mined? From where?"

"I don't know, Ruan. That must have been a long time ago. I have no idea where they came from. Or if they were stolen at some point. I would guess so." She shrugged. "Gems that have been around for a long time, you would think that they might have been stolen at some point, wouldn't you? Spoils of war, maybe?"

"Sometimes from temples," Ruan said. "Offerings to gods or statues in temples."

Reg had seen Indiana Jones. She shrugged. "Yeah, I guess. But there's no way for me to know. And it's... not just a couple of gems. It wouldn't be possible to trace the histories of all of them. I don't know how I would even trace the history of one. They wouldn't be cataloged somewhere, would they? You can't just search on the internet for an emerald pendant of this size and cut and find out where it came from, can you?"

"Internet is an amazing thing," Ruan said with some reverence. "But no, I do not think so."

"What difference would knowing their history make? Would that give me another way to remove the curse?"

Ruan nodded reluctantly.

"It would? How? What would I do?"

"Returning the stones to their rightful owner, or to their birthplace, that could remove the curse."

Reg couldn't even fathom how she would do that. "The last owners don't want them back. I already asked."

"But they did not have them from the source," Ruan speculated. "They are not the rightful owners."

Reg blew out her breath. "No. Probably not." The fairies might have had them for generations. And the Papillons did not even want to talk to her about them. So how would she get the information about where they had come from so long ago? And who would be the rightful owner after so long? If hundreds of years had passed since they were stolen from their rightful owner, then how would she be able to find the heir they were to go to? It was an impossible task.

"Well… you're right. That is probably not possible. Even for the great Reg Rawlins."

Ruan nodded solemnly. "Return them to the piskies," he suggested again. "They will take care of them."

"You make it sound like putting babies to bed at night."

Ruan laughed and nodded. "Yes, like that," he agreed. "The gems need a… different kind of home. Someone who understands where they came from and what they went through. A piskie could take good care of them."

"Well, not if I have any say in it. I'm not going back there anytime soon. I want to be able to get some money for them. What is the point in a treasure if you can't pay for anything?"

"Treasures are… to be treasured."

"Hmmph." Reg didn't know that she agreed. Merely owning a treasure wasn't enough for her. But maybe with the information Ruan had given to her, she would be able to do something.

CHAPTER TWENTY-THREE

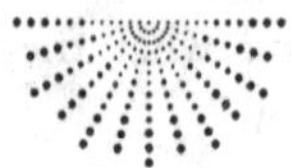

Reg had one small problem with firing the gems. Besides the fact that she wasn't sure if she needed any special equipment or how hot she needed to get them in order to purify them as Ruan had suggested.

And that was, being a newbie firecaster, she was not allowed to "play with fire" by herself.

Because, of course, there was always the danger that she would burn down the house and everything in it. Or, as she had when she was trying to unmake the fairy blade, that she would pull energy from everyone around her and risk burning up half the planet in a massive fireball.

These things were tricky.

Not being allowed to use her power on her own, she had to bring another firecaster into the growing circle of people who knew about the gems. Sarah, Corvin, the Papillons, Jessup—though she might not know that they were real, and Reg was sure she didn't know that they were cursed—Ruan and Calliopia, and now Davyn.

She didn't have to show him the entire hoard. Not initially. They could try firing just a few of the gems, and then if it worked, she could get Davyn to help her with the rest.

"I have a special job today," she told the warlock, who was the head of Corvin's coven. "But I'm going to need help."

"What kind of job?" Davyn asked.

Dark-haired like Corvin, Davyn wasn't nearly as handsome and had a bit of a geeky look when he was dressed for his day job. Which he wasn't, but having seen him at work, Reg couldn't help seeing that sort of "accountant" appearance even when he was in his robes.

"I have these gemstones… but they are, well, cursed, I guess. I've been talking to Ruan, and he said that I could try cleansing them with fire."

Davyn's brows drew down. "You have cursed gems. Where did you get those?"

"It's a long story," Reg said. Although it wasn't. He'd gone with her to the dwarf mountain. He knew all about her helping to cure Calliopia. He'd assisted her in the unmaking of the blade. How hard was it to say that she had received a gift of gems from Calliopia's family after that?

But she didn't want to tell him. That might open her up for questions as to why she hadn't shared the gems with the others who had gone on the quest with her, which she was sure was probably the standard practice. But they all had money. Or most of them. And Reg didn't. It had been her idea, her quest, and she was the one who had provided the firepower to melt down the dagger. The gift was hers.

Besides, if she had shared it with them, then they would all be cursed now too. They wouldn't have wanted that.

Davyn gave Reg a doubtful look. "Well… I know how it works in theory, but I've never tried it myself. And I don't know how reliable a method it is. It isn't as though it's endorsed by the Magical Jewels Association or something."

Reg gaped. "There's a Magical Jewels Association?"

"No." Davyn chuckled. "It was a joke. I was being facetious."

"Oh." Reg shook her head. "I thought you meant there really was. After meeting Julian, I thought there might be all kinds of regulatory agencies out there that I know absolutely nothing about."

"No, there's not really much regulation of practitioners. Usually, it is left to the leader of a coven to address any problems. Or to take it to a tribunal, like we did with Corvin. Magical Investigations is the exception rather than the rule."

Reg nodded slowly. She still really didn't have much understanding of how the paranormal world worked and how they kept it from collapsing into chaos. With all the non-human races, powers, and methods of communication, it was a wonder that things were as orderly as they were.

"Why don't you show me your gems?" Davyn said, bringing her back into focus. "I'll take a look at them, and we can see whether we can purify them."

"Does it really work like that? Burning up the bad stuff?"

"No… cursing doesn't really leave any physical impurities in or on the stones. Which is one reason that I'm a little reluctant to believe that fire will accomplish anything. But fire has other purposes too. It can help with focus and concentration, can magnify other powers, can help to soothe negative emotions. So maybe there is something to it. We won't know whether there is any efficacy until we try it."

"Okay. I'll be right back." Reg withdrew to her bedroom and picked up the little bag with the stones in it that she had already dealt with. It made sense to her to use the same stones for each experiment. It might be that different things would work on different stones, so she didn't want to take the chance of missing the one thing that would work on the stones she had taken to the jewelers on the first day.

She returned to Davyn and put the small bag on the kitchen table, from which she had previously cleared all the wallets and piles of gems and debris. Davyn looked at it.

"Get them out so we can see what we are dealing with."

Reg loosened the strings on the bag and spilled the gems out into her hand. She showed them to Davyn. He leaned closer for a look, but didn't use or ask for a jeweler's loupe. She wondered if he had any more experience with gems than Corvin did. Maybe all that either had ever done was to polish up their family heirlooms.

"Very nice," Davyn proclaimed.

"Can you tell that they're cursed?"

He passed his hand a couple of inches above Reg's, as if feeling for heat. He nodded. "I'm no expert, but I can feel something."

"Okay. So how do I do this? Do I need to heat them to a certain temperature? For a certain length of time? Am I supposed to hold them or put them into an oven safe dish?"

"Let's go with you just holding them. You can withstand more heat than any cookware you have, I would think."

Davyn rubbed his hands together, then started to move them around as if manipulating an invisible ball. The fire started to grow between his hands, a friendly flicker of flames that immediately called to Reg's own fire.

Without Reg even making an effort, a flame sprang up in her hand. She looked down at the fire dancing in the palm of her hand, the gems scattered on her palm beneath it.

"Let's grow the fire a little, but mostly, I want you to make it hotter."

Reg focused her attention on the fire. She grew it into a fireball like Davyn's and watched it rotating just above her hand. She poured more heat into it.

The fireball grew significantly bigger, and Davyn was immediately assisting her, trying to bring it down in size again, to keep it small and compact, while simultaneously allowing her to bring up the temperature.

"That's right," he murmured. "Let's go white hot, but then I want you to hold steady."

It was a struggle. Not to get it hot enough, but to keep the fire small and then to hold at the level Davyn wanted her to. The fire within her, always eager to be called upon, did not want to be regulated. It wanted to burn wild and rampant, consuming everything in its path. What did that say about Reg's nature?

She tried to keep the fire calm and maintain the temperature. She had thought that the way Corvin had referred to the stones as having thoughts and feelings had been funny, but at the same time, she saw her fire as having its own personality, its own thoughts and preferences. And wasn't it just an extension of herself?

"Hold there," Davyn encouraged.

Reg tried to hold on, not letting it get hotter or letting it drop off. She needed to keep a tight focus.

"Now," Davyn's voice was slow and soothing, like he was talking to a wild animal or trying to hypnotize Reg. "Think about the gems in your hand. They are getting warmer. You were able to put power into Calliopia's medallion. Remember how that felt. Start to transfer the heat from the fire to the jewels."

Reg nodded. She looked through the fireball at the gems. The sapphire that had burned Corvin. The ruby that had come back to her. The emerald she had tried to give to Francesca and been refused. A few other gems that she had placed in the bag, thinking that she would be able to cash them all in to get the money she needed to pay her expenses. Had she been naive to think that a person could just own gems and cash them in whenever they wanted to? Maybe owning a gem was more like owning a cat, with extra responsibilities and effort required to maintain them.

She pushed fire into the stones.

Or maybe like welcoming a new child into your home. Reg herself had been introduced to one foster home after another, traumatized by her violent past, unsure what to think of the new parents and family she would have to get along with and be expected to obey.

What kind of harm had the gems experienced in the past? Did they remember all their owners? Everything that had been done to acquire them?

The stones grew exponentially hotter in her hand. She remembered Corvin not even being able to touch the sapphire without burning himself. Maybe the stone had been trying to tell her something. That she could cleanse it not by giving it away, but with her fire.

But even though she could feel the heat, it didn't bother her, didn't hurt her. She was in control of it.

"Now hold again," Davyn suggested.

Reg felt a twinge of doubt. While he had been calm and focused guiding her through the exercise, she couldn't help but notice the uncertainty in his voice. He had been honest with her. He knew how the cleansing should work in theory, but he'd never done it himself. He was winging it.

"They need more," she countered.

"*You* want more," Davyn countered with an amused chuckle. "Stay focused."

Reg obeyed. Despite not being bothered by the heat, she was starting to sweat. Producing a hot fire and holding it steady for so long required exertion. It wasn't like running or jumping rope but, in its own way, it was a physical exercise.

She focused on each of the gems in turn, checking on how they held the heat and if they were changing. Perhaps it wouldn't be possible to tell if there were any change until they were finished with the experiment. She couldn't detect any difference yet.

"Okay." Davyn was looking at his watch. "That should be long enough. Dial it back slowly, and then extinguish your fire."

Reg's instinct was to do the opposite. To let it burn with a stronger furor and intensity. To let it get just a little bit out of control. Davyn was there to pull her back, after all, so she could be a *little* reckless.

"No," Davyn told her.

Reg breathed out in a carefully controlled breath. She lowered the temperature of the fire, then started to reduce it in size until it was just a glimmer above her palm. She extinguished it, feeling a sharp pang of loss as she did so.

CHAPTER TWENTY-FOUR

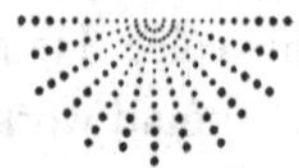

"Good," Davyn proclaimed. "How is the temperature of the gems? Are they still hot?"

Reg rolled them in her palm. "No. They're cooling."

They didn't look any different. But they wouldn't, would they? Reg tried to reach out with her other senses, but found them too difficult to reach.

Davyn went to the sink and started running cold water. He opened and closed a few cupboards until he found a mug. He filled it and brought it to her.

"Rehydrate."

Reg nodded and obeyed, taking the mug with her other hand. Davyn watched her carefully.

"Your control is getting better."

"About time." Reg was impatient with herself. She thought it should be easier to control her powers. If she had special gifts, then she should be adept at controlling them. If she weren't, then it was her own fault.

Davyn shook his head, smiling. "How can you be good at something that you have not practiced? You wouldn't expect to be good at basketball or cooking without some practice. Or playing the piano."

"You're lucky you haven't tasted my cooking."

"It's just an example. Even if you have a talent for something, you cannot expect to be good at it, or even proficient, if you've never had the opportunity to exercise and grow your skills."

"I guess. It just feels like it takes me way too long to learn."

"Keep in mind that children in our community are carefully watched for their talents and once those gifts are identified, are trained up from the time they are very young. Your background is completely different. Your gifts were not identified and encouraged. From what you have said before, they were actively discouraged and beaten down. It takes time to overcome that kind of conditioning. To go from not being allowed to access your powers at all to trying to take control of them and nurture them. It takes a lot of time and effort."

"And in the meantime, I'm like a toddler trying to get his legs. It's so frustrating."

"Like a toddler who is already man-sized," Davyn said, "One of the reasons they are so hard to control is because they are so strong."

Reg looked down at the gems on her hand after chugging a couple more swallows of water. "They don't look any different."

"The difference would not be in their appearance." Davyn leaned closer to peer at them himself. After a moment, he hovered his hand over Reg's, frowning.

"Is it gone?" Reg asked. "Did it work?"

Davyn shook his head slowly. Reg's heart sank. She had guessed as much, but had hoped that he would tell her that it had worked. She was so tired of trying to overcome the curse on the gems. Wouldn't anything work?

"If anything," Davyn said, "I would say they are stronger. They have absorbed some of your energy. But the darkness is still in them. And that's not good."

"Because that means the curse is stronger," Reg deduced.

"Yes. Do you mind? May I take them for a moment?"

Reg held them out to him. "Have at it."

She didn't warn him about the sapphire. Even if it got hot, it couldn't do much harm trying to burn a firecaster. Davyn took the gems from her and handled them carefully. It wasn't long before he was putting them back in her hand.

"You'd better hang on to them."

Reg looked at him, trying to read his expression or his aura. "Why? What's wrong?"

"I don't think... they like me."

Reg raised her brows. "They don't like you?" She gave a short laugh. "Everyone keeps making out like they have thoughts and feelings. But they're stones. They're just... inanimate objects. They don't have feelings."

But she couldn't deny that they were warm in her hand and that she felt a great sense of relief when Davyn handed them back to her. Despite her inability to get rid of them, she found that she had some anxiety over their finding their way into someone else's possession.

But of course she felt that way. They were her treasure. Her way of staying independent and living the kind of life she wanted to, sheltered and protected, off the streets. With friends who cared about her. People she didn't have to leave as soon as she had pulled off a money-making scam.

"It's a bad habit," Davyn admitted. "Ascribing emotions to the gems instead of admitting that they are our own feelings. When I hold these gems, I feel... anger and injustice. They provoke a feeling of dissatisfaction and the desire to... get rid of them and go somewhere safe."

Reg closed her cupped hand around the gems and thought about it. They did not make her feel that way. She couldn't feel any evil or darkness or even anger when she held them. She felt... a sense of longing. An even stronger desire to be kept sheltered and safe.

"Well... thank you, I guess. I mean, yes—thank you! Now we know that fire won't work. I'm disappointed, but I wouldn't have known what to do without you. Now I guess… I try something else."

"Good luck. I hope you can figure it out. I imagine you would like to be able to use them. Or to build a nest-egg for the future. I'm sorry it didn't work out."

"Yeah, it would be nice," Reg agreed with a sigh.

But maybe it wasn't to be. Maybe the only thing she would be able to do was to get rid of them, so that she wouldn't be plagued by any further bad luck. She would be sorry to see all that wealth go out of her life, but it wasn't as though she was losing anything. They had not been of any value to her before, and they would not be after she got rid of them. Her possession of them was fleeting and temporary.

* * *

After Davyn had left, Reg sat down with Starlight to chill out and regain her strength. A bit of ice cream with chocolate syrup would help her to recover more quickly, she was sure. And Starlight liked to lick out the bowl afterward when she had ice cream. Though she'd have to make sure there wasn't any chocolate sauce remaining.

She had the TV on, thinking that she would be able to forget the pressure to supplement her bank account soon. At least the cable was paid for by Sarah, so Reg didn't have to feel like she was paying for unnecessary luxuries. But she found the TV annoying, and shut her eyes to concentrate, thinking over the session with Davyn and her conversation with Ruan. Ruan was the only one of her contacts who seemed to actually know anything about cursed gems and was willing to talk about them. Maybe in pixie society, it wasn't considered inappropriate to talk about cursed gemstones.

Ruan's next suggestion had been to throw the gems into the sea. While Reg had dismissed this on principle, it was beginning to look like her only remaining option. And it wasn't something that she would be able to do by herself.

Getting close to the ocean was one of the triggers that activated her siren instincts. The last thing that she needed while she was trying to get people to forget about her siren parentage was to go on some kind of murderous rampage at the harbor.

CHAPTER TWENTY-FIVE

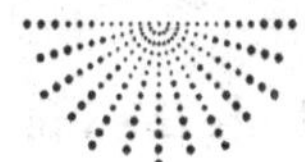

eg knew she was compounding one bad idea with another. She couldn't go to the ocean alone and hope to be able to avoid triggering any siren-like thoughts or actions. There were few people who would be able to help her if that happened. And she didn't want to involve anyone who didn't already know about the gems or to have a whole group of people with her to watch the fun. So she asked Corvin if he would go with her.

"Of course," Corvin purred into the phone, always happy for any excuse for the two of them to be together. "A little jaunt out on the water is just what you need."

Reg tried to figure out whether he was being sarcastic or genuinely thought it was a good idea. "I'm worried about what might happen," she told him. "And you're going to be on the boat alone with me, which isn't a really safe place for you to be. If the water makes me… do things…" She trailed off and grimaced. "We already know that you are… susceptible to sirens."

"But I will be prepared. And you're not a *mature* siren and your blood is more diluted than your mother's. I was able to resist you before."

"Yes," Reg nodded to herself. "That's why I thought… maybe

you would be okay. But I don't want to just invite you and have you come out there, thinking that it's going to be a piece of cake. We don't know what could happen. You're putting yourself at risk."

"I realize that. Just like you realize that *you* will also be at risk."

"Yeah. But the same thing applies. I can resist you, if I'm prepared."

"What an interesting dance this will be," Corvin chuckled.

"Are we both crazy? This is the stupidest thing we could be doing."

"You only live once."

Reg wasn't sure that was strictly true after the things she had seen in the paranormal world. But she wasn't going to argue it.

"We should probably sleep on it," Reg suggested. "You're not supposed to make big decisions like this on an impulse."

"It's not such a big decision to go for a sail. And I can tell you that my answer wouldn't be any different tomorrow, or the next day, or the day after that." She felt like his lips were right against her ear as he whispered into the phone. "The answer will always be yes, Regina."

Reg couldn't suppress the shiver that ran down her spine or the goosebumps that popped up all along her arms. And she was going to trust him?

No, she wasn't. Neither one of them would trust the other, no matter how attracted they were.

* * *

It was getting dark when Reg arrived at the harbor. Maybe not the best time to be going out on a boat, but they didn't want other people to observe what they were doing. Especially not if things got out of hand.

It was a clear night, not a cloud in the sky overhead, although there were some gathered at the horizon, catching the last few pink rays of the setting sun. Reg just stood and drank in the scene before her for a few minutes. She had been keeping away from the water, worried about how she would react to it, but being close enough to see the water stretching out in front of her and to breathe in the salty tang of the water made her wonder what she had been so afraid of. It was beautiful. She felt as though she were coming home.

She should spend every day at the waterfront. Even just a few minutes to walk by the water and breathe in the air, listening to the mewling of the waterbirds flying overhead and the waves lapping against the land. She almost wanted to sleep in the water, it was all so peaceful and idyllic.

Maybe there was no reason for her to worry about the gems after all. What did she need money for? She could sleep on the beach all year long. She would have everything she needed there. Her food within hunting distance. Who needed gemstones?

"Regina."

Corvin had nearly snuck up on her. Reg startled and turned to look at him. He was, as usual, perfectly attired. Not for a dinner out this time, no tux and tails, but casual clothes that would allow him to pilot the boat and have freedom of movement. The black t-shirt he wore clung to his chest in a way that made her want to peel it right off and lay her cheek against him.

Reg resisted the image, trying to wall it off in her mind. She was there for a job. They both had to be on top of their game, aware of every movement and shift in mood of the other. It was not a pleasure-cruise, and letting it become one would lead to her downfall. She would lose her psychic powers to him just as she had once before, and she would be left a hollow shell, the silence echoing in her head, lonelier than she had ever been in her life. Without the voices of the spirits who all vied for her attention, the world was a vast, empty place.

"Did you rent a boat?" Reg asked crisply, taking one step away from Corvin. If she didn't step farther away, she was going to step closer, and she couldn't let that happen. She would stay in complete control of herself, just like she had when she had been firing the gems.

"Of course. I told you that would not be a problem."

"Good. Lead the way."

His gaze wandered over her face, in no hurry to get to the boat. "Maybe a drink first?"

"No. No drinks. I need to stay alert, and so do you."

"Milkshakes?"

"No," Reg said firmly. "This is not a date. This is a job. Trying to get rid of the gems."

He started strolling toward the boats. "I don't see why you're in such a hurry to get rid of them all of a sudden. I haven't had a chance to finish my search of the literature. And you said that the curse hasn't affected you, so it isn't as if you are trying to rid yourself of bad luck."

"Well… maybe I spoke too soon. Without thinking. Because… there has been some stuff lately. I don't know whether it is all because of the gems, or if it's just… the way things would have gone anyway. And if I can't rid the stones of the curse, then I need to rid myself of the cursed stones."

Corvin shrugged with one shoulder as he watched to make sure she was following him. He would obviously rather have her walking with him arm-in-arm, but Reg wasn't about to risk it just for appearances. People who saw them walking together, a few feet apart, without any touching, could think that they were fighting with each other. Or that they were family rather than dates. Or that they were just not *that kind* of friends.

A few of the boats were strung with lights that the owners were turning on as the sun dipped below the horizon. They looked magical, twinkling in the night, the gentle sounds of waves lapping and boats bumping against the dock playing what sounded like a lullaby to Reg.

Corvin pointed to one. "Right there. The White Lady."

"Great."

Reg walked out onto the deck. She felt grounded by the boat

lifting and falling with her breathing. Why didn't she live on a boat? Plenty of other people in Florida did. What had made her rent Sarah's cottage instead of a boat?

She watched Corvin untie the boat. His movements were quick and sure. Familiar with ropes and all things nautical. He jumped aboard and held up the boat keys for her to see. "Let's get this lady on her way."

Reg moved to the front of the boat and stood watching while Corvin pulled it away from the dock and out into the open water. The harbor was protected by a strip of land that ran most of the way around it and, once they got past that, Corvin opened up the throttle and took them away from the lights and out into the deep, dark water.

It was so beautiful. The stars were coming out overhead. The waves were low, slapping against the boat. The wind was a little chilly and made Reg pull her wrap around her a little more tightly. A fine mist of saltwater blew in her face. Reg licked her lips, tasting the salt and the sea.

CHAPTER TWENTY-SIX

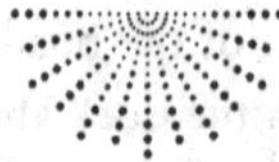

All of Reg's senses sharpened. She could see and hear things she hadn't been able to moments before. Things behind them on the shore. Things under the water. Corvin at the wheel humming to himself, his cologne or deodorant almost intoxicating. Even though Reg had been sure to eat before they headed out, she was suddenly starving.

Corvin shifted his gaze from his navigation to her face and smiled. "How far do you want to go?" he shouted over the noise of the engine.

He didn't need to shout; she could have heard him even if he had whispered. Reg surveyed the water ahead of them. She stretched out her senses and felt under the water. She could visualize the bottom of the ocean in her mind, like a radar map. She pointed to a spot ahead of them and to the right.

Corvin raised his brows, but he didn't argue with her or demand to know why she wanted that spot in particular. He adjusted his course appropriately and slowed so that Reg could tell him where to stop.

Reg watched the water, breathing in the damp spray and growing increasingly restless.

Corvin throttled down still more, and Reg kept her eyes on

the spot she wanted. When they reached it, she raised her hand and Corvin stopped. He looked out over the water.

"Do you want to drop anchor?"

"No, just let it drift."

He nodded and walked out to her. "Enjoying our little trip?"

Reg nodded. "It's beautiful. I could stay out here forever."

"We could come more often."

It was a tempting offer. But Reg needed to remember her purpose. They were not there just to take in the night air and the smell of the sea.

"Ruan didn't say there was any kind of ceremony or ritual," she said, taking out the little bag of gems.

Corvin looked down at it. "It's really too bad… I think we could spend longer looking for an answer."

Reg shook her head. "I want to get it sorted out. I can't wait forever."

"I didn't say forever. But a little longer."

She shrugged and didn't argue the point. Corvin held out his hand, not to take the bag from her, just getting close to it. Feeling the power emanating from the stones. It was strange that Reg had not noticed before how easy it was to feel the power of magical artifacts. When she had met Corvin, she had thought it such a strange talent. She hadn't been able to feel then what was so obvious to her now.

"They're stronger," Corvin said with surprise. "Or are there more of them here than you originally showed me?"

If he examined them for long, he would know the answer to that question. "They are stronger," Reg admitted. "Apparently the fire… increased their power."

Corvin nodded. "That makes some sense. But not the results you were expecting."

"No. So now…" She looked down at the little jewelry bag and addressed them directly. "It's time to say goodbye."

Corvin's mouth quirked up at the corner, amused. "Aren't you the one who said that gems are inanimate objects without thoughts or feelings?"

"Well… maybe someone who looks and sounds like me said that."

He chuckled. "Something like that."

Reg sighed. She loosened the strings of the little bag one more time and spilled the stones out into her palm. "If they're in the ocean, no one will bother them again. They'll be safe from plunder. They can rest."

Corvin nodded. Reg held her hand out over the rail and sprinkled the gems into the water. They fell with little plops into the ocean and sank rapidly to the bottom.

Reg felt the pull of the long, deep trench beneath them. She could dive to the bottom. It would be quiet and dark. She would float there like a baby in its mother's womb. And if she had a mate, she would have everything she needed.

She grasped the front of Corvin's shirt. He jerked back abruptly, eyes widening.

"Come on, Corvin," Reg said in a low, coaxing voice. "Come with me."

"We're not staying out here."

"You will if I ask you." She reached for him again and he retreated several steps. Reg looked him in the eye, pinning him down. She knew he was vulnerable. Even though he was on guard now, she was sure she could overcome any resistance. "Don't you want to go for a swim?"

"And stay under water for the rest of my life?" Corvin asked. "No, I don't think so."

"Don't be so stubborn." She stepped toward him, drawing his scent down into her lungs in a long, slow breath. "You have spent so long pursuing; wouldn't you like to change the game for once?"

Another step. The smell of his body was almost overpowering. The blood pumping through his veins in an endless hot, salty tide. His breath. His sweat. And the smell of flowers. Roses.

Reg's brain clouded. She shook her head, trying to clear the fog. "Stop that."

"You don't want to take me," Corvin warned. "That's not what we came for. You came to get rid of the gems. Remember?"

"I could have thrown them into the harbor. We didn't need to come all the way out here for that."

"Then why did we come all the way out here?"

She took another heavy step toward him and he didn't retreat. Reg drew up to him, nearly touching. Their faces were inches apart.

"Regina." His voice was hoarse. Not pushing her away. She could have what she wanted. Reg took another deep breath and wobbled, losing her balance. She felt as if she'd had too much to drink, when she knew she hadn't touched a drop.

Corvin took her hand. Electricity buzzed between them, jolting Reg back to some sense of reality. Corvin pulled her against him, bending his neck to kiss her. Reg struggled, trying to pull away from him and to push away her desire for his blood at the same time. What had made her think that her siren desires and his hunger for her powers would cancel each other out?

"No." She pushed against his chest; against those perfect pecs she had been admiring under his t-shirt. She could feel the blood flowing through his veins, right under her fingertips. "You'd better stop," she warned.

A war raged within Reg. The desire to take him under the water and satisfy her hunger, the intoxicating smell of the pheromones he exuded, the charms he worked on her, and the little voice in the back of her brain that reminded her she was in danger, both of losing her humanity and of losing her powers. She reached for her powers, reflecting the waves of heat coming from Corvin back at him to fend him off. Corvin stepped back, withdrawing until Reg's hands fell free from his chest and she stood there, almost immobilized, taking in deep breaths and trying to bring her body back under her control.

Galvanized by the space between them, Corvin withdrew,

returning to the ship's wheel. The engine roared to life. Reg's nostrils flared at the choking smell of the exhaust from the engine. Why did humans pollute the environment with their stinking, belching machines? They fouled the water and the air. What other creatures were so enamored with their own technology, their own ability to destroy everything around them?

She grasped the rail, feeling suddenly nauseated. The loss of the gems, the warring attractions, and Corvin speeding away from the place she had selected for his watery grave all converged at once, overwhelming her.

They weren't far from the shore. They would return the boat to its place in the harbor within an hour of having taken it out. So little time had passed, and yet it had been a lifetime. Reg clung to the railing, looking at the water and at the stars in the sky, fixing her eyes on the horizon in an effort to overcome the vertigo. What kind of siren was she, getting seasick?

She saw the lights of the harbor, and then they were there. Corvin carefully returned the boat to its place along the dock. He shut off the engine, threw a rope onto the dock, and jumped out to secure it. He returned to the boat a couple of minutes later and approached Reg warily.

"Are you okay?"

Reg cleared her throat. "Sure. Of course." She still held tightly to the railing, the rise and fall of the boat no longer exhilarating, but barely tolerable.

"You ready to go ashore?"

"I might need a hand."

He looked as though he doubted this was a good idea, and of course he was right. At the best of times, allowing him to touch her was a bad idea. And when she was surrounded by sea water and the smell of the ocean so pungent in the air, it was not a good idea for him to allow her to touch him.

What a crazy, tangled-up world they lived in.

"Just help me off the boat," Reg instructed. Her legs wobbly, she grasped his arm, first with one hand and then both together.

Reg was acutely aware of the buzz of electricity, the heat of his body, and the thrum of the blood in his veins. She closed her eyes most of the way as he walked her slowly toward the dock. He stepped onto solid ground first, then before she knew what he was going to do, picked her up and set her onto the dock next to him. Reg swayed.

"Take a minute to get your land legs," Corvin advised.

"Whew… I don't know what happened… everything just suddenly went wonky," Reg explained.

"Yeah. It's okay. There were a lot of things going on at once there."

Reg leaned against him, appreciating his size and strength and the fact that his body seemed to know which way was up.

"You're getting better," she told him with a weak smile. "You didn't let me seduce you."

Corvin's brows went up. "You don't know how much I wanted to."

Reg smiled in appreciation. But she knew which of them had been stronger. He was the one who had been able to walk away and start the engine of the boat. If it had been left to Reg, they would probably both be at the bottom of the underwater trench she had chosen. And that would not be good.

"How about something to eat?" Corvin suggested.

CHAPTER TWENTY-SEVEN

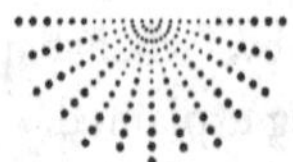

$\mathcal{R}$eg was famished. Which was funny, because she had intentionally eaten before going on the cruise so that she wouldn't be starving when her siren instincts kicked in. And then the nausea had hit. She wouldn't have predicted that having dinner with Corvin would be such an attractive prospect. She hadn't thrown up during her bout of seasickness, so she should still have been full.

"Yeah," she told him immediately. "Let's find somewhere to eat. Is there somewhere close?"

Corvin looked surprised, but he grinned down at her, pleased.

"There is a place just down the road," he offered. "Florida is full of seafood joints, but nothing compares to Seaman Jacks. No seafood more than two hours old. He's got fishermen in the water the whole time the kitchen is open, bringing in fresh catches throughout each shift. It's basically direct from the ocean to your table."

At other times, Reg might have been disturbed by this image, thinking of the live fish in the ocean, minding their own business until they were suddenly caught on a line or in a net. She didn't like to think of the live animals that ended up on her plate and had contemplated the idea of becoming vegetarian like the fairies or gnomes.

But she was starving. And the thirst for blood still lingered. She didn't want salad. She didn't want limp, stringy leaves on her plate. She needed flesh. And next to the smell of Corvin's blood, fish fresh from the ocean seemed the best thing.

"Yes," she nodded vigorously. "Let's go there."

Corvin chuckled. "No need to twist your arm today, huh? Well, let's get something into that bottomless pit."

It wasn't ladylike to have such a big appetite, but Reg didn't care at that point. She just needed to fill the void. Corvin's description was apt.

They walked together to the parking lot.

"Let's take my car," Corvin suggested. "When we're done, I can bring you back here for your car, assuming you're feeling up to driving."

"No." Reg's protest wasn't very forceful. "I should take mine now."

"You're not feeling well. Once you've had something to eat and been able to sit for a while, you'll feel much better. Then you can drive. Right now... I don't think I would trust you not to drive right off the road, maybe straight into the ocean. And neither of us wants that."

"Well..." Reg leg Corvin steer her to the sleek black car that he reserved for dates and special occasions. He walked her to the passenger side and opened the door for her.

"Your carriage."

Reg smiled. She slid into her seat and Corvin carefully closed the door.

* * *

"What should I order?" Reg asked as she looked over the menu. "Everything sounds great, and if it's all as fresh and good as you say..."

"Do you trust me to order for you?"

Reg had previously been furious when Corvin had done so without asking. What he might consider old world manners were, to her, just misogynistic male presumption, and she wasn't having any of it.

"Just this once."

Corvin smiled and closed his menu, setting it aside. Reg closed hers and set it on top of his. The waitress saw that they were ready to order and approached, order pad in hand.

"What can I get you?"

"The next thing that comes out of the water."

The waitress smiled. "Catch of the day," she agreed. This was apparently not an uncommon request at Seaman Jacks. "For two?"

Corvin nodded.

"We should have someone in shortly, so I don't think you'll have long to wait."

She took the order to the kitchen. Corvin picked up his tumbler and had a drink. "You're in for a real treat."

* * *

Reg tried not to give away how hungry she was waiting for their meals. She should have insisted on an appetizer, at least. Something to hold her over until their catch of the day got there. She could still smell Corvin, across the table from her, even though they were away from the water now. Her stomach felt like it was going to consume itself.

What if the fisherman didn't get in when he was expected? What if he hadn't caught anything or his boat had broken down? She couldn't bear to be waiting there for hours.

"Reg?"

Reg tried to turn her attention back to Corvin, who was looking at her with his head tilted slightly to the side.

"Sorry. What?"

"How do you feel? Now that you got rid of the cursed gems. Do you feel any better? Luckier?"

Reg gave a little laugh. "I doubt it works that quickly." She shrugged as he kept looking at her, waiting for a straight answer. "No. I don't feel any different now."

He nodded.

"Do you think I should?" Reg asked. "I never felt like they were bad for me. I didn't feel... cursed or unlucky."

"Well, that's fortunate. Some of the stories that I have heard about people who have received cursed gems... illness and death of family members, terrible accidents, financial ruin. You've had some weird things happen, but it's hard to say whether any of it has been something to do with the stones."

"I don't think so. Don't you think that most of that stuff is just coincidence? People thinking they are cursed, so they start adding up all the stuff that's been going wrong? I mean... I've had lots of bad stuff happen. It didn't just start when I got the gems. Probably the worst things were way before that, when I was in foster care. Or before that, when I was with Norma Jean."

"So you expect bad things to happen."

"Sure, I guess. I don't expect my life to go smoothly, that's for sure. Those stories... they're probably just the worst ones. Things that were really nasty. There are probably lots of other people who held cursed stones who never had any bad luck." Reg thought about it. "Maybe I was too quick to get rid of them. Maybe they wouldn't ever have caused me any trouble. It was people like you who kept saying that I'd better look out. I'd better be careful, get rid of them as quickly as I could before they caused any real damage."

Corvin looked slightly guilty at this. "They can be very dangerous," he said. "Even if yours weren't."

"Hmmph. Maybe I should have waited."

He shrugged and played with the dessert menu on the table. Reg looked away from him, letting her eyes wander over the interior decorating of Seaman Jack's. As with many of the seafood restaurants on the waterfront, it had been decorated with a nautical theme. Lots of nets and ropes and mounted fish. Bit of weathered boards and starfish and shells.

Reg stared at a large net draped over one wall, imagining what it would be like to be in the water when one of those came down. Did mermaids or other sentient creatures ever get caught in the nets? What would the fisherman do if he hauled one of those up?

"What are you thinking?" Corvin asked.

"Just..." Reg broke off when she saw the waitress coming toward her. Making eye contact this time, two plates and a large platter stacked on her hands. She gave them each a plate and put the fish platter down in the middle of the table with a flourish.

It wasn't a sort of fish that Reg recognized, but she wasn't a great connoisseur where fish were concerned. The waitress gave a little introduction about the fish and how it had been prepared. Reg was just eager to get something into her stomach.

The fish had been cleaned and cooked, but the head was still on it, and it was otherwise intact. Reg would have preferred that it not be recognizable. But who was she to complain? She was going to eat it either way.

"Enjoy," the waitress finished, giving Reg a little bow and beaming like a proud parent.

When she was gone, Corvin gave Reg a nod. "Help yourself. First choice is yours."

Reg wasn't sure if there was a particular protocol that he expected her to follow, demurring or asking him to carve it for her or taking a less choice bit so that he could still have the best of it. And she didn't care what he thought. She needed to fill the hole in her gullet. She carved out a portion from the middle of the fish's body and transferred it to her plate.

"Smells great," she commented. She didn't wait for him to dish up before digging into her meal. She forced herself to slow down after the first couple of bites. To enjoy the flavor and texture of the food, the freshness that Corvin had bragged about, rather than just inhaling the whole thing.

"Good?" Corvin asked around a mouthful of food.

Reg nodded, not bothering to swallow before answering. "Great!"

He nodded. They ate in silence for a few minutes. Reg was eyeing the rest of the fish that remained on the platter. There was still plenty more, at least a full helping for each of them. After finishing what was on her plate, she helped herself to more. There was a clink on the plate like a bead falling, and Reg looked to see what had hit the ceramic. It didn't sound like a fish bone or the clink of her fork. As she touched the serving fork to the fish's head to look under and around it for the foreign object, she heard the noise again. Reg turned the platter to get a better view of it. At the very end of the platter, near the fish's mouth, were a couple of bits of rock or glass.

Reg frowned and pushed them around for a better look. Corvin stopped eating and squinted, studying them.

"What did they put in this?" Reg asked. "Is this normal? Some regional dish?"

"No." Corvin poked at them with his fork, and then at the fish's mouth, causing more to fall onto the dish. He and Reg both realized at the same time what they were.

The gems she had thrown into the ocean just an hour before.

CHAPTER TWENTY-EIGHT

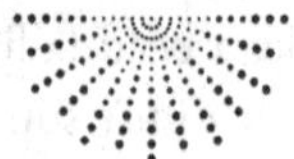

That's not possible," Reg blurted.

"No?" Corvin questioned. "I think it's just been proven possible."

"But no, it can't be. There's no way. How?"

"Apparently the fish caught your gems before it was caught by the fisherman."

"That couldn't happen. Is this all some kind of joke? Did you set this up?"

"It's got nothing to do with me, Reg. You dropped those gems into the ocean yourself. You know that was no sleight of hand. And if you want to gather those up and clean them up, I think you will find that they are the same gems that you threw away, not replacements."

"How would I be able to tell that?"

"You are the one who knows how they feel."

Even with her hand just close to the gems, Reg could already feel their auras. She knew without cleaning them off and concentrating her attention on them that they were the very same gems. Which, of course, was impossible.

There was no way to even calculate the odds that the gems she had thrown into a deep trench in the ocean would be scooped up by a fish, who was then caught by a fisherman and fed to Reg for supper. And that in all of his careful preparations, the cook would not have found the stones himself. They should have been in the fish's stomach or intestines, thrown directly into the garbage, because who would examine fish intestines for gemstones? A fish wouldn't just hold them in his mouth.

"This is crazy," Reg said, shaking her head.

"It is," Corvin admitted. "I knew that the stones were powerful, and that you are powerful, but I didn't foresee that they would be able to make their way back to you after being thrown out into the middle of the ocean."

"They couldn't," Reg agreed, even though they had. She couldn't think of any other explanation.

She gathered the gems and put them onto a napkin, then rubbed them to get the fishy residues off. After making sure that they were as clean and dry as she could get them, she dumped them into the little bag she had tucked back into her pocket. Corvin's eyes followed them.

"So, it would appear that you have been given yet another chance to handle this differently. Throwing them into the ocean is not the answer."

"Yeah."

Corvin shook his head. "You don't need to sound so gloomy about the prospect. If they haven't been causing you any bad luck, as you say, then you don't need to be in such a hurry to get rid of them. There has to be another way to cleanse them."

"No."

"What did Ruan tell you?"

"That they would have to be returned to their rightful owners."

Corvin was silent.

"How could I possibly do that?" Reg demanded. "I have no idea where they came from originally, who they should have rightfully belonged to but were stolen away from. How could I possibly figure out who they should go to now?"

"We could probably figure out some general information to start with," Corvin said. "We may not know exactly which mines they came from, but an expert might be able to look at the composition of the gems, any impurities or other clues, and tell what country or what part of the country they came from."

"How would that help me? Then I could go to that country and advertise, asking them if they were the rightful owner of a bunch of precious gems." Reg's mouth twisted itself into a pretzel, the sarcasm was so bitter.

"I'm not saying that. Identifying the country they came from would be the first step."

"But they're not all from the same place. They've been collected over the years. They all started out in different places."

Corvin sighed. "You don't know that. And there are few enough gems that even if they are from different parts of the world, we wouldn't be totally overwhelmed with the job of identifying what those places were."

Reg slumped back in her seat. Did he really think that she had only the gems she had shown him? He knew better than to trust her and take her word at face value.

Corvin studied Reg's face and body language. The hopelessness of the situation.

"Reg… that *is* all of the gems, isn't it?"

Reg shook her head. "Not even close."

CHAPTER TWENTY-NINE

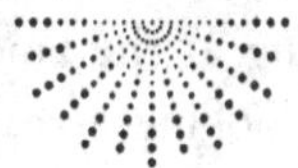

Reg didn't tell Corvin everything he wanted to know about her gems. He already knew too much, more than anyone else. He didn't need to know how many stones she had or exactly where they had come from. Of course, Sarah knew that, so it wasn't like Reg was the only one who knew. She didn't like other people knowing so much about her business but, as the girl at the gem exchange had told Reg, she needed to reach out to her friends for help.

And now, she needed more. She wasn't sure how she would be able to find anything out about where the gems had originated from. And as far as she knew, they could all have come from different places over hundreds of years. How was she going to trace the origin of every gem?

She started thinking about the individual gems on the way home. She had, up until then, been thinking about them only as a collection. Her hoard. Her treasure. But it was made up of individual gems, which had all come from different backgrounds. Like the children she had known in foster care, some of them might be sibling groups who had come from the same time and place, but each individual or group could have a different history. Different damage. Different curses.

Maybe she had made a mistake in considering the whole of the collection and assuming all of them were cursed and that they would all need to be treated the same way. But what if that weren't true? What if the gems and their issues were just as individual as children?

Upon arriving home, she retrieved the small wooden chest and started going through the gems. Not just running her fingers through them and laughing at the amount of wealth that they represented, but actually looking at each gem individually and classifying them.

Chances were that they were all cursed. Why would the Papillons have given them to her otherwise? They had wanted to rid themselves of the curse. Maybe it was what kept pushing Calliopia away from the family. Maybe it had caused them other grief. They didn't want the gems in their home, in their possession any longer. They saw an opportunity to dump them on Reg, and they would not take them back. They were hers for good, until she could figure out the best way to handle them.

But maybe a few had slipped through that were not cursed. Or maybe the Papillons had justified themselves in giving Reg the treasure by including non-cursed stones as well as the cursed ones. Maybe they weren't all bad. As traumatized and damaged as many of the kids Reg had known in foster care were, there were still those who had somehow overcome all their challenges, who had studied and worked hard and pulled themselves up by the boot-straps to qualify for scholarships that would open a pathway out of poverty and homelessness that was closed to so many others. Sometimes those with the worst stories still made it out and got ahead in life. Maybe some of Reg's gems were overachievers and could provide her with a little liquidity while she worked on the others.

She hadn't invited Corvin into the cottage or offered to show him what she had.

Starlight crouched on the kitchen table, watching what Reg was doing with great attention. She had been afraid at first that he would think that the gems were something to play with and would bat them off the table, but he was still and watching her curiously as she scooped and sorted the stones.

Some of them were very powerful, like the ones that she had initially picked out for her trip to the jewelers. It made sense that she had been attracted to the more powerful gems when she had selected which ones to liquidate.

But others were smaller or had less power when she reached out her psychic senses to examine them. Some of them barely stirred any response. So she kept the powerful ones separate from the weaker ones. Maybe the weaker ones would be easier to purify. Maybe if she tried firing those ones, she would have more success.

An idea tickled at the back of her mind that if Davyn had just let her do what she wanted with the gems, that she might have been able to cleanse even the most powerful ones. He had forced her to hold back, and to give up when she felt that she might have been able to achieve her goal if she'd just been given a free hand.

But she couldn't practice firecasting by herself, and she didn't know of another firecaster who could help her. It was not a common gift.

She sorted the larger piles of gems into smaller piles. She couldn't always define what it was she was dividing them by. It wasn't their appearance or the type of stone. Sapphires were mixed with quartz and garnet. Diamonds with zircon and topaz. She couldn't put into words exactly what it was she was looking for or feeling when she considered each of the gems. She didn't stop to think about it too much, not wanting to get derailed trying to figure it out. She just kept going.

Reg was getting tired. Her eyes were itchy, and she could barely see straight, let alone study the gems through a jeweler's loupe. But if she stopped in the middle, she wasn't sure if she would be able to pick up on it again. She didn't trust herself to get back on task once she lost momentum.

Starlight jumped down from the table and prowled around the house, only to return a while later and sit on the table again, looking at all the piles of glittering stones. But not once did he lay a paw on any of the piles to mix them up or to play with the precious gems.

At some point, he disappeared, and Reg supposed he had gone off to sleep for a few hours. It was light out when Reg started going through the cupboards and drawers in her kitchen looking for bags to sort the gems into. She found half a box of zip-top sandwich bags, and used them to segregate the gems, one pile per bag. She was exhausted, but had a great sense of accomplishment as she looked over all of the bags piled up on the table.

She wasn't really sure what she had accomplished. She had sorted the gems based on how they felt to her. Maybe she was drunk. Maybe she was still under the influence of the sea air and Corvin's charms. She was tired, that was for certain. Any or all of those things might have impaired her gifts or influenced her in some way. The gems might just be separated into random groups, and when she'd had some rest and a chance to think, it might all just be nonsense. Like looking back on a bad trip. Knowing that she had believed everything she saw was real at the time, and yet simultaneously had known that it was not.

The sun was already coming up when Reg collapsed onto her bed to try to get a bit of sleep while she still could. Pretty soon, Sarah would probably be coming around expecting to have a chance to visit with her. Jessup might decide she wanted to continue the conversation about the wallets and just what exactly Reg had been doing with them. Corvin might call to discuss the evening and go back over the pertinent details.

She could shut off her phone so that none of them would disturb her, but Reg did not like to be cut off from the rest of the world. She didn't like to think that she was isolated. She would rather be woken up if something happened.

CHAPTER THIRTY

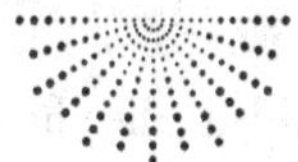

Starlight was curled up on the bed snoring and, pretty soon, Reg was right there with him in dreamland. So thoroughly zonked out that if Sarah had come to the cottage that morning to check Reg's calendar, deliver the mail, and have a visit, Reg had slept right through it. And she imagined that Sarah would probably have woken her up, once she saw the gems, to ask her what was going on.

She had only gotten a few hours of sleep when her body woke her up and she could not find a comfortable position to go back to sleep. Reg dragged herself to the kitchen, promising herself coffee if she could stay awake long enough to brew it. Starlight had been looking out the living room window, and plopped down to sit in front of his food dish and yowl at Reg if she didn't fill his dish in 3.5 seconds.

"Yeah, yeah. I know. It's coming."

She found some tuna, which made her feel queasy all over again, remembering how she had felt on the boat after they had turned around to go back to shore, with no idea that she would see the gems again in just a short time.

That fish had to have grabbed the gems the moment she had tossed them in, and then gone on to find the fisherman who had hooked or netted him. And how could that be, when she and Corvin hadn't seen anyone else close by? It was impossible, just like she'd told Corvin. She knew that magic didn't have to be logical, but it was still an impossibility that it had happened.

Reg just dumped the tuna into Starlight's bowl, not trying to calculate how much he needed. Let him get fat. She couldn't be bothered with fussing.

Starlight happily gobbled the fish, making loud chawing noises that did not improve her nausea.

The coffee had not yet finished brewing when Reg's phone started to vibrate. She looked at it, deciding even before she saw who was calling that she wouldn't answer it. Whoever it was would have to wait until she'd had her morning—afternoon—coffee and had a chance to wake up properly.

But she saw Ruan's picture on the screen and scrambled to pick it up.

"Ruan!"

"Reg Rawlins." The pixie licked his lips. "Reg Rawlins is a deep sleeper."

"Did you call earlier? Yeah, sorry about that. I was up all night…"

"Night is easier on piskie skin," he commented. "The moon's face is better than the sun's burning gaze."

"Yeah, well, that isn't why I stayed up, but you're right. It wasn't nearly so bright and…" she squinted at the bright sunlight in the garden outside, "…so *glaring* last night."

"Better for dealing with gems."

Reg looked around, afraid that she would find Ruan in the house with her. How had he known anything about what she'd been doing?

"What makes you think I was dealing with gems?"

"Reg Rawlins is already finished cleansing her gems?" Ruan asked. "I do not think so."

"Well, no, I guess when you put it that way. No, I haven't

finished cleansing the gems yet. Although… I've been working on it."

"They are difficult?" Ruan asked.

"Yes. I've tried a bunch of different things, based on what you said, but I guess now I'm down to… trying to figure out where they came from. How am I supposed to find their rightful owners when they are hundreds of years old? I don't know how long they were in possession of the—their previous owners. They might have been stolen ages ago. And they might have gone through several different hands after that. I was looking on my phone at some of the gems that people said were cursed, and it seems like they just get stolen one time after another."

She remembered what Corvin had said about warlords stealing them not only for their monetary value, but also for their magical properties. One gem might have changed hands a dozen times in the midst of wars and raids.

"The gems do not belong to you. Or to the one who owned them before you."

"No."

"But you can find a rightful owner."

"I don't know." Reg shook her head to herself. Such a venture felt as though it might take a lifetime. Especially if she had to trace each stone's individual history. Why wasn't there just a depository that cursed gems could be taken to, and someone there could be tasked with the job of finding out where they belonged? "These aren't big gems like you would find in a crown. I mean, some of them are a good size, but not *that* big. How can I find the rightful owner for something like that?"

There was silence from Ruan for a few moments while he considered her question. His answer surprised her.

"I think Reg Rawlins has already started to trace the gems to their sources."

She looked around again, sure that he must be watching her. How else could he know that she had even been working on the problem? She looked at the baggies of gems spread out over the kitchen table. She had done her best to sort them into groups, but she couldn't be sure that the gems she had grouped all came from the same owner or even the same country. It had all been done by feel, and it was completely possible that she had been sorting them based entirely on her own preferences and impulses.

"I've been trying," she said carefully. "But how could anyone do that? Especially someone like me, without any training."

"Perhaps Reg Rawlins would like some help."

"I'd love some help. But I don't know any experts, and I'm not sure who I could trust even if I did."

"You could call Ruan."

Reg laughed. "I'm already on the phone with Ruan."

"Reg Rawlins the sorceress could *call* Ruan."

Reg realized he was talking about transporting him to her magically. She had done it once before, though she had been told afterward that it was extremely powerful magic, and she wasn't sure whether she would be able to do it again. And the first time, she had been calling Calliopia, not Ruan. She had a better psychic connection to Calliopia because of blood magic.

"I don't know. I don't remember exactly how I did it the first time."

She tried to remember the details, but they were foggy. It was incredibly frustrating to deal with the holes in her memory. She had looked in her crystal ball for Calliopia and Ruan. And then she had called Calliopia's name.

Reg walked across the room and set her crystal ball on the coffee table. She sat down on the couch and stared into it. She still held the phone to her ear, which would probably distract her and keep her from seeing anything clearly.

"If I call you… that won't screw up your plans?" Reg asked. "And what about Calliopia? You don't want to be separated from her, do you?" She had been told there was no equivalent of divorce among the fairy and pixie folk. But they also strictly forbade pairings between fairies and pixies. Reg hoped that Ruan had not abandoned the young fairy.

"We will not be separated," Ruan assured her. "You will call us both."

Which was what she had done the first time, when she had called Calliopia and Calliopia had grabbed hold of Ruan to bring him with her.

"Reg Rawlins needs help. We owe for the healing of Calliopia."

"You don't owe me anything." Reg was about to say that she had been paid for the service but, looking at the gems, thought it was probably best not to mention the fact.

But Ruan would probably figure out on his own where the gems had come from, if he hadn't already.

And she hadn't considered the danger that Ruan might try to steal the gems. As far as he was concerned, it would not be stealing, because pixies believed that anything that came from under the earth belonged to them. He would believe that he was simply taking back what was already his. And she didn't think that his gratitude for what she had done for Calliopia would necessarily have anything to do with the decision.

"Ruan, if I call you, you cannot take the gems," she warned. "If you want a few of them, I will give them to you, but you can't take all of them."

If she were going to have to give most of them back to the rightful owners, she couldn't afford to give away all the rest.

"The gems are not thine to give," Ruan countered.

"Maybe not. But they're not yours to take, either."

There was a low chuckle from Ruan. Something that didn't sound as though it should come from the round, childish face. Something deeper and much more grown up than his appearance.

"Humans think they own what they take from the earth, but they do not."

"Pixies can't have everything that comes from the earth just because that's where their burrows are. That doesn't give them ownership over everything."

"Humans do not even know how to access the power of precious stones."

"Some humans know how to access some of the powers," Reg countered. Sarah knew how to access some of the youth-giving powers of her emerald, though Ruan's sister had been able to access much more of it. And Corvin had said that the warlord wanted the powers of the stones. Reg assumed that the warlords he was talking about were human. She was pretty sure they couldn't all be pixies. And there was Corvin himself, who could absorb the powers of other humans and of magical artifacts. She assumed that he could take something from stones of power as well. "If you are going to come and take the stones from me, I'm not going to call you here."

Ruan said something in an undertone that was probably a swear word in pixie. Or maybe a disparaging comment that he made to Calliopia who was undoubtedly there with him, holding his hand, waiting for Reg's call.

CHAPTER THIRTY-ONE

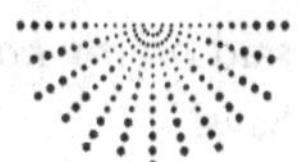

Eventually, Ruan's grudging voice came over the line. "If Reg Rawlins calls, Ruan will not take the stones. But *they are not thine.*"

"Okay." Reg accepted his viewpoint. She knew that they had been given to her and she had accepted them, but it was also true that the stones had probably been stolen and were therefore not the fairies' to give to her in the first place. "Finders keepers" wasn't exactly a legal precept she could rely on. "Maybe some of them have a different rightful owner. That's what you're going to help me to figure out, isn't it?"

"We will find their source," Ruan agreed. Which Reg wasn't sure what quite the same thing.

"So you promise me that you will not take the stones. You *promise.*"

She felt a certain amount of uncertainty that a pixie would keep a promise, even if she wrung one out of him. Pixies and other races had different moral strictures than humans. A pixie would probably consider a promise made to a human to be worthless and unenforceable.

"Ruan promises on his honor."

"And there aren't any loopholes? You don't have your fingers crossed?"

"Why would Ruan cross his fingers?"

"To get out of keeping the promise. You aren't going to turn around and tell me that you're not going to keep your promise because I am a human or because I let you into my house or anything stupid like that."

"No," Ruan huffed. "I said *on my honor.*"

What was this, Simon Says?

"Okay… I'm going to hang up now, so I can focus. Are you ready? I don't know if I can do this again, but I'll try."

"We await."

Reg terminated the call. She slid the phone into one of the pockets of her skirt and breathed out slowly, trying to calm any anxieties or doubts about what she was doing.

She stared into the crystal ball and saw nothing. She kept breathing slowly, forcing the air to move in and out in a focused rhythm, fixing her gaze on the ball.

There was nothing to worry about. Once she was relaxed and focused, she would be able to call Ruan. Ruan would be able to help her with the gems, and everything would work out as she had hoped.

The phone rang again, the buzzing distracting her. Reg hesitated, thinking that she should just ignore it. But what if it were Ruan again, with further instructions? She worked the phone out of her pocket and looked at it. Not Ruan again. Corvin this time. Hadn't she spent enough time with him the evening before? She could use a little breathing room.

But he knew more about her problems than anyone else, including Ruan. Reg groaned and swiped the screen to answer.

"Corvin? I'm kind of in the middle of something here. Is it important?"

"What are you doing that's so important?" he challenged, which Reg thought was more than a little insulting. She didn't have important things to do? Did he think that she just sat around all day and waited for him to call?

"None of your business." Then she bit her tongue and waited for him to state his business. She would not babble excuses and sound like she was his inferior. He didn't have any authority over her, and she didn't owe him any explanation.

"I have been doing some more research on your gems," Corvin said finally, sounding irritated.

"Oh, great. Did you find something in your historical records?"

"Well… no, not exactly. I was looking at some more modern literature."

"What does that mean?" Myths and fairy tales were his usual purview. She had no idea what "more modern" meant. 1800s?

"Scientific literature." Corvin sounded a little embarrassed that he'd had to stoop to reading such things in order to find his answers. "There are some methods for tracking down where gems came from, sometimes right down to the exact mine, if they have enough information in their databases."

"Really?" Reg was skeptical. Science promised a lot of things that it didn't quite follow through on. Whatever futuristic methods Corvin was looking at were probably years away from actually being commercialized and available to someone like Reg. "How do they do that?"

"It's called spectroscopy. They use a laser to vaporize a few atoms of the gemstone, and they can tell by the composition of the vapor—"

"You want to use a laser on my gems?"

"It wouldn't damage them or reduce their value in any way. It would just be a few atoms from the surface of the gem, and they would be able to tell by the elements present—"

"No. No way. I don't want them harmed any further."

"I told you it doesn't do any damage."

"I don't believe it. And I don't want anyone messing with

them. And… I don't know how anyone would test all of them, anyway. The cost of something like that is probably astronomical."

"Well, it might be pricey if you tested every one, but maybe if you tested just a few, you would be able to tell where *all* of them came from," Corvin pointed out, in his ultra-smooth voice, acting as if she were being unreasonable. Just a hysterical woman. She hated it when he got all professorial and acted as if he knew so much more than she did. Reg knew stuff too. It just wasn't the kind of stuff he learned from books.

Reg looked at the bags of gems on the table. All from one place? "They aren't all from one mine. Or even all from the same country. It's not like someone just mined all these stones and kept them together in one collection."

"Well, it's not likely, no. But if you can test a few, and then you could move those stones, then you would have more capital to test the next ones."

"Do you know someone who does this spectral-whatever?"

"Spectroscopy," Corvin repeated, enunciating it carefully. "Not spectral, that would be ghosts."

"Uh-huh." Reg waited. Corvin had a bad habit of not answering her questions.

"And no… I'm just in the research stage. I don't know anyone who does this, and we'd have to be careful of who we approached about your… gems of unknown origin."

The fewer people who knew that she had them, the better. Reg wasn't particularly interested in having some unknown scientist laser off chunks of her gemstones to identify their origin. She had Ruan. With Ruan's skills coupled with her own, Reg didn't think she needed anyone else's scientific crap.

"I don't think I need that."

"I thought you were convinced that tracking the origins of your gems was the way to go."

"Yeah, but I'm on that. I went a different way than spectral analysis."

Actually, what she had done probably *was* closer to spectral analysis. She just wanted to get under his skin.

"Spectroscopy," Corvin corrected, an edge to his voice.

"Whatever it is. I don't need it. And I'm in the middle of something, so if that's everything…"

"I'm trying to help you."

"Yeah. I appreciate it. But I need to go now. Maybe if this doesn't work, we'll try your thing."

Corvin saved her the trouble of having to hang up. She put the phone down on the coffee table and waited for a moment to see whether it would ring again. She didn't expect it to, since he was the one who had broken the connection. After a half a minute of silence, Reg turned her attention back to the crystal ball and refocused her attention on it.

As she tried to breathe calm into her body and consider what she might see in the crystal, she heard Starlight's paws on the floor as he padded over to her. He jumped up beside her, and Reg put her hand on him, petting him as he snuggled close, purring.

He always knew when she could use the boost to her psychic senses.

Reg immersed herself in the warm, sharpened sensations, gazing into the crystal. Gradually, the shapes deep inside began to shift until she could see Ruan and Calliopia. They sat somewhere outside, Calliopia in the sun and Ruan in the shade, with his hoodie pulled up over his head and dark sunglasses on. Fairies needed sunlight and pixies shunned it, but Ruan was willing to do anything for his mate.

It might just have been the effect of the crystal ball, but Calliopia seemed taller than Reg remembered her. She was only an adolescent, so Reg supposed she might still be growing. They held hands, sitting as close to each other as the arrangement would allow. They were talking, but Reg couldn't hear what they were saying as she focused in on them, becoming part of the world they were in, wherever they were. She concentrated on Calliopia, rubbing the faint scar in her hand with her thumb. The bond between the two of them was still there, despite Calliopia's efforts to break it.

Reg saw Calliopia's lips form the word *now* and didn't know whether it was an instruction to her or a warning to Ruan that they were going to be called. Reg took a deep breath, fortifying herself the best she could.

Calliopia, come.

CHAPTER THIRTY-TWO

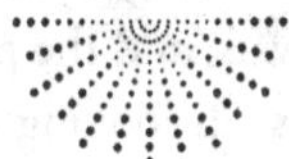

There was a jumble of images, the whole world going sideways. Reg was overwhelmed with a rushing, whirlwind feeling, tripping and somersaulting along through space until, eventually, something large fell onto the floor beside the coffee table. Good thing they hadn't actually landed on the coffee table; that would have been painful. Reg opened her eyes and looked at the pixie and fairy, upended on her floor, looking thoroughly undignified. They righted themselves as quickly as they could, Calliopia releasing Ruan's hand. She brushed at her clothes, straightening her dress and wiping away any dust from Reg's floor. Ruan jumped to his feet, laughing.

"What a ride is that!"

"I imagine so!" Reg agreed. She felt bad about pulling them to her, dumping them in the middle of her cottage like that. But it had been Ruan's idea. His request.

The couple looked around. They had been in Reg's cottage a couple of times before, so it was not unfamiliar to them. Calliopia saw Starlight sitting on the couch and hissed at him. Starlight hissed back.

"Mind your manners," Reg warned the two of them.

Cats and fairies did not get along. Nor did pixies and cats, for that matter, but Ruan had spent some time with Starlight and had grown to accept him, if not to like him. He delved into one of the pockets of his pants and pulled out a small jar. Reg did not look to see what he shook out onto his hand and offered to Starlight as a treat. Probably a spider and, if so, Reg didn't want to know about it. She was better off not seeing that. Starlight eagerly snarfed down whatever delicacy it was, and the pixie downed one himself.

"My gems," Calliopia said, looking at the stones arranged on the table, sorted into bags.

Reg's stomach clenched. While she knew that they had come from the Papillons, she had hoped that Calliopia wouldn't recognize them. She had certainly not expected the fairy to claim them.

"Not your gems," she countered, keeping her voice even. "They were given to me. By your parents. They are no longer the property of your family. If you don't like it, take it up with them."

Calliopia walked over to the table and looked through the bags, her eyes bright and interested. Reg watched her carefully. As much as she had tried to get rid of the gems, she wasn't prepared to let Calliopia just walk away with a bag or two of them. She was getting closer to finding the way to cleanse them.

Ruan joined Calliopia at the table as her hand lingered over one of the bags, fingering a couple of the gems under the plastic.

"Reg Rawlins has been hard at work," Ruan said with an approving nod.

"I have," Reg admitted. She yawned. "Stayed up late last night trying to get them sorted."

Ruan looked carefully over each bag. He pulled one of them toward him. "These ones are not cursed," he observed. "Reg Rawlins cleansed them?"

"No. Those ones were not cursed to begin with. Or if they were... it wore off. I will use those ones to get myself some money." She motioned to the cottage. "So I can pay for the rent and my food."

Ruan nodded. Reg didn't know how much he understood

commerce. She didn't know if he still had a car, but he had once, so he must have had to pay for gas and repairs, if nothing else. She assumed that when he and Calliopia traveled, they must have to pay for at least some of the places they stayed, even if they found free shelter at others. So Ruan understood money and the need for it more than other pixies, living in burrows and eating grubs.

Reg put out her hand and took the baggie of clean gems from Ruan. Even if those were the only ones she managed to hold on to, she had to make sure that he couldn't take them. Calliopia's eyes lingered on them. She gave Reg what looked to her like a pout.

"Those too were cursed."

Reg looked at them through the bag before putting them into a pocket. "These ones? Are you sure? Maybe… the curse wore off over time?"

"No. Curses do not wear off," Calliopia insisted.

Maybe something that Reg had already tried, maybe dropping them all over town in wallets, had done the trick. Only Reg hadn't realized it at the time.

"Well, it doesn't matter either way. I'm just glad that these ones are curse-free so that I can use them. It is all the others that are a problem." Reg eyed the mess. "I sorted them, but I don't know whether it is right. Do you?"

Ruan nodded, while still looking the bags over carefully. Reg suspected that he was itching to take at least a bag or two.

"They hail from many places," Ruan observed.

"Yeah. I don't know how I'm supposed to find the rightful owners for all of them. It's impossible."

He shrugged. "Perhaps not all. Perhaps only some."

"Even that seems… impossible. How am I supposed to figure out who is supposed to own something that was stolen generations ago? I would have to find the original owner, and then find his heirs… over generations… it isn't possible."

"If you do not start…" Ruan gave an expressive shrug.

If Reg didn't at least give it a try, there was no way she would succeed. Not even with one stone.

"So what do I do?"

"Go there."

"Go where?"

"To their source," Ruan said, rolling his eyes as if the answer should have been obvious.

"The countries they came from? The mines?"

He nodded.

Reg sighed, shaking her head. "How can I do that? I don't even know which countries they each came from. And to travel there… I have to cash in the other gems to get enough money, find out what the travel requirements are, visas and identification and all that. I don't even know whether they'll even let me on a plane." What if they identified her as someone with outstanding warrants? What if they fingerprinted her or used facial recognition and decided to hold her for things she had done in the past? "Can you even get on a plane with gems like this? They'll want to know where I got them. And I can't explain it."

Ruan shook one of the bags of gems. He picked at the plastic. "How does it work?"

"Traveling with gems? I have no idea!"

"No," he scowled. "Opening the bag."

Reg laughed. She took it from him and showed him how to separate the two sides of the zipper to open the bag he had picked up. Ruan held the bag up to his face, sticking his nose into the mouth of the bag and inhaling deeply. Reg scratched the back of her neck. Exactly what did gems smell like? She couldn't believe that they had a smell at all. There hadn't been any particular odor when all the gems had been stored together in one chest. There was no mustiness or other smell that Reg associated with old things. Gems didn't rot or disintegrate. That was one of the things that made them retain their value. As stones, they would stay in the same form for centuries without any degradation.

"You," Ruan told Reg, holding the bag up to her.

Reg took it uncertainly. "What? Am I supposed to smell them too?"

He nodded.

Reg inhaled, pulling the smell in and holding her breath, trying to identify a particular nuance.

"And now," Ruan explained, "Reg Rawlins takes us there."

CHAPTER THIRTY-THREE

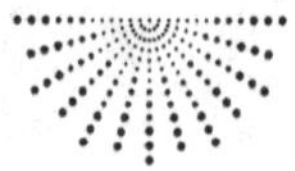

Reg snorted. "I what? I take you where?"

Ruan pressed the bag upward again, toward her nose. "Smell, smell! Take us there! To their source!"

"I can't take anyone anywhere!" Reg protested.

Ruan pushed the bag back up toward her nose again, insistent.

"Reg Rawlins can call Ruan and Calliopia here," he pointed out. "She can take us elsewhere!"

"No…"

Ruan went to Calliopia and took her hand. "We all together. Join together."

Ruan resealed the bag of gems, put it into Reg's pocket and took her hand in his. Reg took Calliopia's in the other. Ruan's hand was moist and bony. Too hard for the hand of a little boy, which was what he looked like but was not. Calliopia's hand was smooth and soft, and her strength was different. Not gristly like Ruan's, but Reg could still tell that she was much stronger than a human.

Reg looked at Ruan, not sure what to do. She had never transported herself along with someone else.

"How do I do this?"

"Close thine eyes," Ruan instructed. His tone was not sharp, but patient, like a parent walking his child through tying her shoes or riding a bike for the first time.

Reg closed her eyes, and breathed in and out, trying to settle herself and feel comfortable holding on to Calliopia's and Ruan's hands.

"See the gems in thy mind."

Reg pictured them, trying to make the image as clear as possible in her mind.

"Smell them."

Reg did her best to bring the smell into her mind. Green and fresh and warm, like spring air.

"See the source from whence they came."

That was more challenging. Reg focused on the smell, felt the weight of the gems in her pocket, and pictured them in her mind. But she had to picture where the gems came from, not the gems themselves. She didn't even know what a diamond mine looked like, other than a vague Disney-esque picture of dwarfs plucking gems from the inside of a dark tunnel. She inhaled again, trying to cement the smell of the place in her mind. Green. Wild. The air thick and hot around her.

"Yes, you see?" Ruan chuckled. "Much smoother when Reg Rawlins is with us."

Reg was reluctant to open her eyes. Ruan let go of her hand, and then Calliopia did the same. There was something buzzing in the air. A bug. Reg swiped at it.

"We are here, Reg Rawlins," Ruan called softly. "Open thine eyes."

Reg didn't want to, but eventually, she did. The cottage was gone. Everything familiar was gone. She was in the middle of a hot green jungle. And it was not somewhere she wanted to be.

"What are we doing here? This doesn't make sense. We don't want to come here. I want to go back home."

"First time traveler," Ruan said with a laugh. "It will get easier."

"I don't want to travel. I don't want to be here. I'm doing just fine without any more gems. We can just leave these ones here and go home." Reg took the baggie of gems out of her pocket and looked around. If she left them there and transported herself back home, the gems would be sure not to follow her again. It was much too far for them to go. She would just dump them and run. Someone else would find them, and his life would be blessed because of them.

"Hold, Reg Rawlins," Ruan said, putting his hand on her arm, his words pitched low and soothing. But Reg was not a horse or whatever other kind of animal might be spooked by sudden movements. She was a human, and she didn't want to be stuck in the middle of a jungle she had never seen before.

She started to flash back to the Everglades. Lost in the midst of the swamp with no idea which way to go to get home. Predators around her, both of the magical sort and the conventional kind that would just tear her to shreds and eat her. She panicked, remembering being tied up and drugged or enchanted. Seeing the rows of human skulls in Tybalt's vault.

"No," she insisted. "I have to go home."

Ruan patted her arm. "Shh. No danger here. Let us look around and find the source."

Having a job to do made Reg feel a little bit more stable, but she still wanted to go home where she knew she was safe. She looked around for a mountain with a hole in the side of it. A mine, like she had seen on TV. If she had transported them there based on what she had learned from the gems, then they must be close to the entrance of the mine.

"This way," Ruan suggested. "We will follow the water."

CHAPTER THIRTY-FOUR

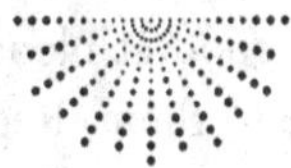

Reg stuck close to Ruan as he led the way. No way was she going to be left behind, fending for herself alone.

The canopy of trees shaded them from the hot sun. Ruan adjusted his sunglasses on his nose and tugged his hood down farther.

Calliopia looked back at Reg, her irritation clear. "Try not to crash through the jungle like a buffalo."

Reg's face heated. She tried to step quietly. The pixie and the fairy seemed to have no trouble slipping silently through the vegetation, but every step Reg made seemed to broadcast her presence to anyone who was nearby. Calliopia didn't criticize her further, so Reg hoped that she at least only sounded like a *small* buffalo.

They were on a slight downhill slope. It was a while before Reg's dull human senses could discern what the pixie's already had. The sound of water splashing somewhere close by. As they got closer, she could smell the water. She hesitated, worried about triggering her siren instincts. Ruan and Calliopia didn't know about her parentage and how she might react. Would a siren attack a pixie or a fairy? Or only a human? She didn't imagine her instincts were that discriminating. Blood was blood.

As they drew closer to the water, she could hear voices. More potential victims. Reg resolved to stay well back from the water, which would hopefully keep her from being triggered. The others were going more slowly as they reached an embankment that was just above the river. There was a sharp drop-off of eroded earth and rock. They followed the embankment downriver, toward the voices, staying just under the edge of the trees, hopefully out of sight of the people down below them.

Fairies and pixies were good at blending with their surroundings. Even walking so close to them, Reg lost sight of Calliopia or Ruan as Callie's green dress and Ruan's dirty brown clothes blended with the jungle. Reg was sure that she, on the other hand, stuck out like a sore thumb.

She wanted to ask Ruan where this mine was that they were supposed to be visiting. Had she taken them to the wrong place or was it close by and she just couldn't see it because of the denseness of the jungle vegetation? Did Ruan have any idea where he was going?

They reached a place where they could see men down in the river. They stood in water up to their mid-thighs and called back and forth to one another as they worked. They had shallow boxes and they stooped into the water to fill and then held up high, shaking them slowly back and forth.

"What are they doing?" Reg whispered. "Panning for gold?"

Ruan raised an eyebrow at her. Calliopia scowled and held a finger to her lips.

Reg shook her head and turned her attention back to the men in the river. They were tall and very dark-skinned, their bodies impossibly thin, dressed in clothing that was almost as ragged as a pixie's. They continued to fill their boxes and to shake them. It didn't take long for Reg to realize that the bottom of the box was a screen, so that the boxes acted as sieves, allowing the men to strain the mud from the river bottom, looking at the larger bits of stone and debris. Reg still had in mind that they were looking for gold. She'd seen old Western movies where prospectors had panned for gold.

One of the men moved differently from the others and, at the distance Reg was from them, it took her a few moments to realize why. He handled his sieve differently because he had only one hand. The other arm ended in a stump. Reg was about to point this out to Ruan, then decided that he had probably noticed the fact before she had and kept her mouth shut. The man used his stump to hold the sieve against his body and plucked something out of it. He put it into his mouth to clean it off and held it up to the sun with a shout to the others.

They moved closer to see what he had found, and high-fived each other, their voices rising excitedly. Reg leaned closer, trying to get a better view of what was happening. Ruan glanced at her.

"A diamond," he told her.

"Really? People get diamonds out of rivers? I thought they had to go down mining tunnels, really deep."

Ruan shrugged. "Sometimes. And sometimes, like here, they have a river mine." He looked over at Calliopia and said something to her.

Calliopia considered for a moment, then offered, "Alluvial."

Ruan nodded. "Alluvial mine."

"So all they have to do is come over here and strain the muck to find the diamonds? That sounds a lot better than going down some hole in the ground."

Ruan did not say anything. Reg turned her attention back to the men congratulating the one-handed man who had found the diamond. She didn't think that they would have been so excited if it had been a common occurrence. Maybe they pulled only a few diamonds out of the river each day, so each one was reason for celebration. Maybe it only came out to one diamond each at the end of the day. But Reg knew what diamonds sold for. That would still make each man a very good living.

There was a shout from the shore. Reg had to lean out over the embankment to see the man standing beside the river. Unlike the men in the river, he was dressed in army fatigues, and in his hand he held a large gun. Reg couldn't see it very well and she didn't have much knowledge about guns, but she knew enough to iden-tify it as a machine gun. Something big and very deadly. He held it pointed at the group of men in the river. They turned and looked at him, each of them falling back a step or two and raising his hands in the air, separating from the man who had found the diamond. The man with the gun barked orders, gesturing at the one-handed man.

He was, Reg supposed, asking for identity papers or a permit to mine in that river. Some law enforcement officer who patrolled the river to make sure that everyone was properly authorized and behaved fairly.

The tall man who had found the diamond walked slowly through the water toward the army man, protesting or explaining, his words quick, asserting his rights. The man with the gun was insistent, repeating his demand. Eventually, the man with the diamond reached out and handed it to the soldier on the shore. The soldier folded it into a piece of paper and put it into a pocket, grinning. He motioned with his gun to the man who had found the diamond, threatening.

Reg realized with a sick heart that the soldier wasn't there to enforce some regulation, but to steal the man's treasure. His means to make a living.

CHAPTER THIRTY-FIVE

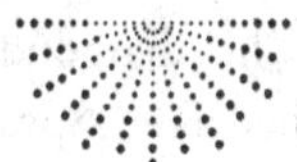

Reg turned to Ruan, her mouth dropping open. She tried to put together the words to express how she felt about this injustice. Nothing came to her. Ruan shrugged.

They continued to watch. The mercenary walked away from the river. It was some time before the men resumed their search for diamonds. Reg hoped that they would find enough by the end of the day to make up for the loss. Ruan and Calliopia stood there watching with Reg, their faces somber.

"Can we go talk to them?" Reg asked. "Do you think it would be safe?"

Ruan rubbed his chin. "As long as Reg Rawlins can touch us, we can return home."

They were relying upon her for their transportation back to Black Sands. If they got separated, Reg would not be able to take them back. She wasn't completely confident in her ability to return to her cottage at will, but Ruan seemed to take it for granted that she would be able to.

Reg nodded her understanding. "We'll stay close together."

They started to pick their way downriver again, getting closer to the men and the place where the soldier had stood and made his threats and demand. She wasn't sure how she would introduce herself to them, but they spotted her little company and started to talk excitedly again, pointing her out to each other and chattering in their native tongue. Reg had second thoughts. She hadn't even thought about the language barrier. She could sense the men's emotions and read what she could from their actions and body language, but it would take more than that if she wanted a conversation with them.

The man who had lost his diamond walked up the shore out of the water and approached Reg. Speaking, he touched her red hair, done up in tiny box braids, and motioned to his own face, almost black in comparison with her pale white skin. He had probably never seen a white person before, let alone a white woman with red hair. It would be something to tell his children and grandchildren about.

"You don't... do you speak any English?" Reg asked.

He said a few more words that she didn't understand, then addressed her. "My grandmother teach me. She work in big house for white man." He smiled proudly, a broad, toothy grin.

Reg breathed a sigh of relief. "We saw what happened. That man who just stole your diamond."

He nodded, face falling. "First stone we find in... five weeks." He held up the five fingers of his remaining hand to make sure she understood.

Reg quickly revised her ideas about how much money the men would be able to make searching the river for gems. One diamond in five weeks, split among—she did a quick head count—six men. Far less than she had speculated. It would be much harder to support themselves and their families on that. But depending on the size of the diamond, they could still make a living.

"I am Joseph," the man said. He looked at his friends. "We will go back to the village. Show you to our families. It is a great honor to be visited by a witch."

"I'm not..." Reg decided that it would be too difficult to explain to them that she wasn't really a witch, just a psychic, who happened to have parents who were... she didn't want to get into all that. She would let them call her a witch, just as she had stopped protesting Ruan calling her a sorceress. She had red hair, she had appeared there magically, she wasn't sure what the right word was to describe herself simply in his language. Or in English, for that matter. Sometimes it was just easier to take the path of least resistance. They were offering to show her hospitality, and she wanted to talk to them further, to get to know them. "My name is Reg. And this is Ruan and Calliopia." She motioned to the pixie and fairy.

Joseph's eyes got wider as he studied her two companions. He bowed low to them, muttering something to his friends. They all followed him out of the water and bowed to both Reg and the others. Ruan gave a low bow back, his eyes glittering. Calliopia gave a scarce nod, her head held high. Reg nodded and shrugged, unsure how to respond to their actions.

The men led them back to the village. It felt as though they went a mile or two through the jungle, following no pathway that Reg could see. But it might have been much shorter than that and she was just out of shape and not used to walking through such heavy vegetation. At least she didn't have to try to walk quietly anymore, which helped. Though she couldn't help noticing how quiet and catlike the men were.

Eventually, they reached a small clearing with several shacks or huts clustered together. Young children, tiny, with arms as thin as sticks ran to greet the men, who smiled and lifted them up and spoke with them. Women in colorful dresses, many with head scarfs, stood back, watching Reg and the other visitors with wary, distrustful eyes. Reg knew fairies and pixies stole young children, so maybe they had reason to be wary.

The men sat down on the ground, motioning for Reg and her companions to join them. Reg felt a little awkward at first. She clearly stood out, and the women and children watched from a distance, fascinated with the white woman with the red hair. But Reg soon became engrossed in the conversation with Joseph and forgot about everything else.

She couldn't help but notice that Joseph was not the only one who was missing a limb or part of one. She wasn't sure whether it was a birth defect, common to this village because of their isolation from others, or perhaps a disease or bacteria that had resulted in their having to be amputated. There were some in the village missing both hands, and even one man missing both arms with only stumps extending from his shoulders.

Joseph caught her looking at the man. He tapped his own stump with the other hand. "Mbombo's army," he explained. "Cut off, prevent men from joining the rebels against him."

Reg's eyes widened. She couldn't imagine someone having men's hands amputated just to prevent them from rising up against him. And clearly, it was not only men who had been maimed. A number of women and even little children had been victims as well.

"How could he do that?" Reg shook her head in disbelief.

"Machetes," Joseph explained, making a chopping motion. He had mistaken her horror for a query as to how it had been done. "Many people, very fast. Must bind them up quickly, see doctor, or..." He rolled his eyes and made a slumping motion, indicating death.

"That's horrible!"

He nodded his agreement and conveyed her comment to the other men, who talked among themselves and nodded. Reg looked at Ruan and Calliopia, gauging their reactions to this news. They nodded as if it didn't come as a great surprise to them. Reg supposed that if they had lived for hundreds of years, they had probably witnessed all kinds of barbarity. Despite media coverage of mass killings at schools or nightclubs, the world did seem like it had become more civilized in the last few centuries. In Reg's world, she did not expect to encounter villages filled with people who had been mutilated by a warlord.

CHAPTER THIRTY-SIX

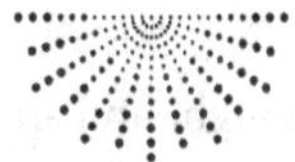

"$\mathcal{A}$nd I am sorry that man took your diamond," Reg said. "Does that happen a lot?"

Joseph nodded. "Very difficult to hold on to a stone until you can sell it," he admitted. "Hide it under your tongue so no one sees it… we should have been quiet and not given ourselves away. But it is very hard when you have been looking for so long without finding a stone."

Reg remembered their cheers and high-fives. Relief and joy that they had finally found what they had been seeking for weeks.

"How much would you get for a diamond like that?"

Joseph looked around at the others in the circle. "The last one we got eight hundred dollars." He indicated himself and the other men. "For six men."

Reg was not great at math, but calculated that to be just over one hundred dollars per man. For five weeks of work. She was quickly realizing that her initial thought that it would be an easy life, just pulling diamonds out of the river, was totally off the mark. A hundred dollars to support a family for a month. All around her were indicators of the poverty they lived in, from the shacks to the children with arms like sticks and swollen, malnour-ished bellies.

"How much would someone pay for it?" Reg asked.

"Pay for it?" Joseph looked confused, having just told her what they had gotten for it.

"I mean… the man or the woman who buys it to put in a ring on a necklace, what would they pay?"

"Oh." He shook his head. "I do not know that." He relayed the question to his friends, who mostly shook their heads in response.

One leaned forward though, and spoke to Joseph with his eyes fixed on Reg. He was older than most of the others. His chest looked as if it were collapsing inward. He had a lot of scars on his face.

Joseph looked back at Reg. "He says his nephew lives in the city, and that he talks to the diamond brokers and the men who sell the stones when they are cut. He says ten thousand." Joseph shrugged and shook his head. "I do not think that can be."

"If it go to a jeweler," Ruan told Reg. "But maybe to a wizard, if a stone of power."

"For more money?" Reg demanded.

"For more…" Ruan's mouth twisted as he searched for the right English words and construction. "…other trade. Slaves, crops, weapons, sorceries."

Reg didn't like the sound of that. She put her hand to her head, which was aching with the heat and with the weight of the village's sorrows.

"You are tired," Joseph observed. "You have come a long way. You will come into my home and rest."

"Oh, no…" Reg protested weakly.

"You should come," Joseph told her. He stood up and extended a hand to her. Reg rose to her feet. She looked at Ruan and Calliopia.

"What about you? You'll want to go back."

"We wait," Ruan told her. "Reg Rawlins cannot travel unless rested."

"Well… you're probably right." Even just a psychic reading for a client could tire her out. Traveling across the ocean must take more energy than that.

She conceded and let Joseph lead her to his shack, where she met his shy wife and was shown to a mat on the floor where she could sleep.

Reg had slept on the streets before. She knew that if she were tired enough, she could sleep practically anywhere. It didn't need to be a comfortable soft bed in a darkened room. So she lay down on the mat, turned on her side with her back to Joseph and his wife, and listened to them conversing in a language she could not understand as she drifted off to sleep.

* * *

She awoke disoriented, unsure of where she was or what had happened. She listened to the noise of a fly buzzing and children's voices in the distance and tried to reconstruct her day and how she had ended up there. She couldn't help worrying about losing significant chunks of her memory, but it all came back to her quickly. Ruan's arrival, traveling around the world to the river mine, Joseph's village.

Reg got up from the mat slowly and looked around. Joseph and his wife were gone, and she was alone in the little shack. She took a quick look around, not wanting to be caught snooping. There was a fire pit in the middle of the floor. A small supply of grains and roots on a counter. There was a plastic basin, but no sign of plumbing. Water was probably carried in from the river, or a smaller stream closer to the village.

She walked out of the shack and looked around for the others. Ruan and Calliopia sat under a tree as they often did at home, with Ruan shaded and Calliopia in the sun, which was starting to descend. A lot of children were gathered around them, looking at them curiously, talking to each other and occasionally approaching the couple, then withdrawing in alarm if either of them moved or looked at them.

Reg approached them, smiling at the children who swarmed around her, touching her white skin or reaching up to examine her red hair. They were older than the children they had seen earlier.

"You must have all been at school," Reg observed. She didn't know whether they knew any English. But maybe they taught a bit at school, or the children had learned some from American music or TV.

One of them, a boy who Reg thought might be about ten, laughed. "No school. We do not go to school."

"Oh. You were out...?" Maybe they worked in fields or gathered fruit or did some other chore for their families.

"In the mine. All must help in the mine."

"In the river?" Reg asked in confusion. She had only seen the grown men working in the river. There hadn't been any children around. But maybe they worked another part of the river, where the water was shallower or the adults could watch over them and keep them safe from soldiers.

"No," a little girl with big black eyes shook her head at Reg and wound one of Reg's red braids around her finger, looking at it raptly. "Under de ground."

Reg looked around at the children to see whether she was being teased, or whether they supported what the little girl said. Several of them nodded. A few commented, but none of the others in English so she could understand.

"You work in an underground mine? All of you?"

They nodded. "We are small," the boy said, "we can go in holes too small for grown-ups."

"You are too big," the girl told him, poking him in the shoulder. "You getting too old."

The boy nodded, lowering his eyes. "Yes. I go soon to the river with the men. Or join the army."

"The army? You're too young for that," Reg laughed.

He shook his head vigorously. "The other boys, they already go. I stayed here because my leg hurt." He pointed to ugly, puckered scars on his leg. "But I am strong now. Big enough and strong enough to go."

Reg looked around for the adults, hardly able to believe what the children were saying. Was it all a big joke? Were they seeing how long they could string along the strange white lady? She had heard of child soldiers, but she thought that UNICEF and all the other organizations had lobbied to have such practices banned. They were well into the twenty-first century. How could such barbarity still be going on in the world?

She looked back at the scars on the boy's leg. She had a sneaking suspicion that they were from bullets, but she was afraid to ask. She knew about blood diamonds. Conflict gems. But she had never really pictured what that meant in terms of human life.

Reg walked over to Ruan and Calliopia and sat down with them. For a while, none of them said anything.

CHAPTER THIRTY-SEVEN

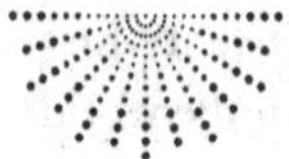

*T*he stones came from here?" Reg asked eventually.

Ruan nodded.

"From the river or from the underground mine?"

"They are the same source," Ruan explained. "The water pounds the rock and gathers the stones that wash out of the ground. Two mines with one source."

"And just the diamonds, or the other stones too?"

He shrugged. "They come from these people. Whether out of the same mine or nearby."

Reg looked around at the children still gathered close to them, so curious about the strange visitors. Who knew how much English they understood? "Can we talk without little ears listening?"

Ruan looked at the children. He suddenly bared his sharp teeth and let out a snarl that sent all of them running away, shrieking. Reg giggled and hoped that they hadn't been too traumatized by the sudden show of aggression.

"Children everywhere are the same," Ruan advised with a shrug.

"You're pretty scary. I nearly ran away myself."

"The first day Reg Rawlins met Ruan Rosdew, she was afraid."

Reg thought back to that first day. Not as afraid as she should have been. She had almost let him mesmerize her. She was lucky that he hadn't harmed her. Strong as pixies were, he could have done her damage. If Calliopia's blood had not burned him.

"You are very strong and dangerous," she told him.

Ruan looked pleased.

"So…" Reg touched the bag of gems in her pocket, which drew both Ruan's and Calliopia's immediate attention. "If these gems came from here, then can I give them back? I don't know who they were stolen from originally, or how long ago. But these people… they are the rightful owners. Just like Joseph and his friends are the rightful owners of the diamond the soldier stole today."

Neither of them agreed. Reg supposed that was a bit too much to expect from them. Ruan believed that the pixies should own anything that came out of the earth, and Calliopia had been part of the family that owned them before they had been given to Reg.

"They are the rightful owners," Reg asserted, looking at both of them for some sign of disagreement. It was too much to expect them to agree, but maybe if they didn't disagree, that was confirmation enough. "How do I give them back? Is there a ceremony? A spell? And…" Reg searched for the words to express what she wanted to say. "If I give them back, how do I make sure that they make things better for these people? That they won't just get stolen by the guys with guns and then the people are beaten down and worse off than they were to start with?"

* * *

Reg approached Joseph after the evening meal had been served. She and her company had refrained from eating anything, knowing they could eat however much they wanted when they got home. The villagers needed every bite of food they could get. Reg despaired over the little children, some of whom seemed to have no energy and who were, she feared, already at death's door.

Mothers looked away from the children they held, maybe off into a future they hoped might exist, and not down into their dying children's eyes.

"Do you have… a medicine man or a holy man?" Reg asked Joseph. "Or woman?"

Joseph nodded slowly. "Yes. We have Benji Kongolo. But… his power…" Joseph was apparently looking for a polite way to say that the elder wasn't able to perform the protective or healing rites that they hoped for. "It is *limited*. He is not powerful like you." Joseph indicated Reg, sweeping his hand down and up to indicate Reg's entire body.

Reg wanted to protest the declaration, but she kept her mouth shut. If she said she had no power, then why would Joseph let her see him? Why would Benji want to see her?

"I would like to talk to him."

"He does not speak your language."

"Then I would like to sit with him. Privately."

"I could translate for you."

Reg shook her head. "No. I need to see him alone."

Joseph nodded, accepting that Reg might have good reason to talk to the holy man on her own. "I will take you."

He got to his feet. Reg followed suit. Joseph led her beyond the small circle of huts, into the jungle. Reg kept her mouth shut and followed. She was sure it was not safe to be outside the village as night fell. Besides the night predators who might be stirring, there were also humans out there. They type of humans who shot at or recruited young boys to fight their wars, and girls to be their wives and slaves. Who stole gems at gunpoint and would be delighted with the haul they would find in Reg's pocket. Both Corvin and Ruan had warned about supernatural warlords wielding gems of power. Where were they? In the cities where they had all the modern conveniences? Or in the jungle, close to nature, able to hide in the shadows and watch unobserved?

Reg had thoroughly freaked herself out by the time they reached a camper shell in the middle of the jungle. A camper shell there in the middle of nowhere? Joseph walked Reg to the door of the cabin and stood to the side of it, knocking and raising his voice to say something to the occupant.

Reg waited anxiously for the answer. Eventually, a gruff man's voice responded. She looked at Joseph, who nodded. Reg stood there for a moment, unsure how to proceed. Gathering her courage, she stepped forward and tried the door handle. It moved when she turned it. The door clicked open.

"Mr. Kongolo?" Reg looked into the camper, then poked her head in to look down the length of it. "I'm sorry to bother you, but…"

He said something to her from within the darkness at the back of the camper. Feeling only slightly encouraged, Reg forced her feet to move, stepping farther into the home. It was getting dark outside, and it was pitch black away from the small windows at the front of the camper. Reg walked toward the sound of the voice. In a few steps, she reached the sleeping area, an upper and lower bunk. The upper bunk was filled with boxes and books.

On the lower, she had to squint to make out the shape of a man. She couldn't see any of his features, only the dark shape against the lighter sheets.

A voice encouraged her again. Old and gravelly, but friendly. A pat at the edge of the bed, close to where Reg stood.

Sit down.

Reg sat awkwardly, feeling like it was too close, too intimate to be sitting on the man's bed, only inches from him.

"I'm… I'm Reg," she told him, pointing to herself. "Reg."

"Benji."

"Joseph said that you are a holy man."

"Joseph."

"Yeah. So. Here's the thing…" Reg touched the bag of gems in her pocket. "These belong to you." She hesitated for a moment, then drew the bag out. He wouldn't be able to see it, so she didn't know why she bothered. Were there no lights? Lanterns? Candles?

She put them down on the bed, next to his hand. They glowed slightly, seeming to produce their own light.

"These stones are not mine," Reg said. "They are from your people. They belong to you."

Knowing that he could not understand her words, she concentrated on projecting her feelings to him, and trying to read his in return. She pushed the gems toward him in her mind, showing them to him, offering them.

He reached over and grasped the bag. He pulled it in to his body and hugged it against himself. The whole camper shell began to shake. Reg wondered briefly whether Joseph, still outside the camper, was shaking it for effect. Maybe some of the children from the village had followed them and thought it would be funny to scare the stranger.

But she knew that wasn't what was going on. The shaking originated inside the camper, not outside of it.

The holy man began to hum. Reg looked around her, wishing that she could see something in the dark interior of the camper. The stones glowed more. Reg focused her attention on them, on magnifying the light, and it increased again. She could see the bottom portion of Benji's face, lit up in grotesque detail by the underlighting. He was older than Joseph, but not a grizzled old man with gray hair and no teeth. And not, she didn't think, someone who had seen the centuries pass, like Sarah or others that Reg knew. Magic seemed to slow the progress of time in those people, but Reg felt like Benji's aging process had been sped up rather than slowed down.

Will you accept these stones? Reg tried to convey the thought to him.

He began to chant. Reg closed her eyes, listening to the syllables and rhythm of the chant. She couldn't understand it, but she wasn't sure she was meant to. Maybe it was words, and maybe it was just meaningless syllables, and the magic was contained in the cadence and tones. She could see colors in the darkness behind her eyelids, flashing and changing and growing with the chant, becoming more and more clear.

She saw brown hands of varying different sizes and tones pulling gems out of the river, and gems catching the light in the rock walls of underground tunnels.

And she saw the people in the village, but they were different from what she had actually seen with her own eyes. Whole families were together, the babies, children, and teens with their parents. Their bodies whole, not scarred from bullets or missing limbs. Their faces were happy, their eyes not hollow and sad. The mothers smiled and gathered their children in rather than staring off into the distance, looking for something to hope for, anticipating the next death.

Reg's cheeks were wet. She didn't rub the tears away, but let them fall, listening to the man's chant.

Can you use them? Reg wanted to know. *I don't want them to bring more suffering, more death.*

She opened her eyes. Benji pulled open the zipper on the bag and put his hand into it, running his fingers through the gems. He pulled out one stone and held it toward Reg. Reg hesitated, then took it from him, wondering why he had given it to her.

She let it warm in her hand. She closed her eyes once more, feeling the stone. It was a diamond. One of the largest stones. Why had he given it back to her? What did it signify?

Reg saw a man. He was unlike any of the men she had seen so far in the jungle. His skin was dark like those of Joseph and the other villagers. He wore army fatigues like the soldier who had stolen the diamond from Joseph. And he was fat. Everyone she had seen there had been thin, accustomed to eating meals that were scant with long periods of hunger between them. Someone who was that fat clearly had no trouble getting enough to eat.

Who is this?

You will find him. They were the first words that Reg had felt from Benji. They were strong and resonant, and she had no doubt that he spoke the truth.

He pulled another gem from the bag and put it in her hand. Reg concentrated on it. Not another diamond, but an emerald. Rich and green and warm. Like the lush growth of the jungle. A picture of Joseph came into her mind. Reg didn't have to ask questions this time. She would give the emerald to Joseph. That would be easy, and she felt confident that he would know what to do with it, how to use it to the best benefit of the village. He wouldn't let anyone take that stone away from him.

Benji ran his fingers through the gems that remained in the bag. There were still plenty of them. Enough to sustain and bless the village for a long time, if they were carefully guarded and used the right way. Benji drew a third gem out and put it into Reg's hand with the others.

A ruby this time. Red like Reg's braids.

For you.

"No." Reg tried to give it back to Benji. "No, these are for you. They belong to your people."

For you, he insisted firmly.

Reg didn't argue. She felt the three gems in her hand. Each different. Each very valuable. Each with a different purpose, though she wasn't one hundred percent sure what each purpose was.

Benji did not remove any more of the gems from the bag. His fingers worked to close the zipper at the top to seal them up again. He would, she hoped, find a suitable hiding place to store them in to ensure their safety. She wouldn't want them to be stolen from the villagers again.

Benji nodded reassuringly. He hummed some more, and then the sound gradually died away.

CHAPTER THIRTY-EIGHT

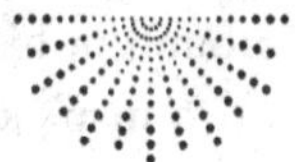

Reg turned the handle and pulled the camper door open, letting in the cooler night air. It was quiet, the sounds of bugs and birds and activity that she had become accustomed to quieted. There were a few unfamiliar night sounds, which made her anxious to return to the village, where she would at least have some protection from predators that slunk through the jungle looking for the weak and vulnerable.

There was a movement to her right and she turned quickly, panicking. But the tall, slim shape spoke in a reassuring voice.

"It is Joseph."

"Oh." Reg blew out her breath. "Thanks for waiting for me. I'm glad you didn't go back to the village."

"Of course not. You are ready?"

"Before we go…" Reg pinched the emerald between her fingers. "Put out your hand."

It sounded like a game. Or like one of those tortures that fellow foster children dreamed up. "Put your finger here," one would say, displaying an empty palm. Curious, Reg would do so, only to have the child close his fingers around it and give it a sharp jerk or twist, forcing her to her knees in pain.

But Joseph did not suspect any deception on her part. He put out his hand obediently. Reg placed the emerald in it.

"You must keep that safe. Find a way to sell it in the city, where you'll get a good price for it. Buy food, build a water pump, get the other things the village needs."

Joseph looked down at the gem, his night vision clearly better than hers, used to navigating at night without a light. "Where did you get this?" He rolled it around in his palm. "I have not seen a cut stone before, except in a rich man's jewelry."

"It is yours. It belongs to your people. If you have questions, you can talk to Benji, he can tell you what you need to know."

Joseph slipped it into his mouth, placing it under his tongue, where he had told her that he should have hidden the diamond instead of advertising its existence to the soldier.

"I will keep it safe."

Reg nodded. "Let's go back to the village."

They went slowly, Joseph quickly figuring out that Reg couldn't see where she was going. She remembered Ruan addressing her as "oh blind one" on their previous quest to the dwarf mountain and she smiled to herself.

"Is there a man around here, not in your village, a man who wears army fatigues and is very fat?"

Joseph turned to look back at her curiously. "How do you know of General Mbombo?"

"Benji—" Reg started to motion back to the camper and to explain, then remembered that Benji could not speak English and it might be difficult to explain the matter to Joseph. "Well… I heard of him. The General. Is he…" Reg cast about, finding it awkward to ask the question. She didn't really understand the politics and factions in the area. "Is your village for or against him?"

Joseph didn't answer immediately. They continued to walk through the jungle, Reg regularly stubbing her toes, tripping over something, or having a branch slap her in the face.

"The people in my village are not… aligned with the army or the rebel groups," Joseph said finally. "But the rebels often recruit them to fight, and some choose to join one side or the other. And sometimes they switch sides, if they are left behind or captured. It is not easy to answer."

Reg nodded thoughtfully. "But he is not good for your village. He does not protect you."

"No." Joseph gave a sharp laugh. "The General does not help anyone but the General."

Then why had Benji asked her to give one of the gems to the General? And how was she going to find him and get him to meet with her in order for her to give him the gem? Reg tried to think of a story that would make sense. How she had heard of him and wanted to help his cause. But she was sure that wouldn't make any more sense to the General than it did to Reg herself. A white woman showing up out of the jungle and offering him a large diamond? There was no reason for her to even be in the country.

She frowned, pondering on this while she trudged after Joseph. She swore as she barked her shin on a log that jumped in front of her. Joseph looked back at her. She could see little but the whites of his eyes.

"Are you okay?"

"Yes. Just a klutz."

"Klutz," Joseph repeated.

"It's… someone who is clumsy."

"Ah." He didn't argue that she wasn't clumsy, just blind as a bat. Reg wondered how much farther the village was.

* * *

She didn't know how much of the story she should tell to Ruan and Calliopia. Neither one was particularly happy with her returning *their* stones to the country they had come from. If they knew that she had been given a ruby in return, they would probably try to steal it from her. Since she'd been given it by the rightful owner, Reg assumed that she would now be able to use it as she pleased. She didn't want to lose it to a quick-fingered pixie or fairy.

So she gave them a brief description of the camper and the man she had found there. As much as she could tell them about the little she'd been able to see. She told them that she had given him the gems, but not that she had been given any of them back again.

"We go home now?" Ruan asked.

"Uh… I still have something else to do here. I guess that means sleeping here tonight, and then hopefully… tomorrow…"

"Something else?" Ruan lowered his brows, looking suspicious. "What else?"

"I can't discuss it. Something that the holy man wanted me to do."

"We should go home."

"You and Calliopia are nomadic. Why does it matter to you where we spend the night?"

"Reg Rawlins gave him the gems, we go home."

"He asked me to do something for him."

"Dangerous." Ruan shook his head. "This be a dangerous place. Not a good place to sleep, and Reg Rawlins should not make promises to medicine man."

"Why not?" That feeling in the pit of her stomach again. The beginnings of dread. How was it she kept making these mistakes over and over again? Don't take gifts from fairies. Don't go out with men of Corvin's ilk. Don't go to the Everglades looking for a lost wizard. There should be a rule book somewhere.

"Why does medicine man need Reg Rawlins to do something?" Ruan asked. "Medicine man has his own magic. And all of the stones. Why does medicine man not do his own magic?"

Ruan had a point. Reg shrugged and shook her head. "I don't know. I didn't ask. We didn't exactly have a detailed conversation.

I gave him the gems, he asked me to do something for him. I didn't think… that it might be a problem."

Calliopia looked around them. The jungle was dark. The shacks were darker blots in the night. There were a few flickering lights; candles or lanterns inside the huts. They cast long, flickering shadows across the central clearing where Reg talked with them. Reg could feel Calliopia's anxiety at the shadows. She remembered Calliopia's fear of being attacked by shadows in the night. And she had been attacked in the night. She clearly hadn't gotten over it.

"I'll ask Joseph where we can stay for the night," Reg said. She was surprised that they hadn't been asked. Weren't poor villagers always supposed to be hospitable? Inviting strangers to share their food and homes? It wasn't very hospitable to leave Reg and her company with nowhere to sleep.

And Reg was hungry. She had thought they would be going home right away and hadn't wanted to take food out of the mouths of the children. But now her stomach was growling, and it hurt, and there was nothing to eat. She hadn't even managed to bring her purse with her, where she always stowed a couple of granola bars or some food she could eat in an emergency. She'd had too many hungry nights herself as a child to take it for granted that she would always have something to eat.

She found her way, mostly by feel, to the shack that she thought was Joseph's, the one that she had napped in earlier in the day. She knocked quietly on the door, hoping that she wasn't disturbing anyone's sleep. Like the other men who had been digging in the river, Joseph had at least a couple of young children.

The door opened a crack. Joseph put his face to the door. "What is it?" he whispered.

"My friends and I… we need somewhere to sleep."

"Yes?"

Reg stared at him. He didn't invite her in.

"We are strangers here. We don't know the area. Where can we sleep?"

He gestured to Ruan and Calliopia and nodded. "There is fine."

"There is not fine!" Reg disagreed. "It's dark and we can't just sleep in the dirt."

"You can light a fire."

There was a pit in the middle of the ground, where some families had cooked and shared their dinners. Reg supposed there was enough fuel stacked nearby that she could light a pretty decent fire. It would provide some light for Calliopia. It might not be enough to banish her nightmares, but it was the best they could do.

"Do you have some blankets or sleeping mats we could use?"

"One moment."

He shut the door. Reg waited outside impatiently. Hospitality. They should be taught a lesson on hospitality. In all the TV movies she had ever seen, poor villagers had been welcoming and helpful, giving up their own food and beds for strangers.

But that was TV, and she was now confronted with real life. And real life had plenty of bumps and unexpected turns along the way.

After a few minutes, Joseph opened the door again, and he pushed a few blankets into her hands. Reg had expected them to be hand-woven, like the Mexican blankets she had seen in craft sale stalls and roadside tables in the south. But they were more like the rough blankets that she had slept in when sent to summer camp in the hopes that she would behave herself and stay out of everyone's hair.

"Thank you. And—"

Joseph shut the door and Reg heard him latch or bolt it on the other side.

She could probably still get the door open. Failing that, she could probably just kick a hole in the side of the shack. But she was supposed to be a good guest, and good guests didn't do that, even if their hosts didn't think to provide them with pillows and more comfortable bedding. Reg took the blankets back to Ruan and Calliopia. She put them down on the ground in a pile without any comment. She went to the fire pit and started to stack bark and wood in it.

CHAPTER THIRTY-NINE

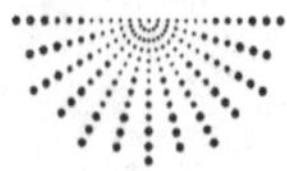

We are staying here?" Calliopia asked.

Reg nodded. "It will be fine. I'll get a fire going, and we'll be nice and toasty."

Ruan took Calliopia's hand and murmured to her.

Reg knew it wasn't the first time that they'd had to sleep under the stars. It had taken a long time before Calliopia had been able to sleep under a roof, worried about being ambushed in the night as she had been when she was kidnapped. She had needed to be outside, under the sun and the stars. So there shouldn't be any reason for her to be averse to sleeping outside in the village. She wouldn't have to worry about anyone coming in through the windows, since there were no windows.

"Do either of you have any food or any way to get food?" Reg asked.

In *The Hobbit* the elves had Lembas, a kind of cracker that never got stale. Shouldn't Ruan and Calliopia be carrying something like that with them? They were the ones who had chosen a nomadic lifestyle. So they should be prepared for unexpected travel or to occasionally run into a few bumps.

She looked over her pile of wood. It was a nice big pile. It would burn all night and keep away the jackals and lions and whatever else roamed the dark jungle at night.

"We have no food," Calliopia said, her tone accusing.

"Well, I'm providing the fire. You see if you can think of a way to get some."

"There is not much to steal," Ruan said logically.

"I don't want you to steal it. Aren't there all kinds of foods that grow in the jungle around here? Fruit and nuts and leafy things?"

Not that Reg liked to eat leafy things. But her stomach was really hurting. If it were all she had, she might break down and eat even leafy things.

"We cannot find them at night," Ruan said scathingly.

"You're the one who can see in the dark. What does it matter to you whether it is day or night?"

Ruan looked around. "Not safe to wander in the jungle at night."

"What could happen? You can make yourself disappear. And Calliopia…" Reg couldn't think of what Calliopia could do. "She has magic."

"We will not hunt at night," Ruan said firmly. He looked at Calliopia, who looked as though she might argue and order him to go find her something to eat anyway. He shook his head and said something to her. Calliopia looked away, arms folded, and scowled.

It amazed Reg that Calliopia could scowl and still look so beautiful. In the dark, with shadows flickering across her face. What would it be like to be that beautiful? Reg had always thought herself quite plain, even though Corvin and others had told her she was pretty. Corvin was just attracted by her powers, not her looks. Or if he was attracted to her looks, it was just the influence of her siren parentage. Sirens always looked beautiful to their prey. That was how they attracted them. As a child, Reg had been skinny and gawky and awkward. Not very impressive.

"Well, if you won't gather any fruit at night, then you might have to go hungry."

Reg rubbed her hands together and then began to form a ball of fire between her palms, gradually making it bigger and pulling her hands farther apart. It was so warm and friendly; it instantly made her feel better. She could banish the darkness and gloom. They would have a pleasant night, sitting by the fire. There was nothing as relaxing as staring into the flames.

"Big enough to light the wood, Reg Rawlins," Ruan warned.

Reg pulled back, becoming aware of the size of the fireball she had created. She squeezed it back down to baseball size, then reached into the wood and let it go, lighting the prepared fuel quickly.

The wood was dry and burned bright and hot. Reg basked in the glow. She went over to the blankets she had put on the ground and picked one out.

It was one night. It wouldn't hurt her to sit or lie on the ground for one night in the open air. It was still warm. But she was hungry. Where was Harrison and his chocolate cake when she needed him?

"Harrison," Reg whispered, and looked around, wondering whether he would come to her. Even though she knew that he was an immortal and his powers were beyond her comprehension, she was still surprised to have him appear somewhere other than Black Sands.

Harrison sat next to her, his long skinny legs encased in chaps and a large cowboy hat on his head. His shirt, rather than one of the prints or styles that Reg associated with western wear, was a bright blue and orange Hawaiian print. Harrison's long fingers strummed a banjo. She wasn't sure if it was a child-sized banjo, or if it just looked small because of how long his arms and legs were.

"A camp out," Harrison said enthusiastically. "You have not done a camp out for many years."

Reg opened her mouth to answer him, but he cut her off.

"You have slept outside, though. Is it a camp out when you don't have a campfire?" He looked thoughtful, considering this. "Or if you don't sleep in tents?" He looked around at the shacks, shaking his head. "These are not tents. But sleeping in a blanket on the ground... that *and* the campfire make it a camp out, right?"

"Uh, right," Reg agreed. "We are having a camp out."

"Oh, good. I love a camp out."

"You know what we need, though? Wieners to roast. And marshmallows. *Not* together."

"Wieners and marshmallows," Harrison agreed. "Yes."

Reg found a package of wieners and one of jumbo marshmallows at her feet. She looked around for a stick to roast them. Ruan picked up the package of wieners and smelled it.

"Meat? What kind?"

"We never ask."

"Oh." He nodded. "And what for Calliopia?"

Reg had forgotten that fairies didn't eat flesh. She thought about other traditional campfire foods. Most of them seemed to involve roasting meat.

"These fruits?" Ruan asked, tearing open the bag of marshmallows and pulling out one of the marshmallows. He squished it between his fingers several times, apparently fascinated by the texture. He took a small bite and looked surprised.

"Uh, no, they're not fruit. But they're good. I don't know whether they're vegetarian, though. How about... bananas or potatoes? Those are good roasted in the fire. Or... pineapple. Or some kind of stew. Those brown beans—cowboys ate those, didn't they?" She looked at Harrison in his *unique* cowboy getup.

"Beans," Harrison agreed with a nod. He moved a bubbling pot of bubbling baked beans closer to the fire. Reg wasn't sure why they needed to be move closer to the fire if they were already bubbling. Calliopia leaned forward and sniffed at the pot delicately. She looked back at Reg as if suspicious that Reg was trying to fool her.

"This is good human food?"

"Yes. Beans. You've eaten beans before, haven't you?"

"Not this kind."

"They're really good. Grab yourself a plate and a spoon and have some," Reg suggested.

Still looking dubious, Calliopia picked up one of the provided tin plates and ladled some of the beans into it.

Ruan looked at Harrison. "Energy drinks," he said distinctly, as if speaking to a computer that wasn't very good at voice recognition.

"No!" Reg objected. She remembered what Ruan was like after a couple of cans of energy drinks. "Fruit juice. Or milk. Or pop."

"Milk," Calliopia echoed. She dipped her spoon into the beans and delicately ate a few. She didn't look pleased, but she didn't spit them out either, so Reg figured that counted as a success.

"No energy drinks?" Ruan asked, looking disappointed.

"We won't get a wink of sleep. No."

Harrison passed out glasses of milk. Reg passed a couple down to Calliopia and Ruan, and then ended up with one in her own hand. She didn't like milk. She hadn't thought when she blocked Ruan's request that Harrison would give them all the same thing.

"Can I at least have chocolate?" she asked Harrison.

She was left holding a chocolate bar, which was ten times better than chocolate milk, so Reg was okay with that.

"I want candy too," Ruan insisted.

Before long, every demand had been satisfied, other than the one for energy drinks, and everyone was quiet as they ate.

"Do you remember camping out?" Harrison asked Reg. "Your brain is not holding as much lately."

Reg choked on her wiener covered with ketchup. That was one way of putting it. She knew that Harrison didn't mean it in an insulting way, he was just having a normal immortal-type conversation.

She cleared her throat. "Yeah. I remember a few camp outs. Mostly being sent away to camp."

He nodded agreement.

"Some of those were okay. I liked it when we did crafts or hiking or swimming. But *not* getting up early or having to go on runs or do calisthenics." Too many of those camps had been intended to reform the troubled and the troublemakers. Inevitably, that involved trying to work them so hard that they didn't have the energy to get into any trouble.

Which inevitably failed. At least with Reg.

"And the food," Harrison suggested. "Always lots of food. Tables piled high with it."

Reg nodded, remembering. For someone who had been through several periods when food had been scarce or nonexistent, that had been very important for her, and she had not overlooked it. "Pancakes and bacon and eggs," she remembered, salivating even though they already had too much food for all of them to eat before morning. "Sausages, macaroni and cheese, sub sandwiches filled with whatever you liked. The food was great."

* * *

They all ate until they were stuffed. Reg lay down, her hand over her bulging stomach, and felt guilty for eating so much when the children in the village had probably never had the opportunity to fill their bellies until they were full. If they tried to eat all the food that Harrison had provided, they would probably go into shock. She'd heard about that happening after WWII. It could kill someone who was starving to suddenly eat normally.

Ruan and Calliopia were talking together, speaking pixie or fairy so that Reg could not understand them. She kept her voice low and spoke to Harrison.

"Do you know the General?"

"The General?"

"There is a man who lives somewhere close by. He is not skinny like the people who live in this village. He's fat, and wears army fatigues, and he is called the General. He probably lives in a palace. Or at least a bigger house than any of these." Reg gestured to the shacks around them.

Harrison nodded.

"Does that mean yes, you know him?" Reg demanded.

"I could," Harrison said obliquely.

Reg shook her head. "Do you or not? Can you tell me where he lives?"

Harrison waved in the direction Reg thought the river was. "It is not far."

"I need to see him tomorrow. I have something to give to him. Do you think I could walk there? Or he might come here to me?"

"Human time is very linear."

"Yes. It is. Do you think I might see him?"

"You might."

Reg wasn't satisfied with the answer. But she didn't want Harrison to magically transport her to the General or to transport the General to her. Using magic on him would probably just cause trouble. Reg was hoping to avoid as much trouble as she could. Get to the General's house, give him the diamond, and then return home with her companions. Quick and simple.

"I don't know whether I'm going to get to sleep tonight," Reg said with a yawn. "With everything that has happened today, and what else I have to do. My stomach hurts and I don't even know what time it is supposed to be."

"Humans don't know anything," Harrison said agreeably.

CHAPTER FORTY

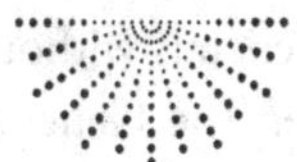

Despite her worries and her grossly overstretched stomach, Reg was able to sleep. Maybe Harrison had put a spell on her to stop her from talking to him and asking more questions. More likely, he just got bored and disappeared. He was nowhere in evidence in the morning.

Sometimes when he disappeared, all the food disappeared with him, and sometimes it did not. This time, perhaps he had seen the need of the villagers, and he had left the food behind. The children gathered up all the scraps and leftovers and divided them up. There was no fighting and competition, they just split it up and took it to their various homes, to eat or to share with their families.

Joseph and his men were up before the sun had risen much over the horizon and were preparing to leave. Back to the river to look for more gems, Reg assumed. Had Joseph hidden the emerald somewhere safe, or was he still holding it under his tongue?

"You are still here," he said to Reg, seeming a little surprised by this. Maybe his inhospitality of the night before had been designed to make her go home. Reg folded her blanket carefully and offered it to him.

"I am still here. I need to see the General today."

"The General. You do not want to see him."

"I need to."

Joseph shook his head. "That is not a good idea."

"Even if it is what your holy man wanted me to do?"

Joseph's eyes went to her face, surprised, then he looked down at the ground. "I am not a holy man. Or even a good man. But… I would not see the General without protection. Will your companions keep you safe? The General is a powerful man. Not just in politics."

"Well, I guess I'll have to do my best." Reg wasn't nearly as confident as she tried to sound. She did not want to face a powerful warlord. She wanted to go back home and forget that she had ever been there. Benji could have the ruby back. Or she could give it to Joseph or to one of the women in the village. That would be more equitable. Why did it have to be the men who held the gems?

"I cannot help you with this thing," Joseph said. "We go to the river to dig."

He nodded to his companions, and with their screens in their hands, they started on their trek back to the river to search for precious stones.

Reg looked around at the villagers who were watching her, though they dropped their eyes or looked away and pretended they were not.

"Can somebody tell me the way to the General's house?"

None of them offered anything in response. Of course, they probably didn't speak English. It seemed that only a few had any fluency. Though maybe they understood more than they pretended to, and it was just a good blind. It was always a good idea not to give too much away. Let your opponent underestimate you.

Joseph didn't want her to go to the General. Ruan and Calliopia didn't want her to go to the General. The villagers didn't want her to go to the General.

And Reg didn't want to go to the General.

She closed her eyes and pictured the man that Benji had showed her in her mind the night before. She focused on making the picture very clear, seeing every detail of his face and body, the way his clothes stretched around his fat middle. Then she expanded her view out, looking at the room around him. Then waiting, feeling for a tug in a certain direction. He was there. She could feel him. Reg started to walk.

She'd been pushing her way through the jungle for a while before she realized that she was being followed. Reg looked behind her and saw that Ruan and Calliopia were a few paces back, walking silently in her footsteps. She was crashing through the bush like a buffalo and hadn't even heard them.

There wasn't anything to say that hadn't already been said, so Reg just kept walking. Eventually, she stumbled into a clearing.

It wasn't just a natural break in the trees, a natural little grove. It had been clear cut, maybe even burned, so that all the space around the compound was flat and empty. To prevent anyone from being able to sneak up on them. Anyone approaching the buildings would have to make themselves visible.

Unless it was someone like Davyn, who could cloak himself. Or a pixie. Reg turned to the others. "Ruan... can you go to the world of shades?"

Maybe it was surprising that he hadn't already.

"And can you take Calliopia with you?"

Ruan studied Reg. "Calliopia can no longer enter that world. She is full fairy now."

"I thought maybe if you were holding on to her, it would work like it did when I called her and got both of you."

"No."

"I can hide," Calliopia offered. She made a motion that was half-shrug, half-indicating the greenery around her. "A fairy can easily hide from human eyes."

Being as blind as they were.

"Yes. The two of you. I want both of you to hide yourselves. I don't know what will happen, but we have an advantage if they don't know that you are here."

Calliopia nodded. She withdrew from them and, in a moment, Reg could no longer follow her movements. Her dress and hair and even her pale face blended in with the dappled light and she was gone. Reg nodded. She looked at Ruan. Ruan spun in a circle, gaining speed and, in a moment, he too was gone. In the right conditions, Reg would still be able to see his shadowy shape, but with the contrast of the dark jungle and bright sunlight in the clearing, her eyes couldn't adjust well enough to make him out.

"You two wait here," Reg told them, talking to the air. "I will… hopefully not be too long."

She began her walk across the empty space, knowing that she would be spotted by the soldiers immediately.

The insects continued to buzz, and the birds continued to chirp and sing. Nothing had changed. But Reg felt as if she were walking into a void. Everything was different.

She was not approached, but could feel eyes on her. She strained to see anyone in the compound up ahead, but if they were watching her, it was through viewing slots or peepholes or hidden cameras. Or maybe some of them were in the jungle behind her, watching from high perches or dark shadows.

The compound was enclosed by a wall and the outer walls of the buildings. Reg aimed for a large gate, where she assumed there was a checkpoint where they would want to see proper ID or credentials. How was she going to get past there? She was a con. She would try to con her way in.

It seemed as if she would never get there. She covered the first half of the distance, and then half again, and again, each fraction seeming to take longer and to be more difficult. Even though she was walking on flat ground and then pavement, she felt more tired than she had been walking in the jungle, climbing over obstacles and pushing her way through dense brush.

CHAPTER FORTY-ONE

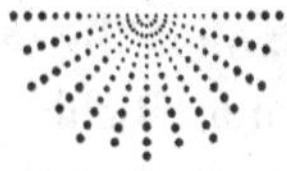

Finally, she was at the gate. A soldier was there waiting for her, his weapon cradled in his arm. Was it the same man as had taken Joseph's diamond the day before? Reg wasn't sure whether it was him or just another with the same uniform.

He looked her over with hard eyes. Eyes that looked on all the suffering in all of the villages and were not moved. He had grown up in a war-torn country, and he'd had to be strong and hard to earn his place in the General's forces. Like the children from the village, he had probably been recruited when he was a young teen and had worked his way up the ranks to gain a position where he always had enough to eat and could, as a bigger predator, live off of the people beneath him.

But he couldn't hide his surprise at seeing Reg. Her white skin and red hair were enough to make her stand out anywhere. They certainly did not belong in the jungle or in the General's citadel.

"Who are you?" he demanded.

Reg tried not to betray any surprise over his use of English in addressing her. His accent was heavy, but his words and meaning were clear. "Reg Rawlins. I am here to see the General."

"What about?"

"That's between me and him."

"You have no business here."

"That isn't for you to say. Take me to see him. I am sure you will be rewarded if you do."

"Rewarded." His eyes glittered. "By you?"

Reg's skin crawled. She couldn't wait to get out of there. To get back home where she was safe and didn't have to deal with predators. At least, not ones like him. "By the General. He will reward you for bringing me to see him. Richly rewarded."

"Why? What makes you think this?"

"Because I have brought him something of great value."

The guard looked skeptical. "What?"

"If I showed you, he would probably kill you. He will not want anyone else to see what I have."

Not a bad bluff. She could see his concern over this dilemma. How could he know if Reg had something that the General would want to see if he couldn't see it? But insisting that he see it could lead to losing his life, which wasn't high on his to-do list. Could he take her word that she had something of value? Or should he insist on seeing it? Even take it from her and deliver it to the General himself? That would earn him points.

Then again, if she had something of great value, maybe he could take it for himself and, with enough money and power, he could overthrow the General and take his place. It was always a possibility.

"Not a good idea," Reg told him. She pushed emotions toward him. Fear and anxiety, worry about his precarious position in the organization. He was the first line of defense, but the first line of defense would always be the first to fall. The higher-ranking men were not placed at the outer doors, but inside where they were better protected. With the General at the center of the citadel like a spider in the middle of his web.

The anxiety took hold quickly. It was a familiar feeling for the man. Something he fought off every day, worrying that he was not good enough, that he had risen as far as he could go. That he had left behind his mother and his brothers, betraying them to work for the man who would happily kill every villager in the country if it brought him more money and power. And so far, he was succeeding.

"You don't want to make him angry," Reg warned. "If he finds even that you have delayed, he'll have your head."

"You do not know anything. You are not from here."

"I know things that you do not. And I know what I have."

"You will wait here," he said abruptly, turning away from her.

Reg watched in surprise as he retreated to a guardroom. Maybe to consult with a superior? To make a phone or radio call outside her hearing? There were other guards in the hall beyond the guardroom, watching Reg carefully with their guns on their hands. Thin rangy men like coyotes.

In a few minutes, the guard was back. He had a wholly different aura. Instead of the fear and anxiety, he was angry, heedless, confrontational. Reg wasn't sure what had changed, but he was not the same man as he had been when he had disappeared into the guardroom.

"You don't frighten me," he blustered. "You don't know anything about the General. You aren't from here."

"That doesn't mean I don't know anything about him."

The guard leaned closer to her, getting into her face, intentionally invading her personal space in order to intimidate her. She stared into his eyes. A sea of dark brown that she couldn't even see the pupil in. Reg tried to keep her own anxiety at bay. This was more what she had been expecting to run into. Angry, violent men who didn't have the same rules and morals as the law enforcement back home. Men who wouldn't hesitate to go way over the line.

He sniffled and wiped at his nose, and Reg suddenly understood the pinpoint pupils. He hadn't gone into the guardroom to talk to a superior, but to work up a little courage through other means. And whatever he had snorted had done the trick. He would not be intimidated by a strong woman who pretended she knew more than she did now.

"Well, if you won't take me to him…" Reg shrugged, pretending to withdraw. When advancing didn't work, retreat was always an option.

He glowered at her suspiciously. He'd expected her to fight more. To insist that he would regret it if she didn't let him see his boss.

"Tell me why you want to see him."

"I told you. I have something of great value. I thought… never mind. There are others I can offer it to. Your General is not the only powerful man in the country."

He grabbed her arm, holding it tightly. "You're not going anywhere."

She didn't pull away, just looked at him. "It doesn't make much sense for me to just stand in the door, does it? Either in or out. Which is it going to be?"

He looked undecided for a few seconds, then his lips pressed together into a straight line, and he jerked her toward him. Over the threshold. Reg could feel herself slipping through an invisible barrier as she allowed him to pull her in. It was a good thing she hadn't tried to just walk in while he was in the guardroom and had not tried to sneak through a back gate. She would not have been able to get through the magical protection and they would have had her for trying to break in rather than just asking at the door.

Reg let him pull her along, and eventually he decided that dragging her wasn't giving him the upper hand and he let her go, allowing her to walk beside him. Reg looked around at the building as she walked through the various passages. The walls were bare, not adorned with all manner of rich art and tapestries. Despite his apparent power and wealth, the General wasn't living in a kingly mansion. It was utilitarian. A stronghold.

They went through many twists and turns, moving from one building to another until they reached a waiting room or antechamber where the soldier stopped and spoke with another guard. He was deferential, but his face and his movements still gave away the fact that he was high on some kind of opiate. Reg was sure the inner guard could see that as well as she could. They spoke together in low voices, and eventually the inner guard approached Reg.

"Who are you?"

"My name is Reg Rawlins."

"But who are you?"

"Someone with something of value for the General."

"Show me."

"He will not want anyone else to see or know about it."

The new guard thought about this. He knew, of course, that his boss had secrets. Anyone who had attained that kind of standing had to have secrets. Dirt on other people, leverage, booby traps, secret plans, powers, and weapons. Secrets were the currency of power.

"He was not expecting you."

"Of course not."

"I could beat it out of you." The guard's eyes traveled up and down Reg's body, assessing her, imagining what he would do to her.

Reg suppressed her reaction to him and stuck to the same line. "He wouldn't want you to know about it. What good would that do?" She laughed. "Is it worth it to beat a defenseless woman so that you can see something secret before you die?"

She wasn't defenseless, of course. He might be stronger than she was physically, but Reg could overcome him with magic any day. She didn't sense that he had any powers himself. He was a physical being. Someone used to using his physical strength and intimidation to get what he wanted. Maybe he was wily and smart too, to have achieved a high standing among his peers, the last guardian of the General, but he didn't have any magic that she could sense.

He stared at her boldly before finally making his decision. "You will wait here." He pointed to the guard who had brought Reg from the front gate. "And you will watch her. Make sure that she does not try anything."

At the nod of agreement from the front gate guard, he turned and withdrew into the chamber behind him. The General's office? Or was there yet another layer of protection before reaching him? He was very well-protected.

Reg didn't say anything. The high guard didn't say anything, but jittered and vibrated as he walked around the antechamber, looking for something of interest within its bare walls. Reg could hear him grinding his teeth, and it set her own teeth on edge like fingernails on a blackboard. She tried to wall off his emotions to keep them from affecting her. She needed to stay sharp during her conversation with the General, if she got in to see him.

CHAPTER FORTY-TWO

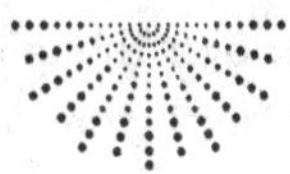

The door opened, and the inner guard stepped out. He nodded to Reg.

"Enter."

She walked by him, into the final room.

The General sat behind a desk. Exactly as she had seen him. A pristine camouflage uniform that did not appear to have ever seen the battlefield or a hike through the jungle growth. Plenty of meat on his bones. It wasn't all fat; she could see that. He undoubtedly worked out as well, lifting weights or wrestling or doing something else to help him to increase his muscle size. A powerful man, both politically and physically.

"Has she been searched?" the General barked.

The guard, who had entered behind Reg, shook his head. "She said… she has something for you that you would not want us to see."

"And you just took her at her word? Assumed that she does not have a knife or a gun? Or enough explosives to blow this building sky high?"

The soldier nodded stoically. "Yes, sir."

"Is that really wise?"

"If she has something you would not wish us to see, then it

would be unwise for us to search her."

The General laughed. "And you feared me more than the possibility she might set off a bomb?"

"Yes, sir."

He chuckled again. "Very wise," he agreed. "You are dismissed."

The guard withdrew and shut the door, leaving Reg alone with the General. He looked her over thoughtfully. Reg wondered if he had ever seen anyone like her before. A white woman, certainly. But a redhead? A powerful psychic, firecaster, and part-siren? There was a lot more to her than met the eye.

"What is your name?"

"Reg Rawlins."

He considered this. Reg waited for him to think through whether he had ever heard of her or should have.

"And have you brought a bomb to blow us all up?"

"No. I have brought you a powerful stone."

The General's brows went up, and he leaned forward on his desk, studying her intently. "A powerful stone?"

Reg stayed where she was for a few minutes, then decided to approach him. He didn't draw back or tell her to stop. If she had a weapon, then now was the time to pull it and see whether she could get the drop on him.

But Reg didn't.

She stopped right in front of his large, heavy desk and delved into her pocket. She withdrew the large diamond and displayed it to him, pinched between thumb and forefinger. The General's eyes were greedy.

"Give it to me."

"I have to warn you, before I give it to you…"

"Warn me what? You think you can intimidate me? I am not afraid of a little girl like you." He shook his head. "You may think you have power, but you have nothing. I have had more power than you from the day I was born. A girl like you? You can't even comprehend the kind of power I have."

Reg tried to keep a straight face. Despite his bluster, she didn't sense much magic from him. Maybe he could keep his gifts hidden to an extent, but she didn't think he would be able to keep very much hidden. Maybe he was strong in the family he came from, in his own village, and he had amassed enough soldiers to be able to command what he wanted. But that didn't make him a powerful warlock or wizard.

"This stone is cursed. If you accept it, you will take that curse upon you."

"Cursed?" He laughed. "I am not afraid of your little trinkets. Let me see it."

Reg handed it to him. It at least didn't burn his palm when she placed it in his hand. Better if it behaved itself until he acknowledged that he accepted Reg's gift.

The General turned the stone in the light, examining it. He didn't pull out a jeweler's loupe to examine it. Reg didn't know whether he just saw a large, precious stone, or whether he could feel the magical potential it had. Either one was fine, as long as he accepted it. He would run into problems if he tried to sell it, just as she had. And Reg had no doubt that he would feel the full force of the curse. The man was oppressing the land that had produced the stone. He was terrorizing the people who were the rightful owners of the gem. There was no distance between the gem's past and the General's actions, as there had been with Reg. He was, by his position in the power structure, the one who had stolen the gem from its rightful owners, and it was the holy man's intention that he should suffer the consequences of those actions.

"It is beautiful. Is it real?"

Reg stared at him. He couldn't even tell whether it was real? How would he know whether it had any powers if he couldn't feel it?

"Yes. It's real. Do you need an expert to certify it?"

"I normally only see uncut gems in these parts. Sometimes they fall into my hands, and I sell them in the rough. I don't usually get to see them after they have been cut like this." He turned it in the light to catch the light, sending a shower of reflected light on his desk.

Reg looked away from him. There was a window behind him, and she tried to figure out what direction she was facing. The sun was shining directly in, so it must have been mostly east facing. She tried to remember which side of the citadel Ruan and Calliopia were on. How long would it take her to get back to them once she was done? She wanted to get home. She'd had enough of the poverty and fear. She needed to get out of there before something really bad happened to one of them. It was tempting fate to think that they could stay there and be fine.

"Why did you bring this to me?" the General asked sharply.

Reg looked back at him, startled out of her own thoughts. She considered her answer. "I was asked to."

"Why? A bribe? Who is it from? I've never even heard of you before."

"No, it's not a bribe. I don't think so. One of the villages… they wanted to make a gift to you. But I wasn't given any explanation. I guess they just… felt you deserved it. Maybe it is a thank you."

He shook his head. "Somebody wants something of me. And you have to know. You're the one who brought it."

"You can take it or refuse it," Reg said with a shrug. "It's up to you. Do whichever you want. If you don't want it, I'll take it back away with me. If you want it… it's your choice how you use it. Maybe you want to sell it. It would fetch a king's ransom. Or maybe you want… to put it in a ring and wear it. Or use it in some other way."

"Yes? Like what?"

"I don't know."

The General's expression was hard. He looked at Reg fiercely and, though she tried to avoid his accusing eyes, there was nowhere to go. The room was without adornment; there wasn't even anything interesting to look at, other than the window. Reg stared down at the diamond in his hand instead.

She could feel the General's mind in hers, looking for a way in, probing and pressing and looking for the answers he needed. She could resist him. She had defended herself against much stronger attacks in the past. She didn't know whether he was aware of what he was doing, or if he were just trying to read her face and, in doing so, probed her mind. Or maybe he was aware, but was trying to do it covertly and not to tip her off. She hoped that it was the third option—that he didn't have any powers to speak of. He was just powerful because he had money and a lot of fire-power behind him.

"How could I use it?" the General pressed.

Even though he was on the other side of the desk and wasn't touching her, she felt as though he held her pinned. He was stronger than she had given him credit for.

"I was told it was a powerful stone," Reg said. "I don't know what that means. I don't know what you can use it for."

"I think you do."

Reg was itching to get out the door and away from him. What was he going to do? Have her arrested for bringing him a gem more expensive and powerful than anything he had ever seen before? He didn't have any reason to detain her.

"Do you accept the stone? Or should I take it back?" Reg didn't put out her hand to take it from him, but her intention was clear.

The General's lips pursed. "I accept," he agreed finally.

Good. Reg relaxed. She breathed out a long stream of air, relieved. She had been afraid that he wouldn't. That he would send her away with it.

"Then I am done here," Reg said. She nodded to him and took a step back, toward the door. She felt her back hit something and stopped, startled. She hadn't realized she was that close to the wall. She glanced over her shoulder to confirm her position in the room but, in doing so, saw that the wall was still several feet behind her. She had run into nothing.

CHAPTER FORTY-THREE

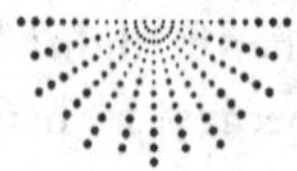

Reg reached out all of her senses, trying to verify what was going on. She had run into something, and yet there was nothing to run into. She was standing in the middle of a nearly-empty room. She wasn't against the wall. The General or someone else in his staff had put a force field there to prevent her escape.

"You have the jewel," she told him. "I am leaving now."

"I have the jewel," he agreed. "I would have gotten it out of you one way or another, so you haven't done me any favors. This *gift*, this bribe, is something that I would have gotten anyway. And now I want to know what else you have. What weapons. What valuables. What *power*."

Reg again tried to step back, but her feet felt as if they were glued to the floor, and she still couldn't move past the barrier behind her.

The General heaved his bulk up, pressing his hands against his desk for assistance. Reg struggled against the force that held her in place. Was the General doing it himself or was there someone else she didn't see who was holding her in place? She was strong. She could break free. But it would help her to know who it was that held her.

He walked around his desk to her. He touched her face. "You are very white. I don't think I have ever seen someone with such white skin."

Reg pulled away from him. She could still do that, at least.

"And you braid your hair. Your *red* hair." He ran one thin braid through his fingers. "Is it naturally that color? Or do you color it?"

Reg didn't bother to answer. She didn't see or sense any other opposing force in the room or close by. So he must be acting alone, using his own powers. She tested her powers against his consciousness. He had already opened the door between them, which made it that much easier for her to work her way inside unimpeded. He looked momentarily uncomfortable as she slipped past his defenses. Like he didn't know whether to burp or sneeze. When she was in his mind, he made a snuffling snort and shook his head, then continued as if nothing had happened.

"You come in here, a little girl like you," he sneered, still trying to physically intimidate her. "Against someone like *me*! Didn't they tell you anything about me, these friends of yours? Did they send you in here like a lamb before a lion, as a sacrifice? So defenseless."

Reg ignored his words, exploring his mind instead. She wasn't particularly careful. She knew that it was against the magical community's rules to invade someone's mind without their permission. At least, it was in Black Sands.

But she wasn't in Black Sands anymore.

His mind was full of dark places, fractured and broken. Not the mind of someone who was strong and powerful, but a bully who had been able to make everyone think he was something he was not. He was happy to take the diamond, to magnify his power. Reg wasn't sure, as Benji had been, that it was a good idea. Giving a man like the General more power did not seem like the way to bring him down. He wouldn't stop recruiting the villagers' children and using them to fight the rebel forces. He would keep putting weapons into their hands and seeing how much destruction he could cause. Because he wanted more power and more of everything.

Reg did not like violence. And violence against the General's mind seemed even worse than violence against his body or the security of his fortress. She should not have let anyone put her in this position. She should have told the holy man no. She should never have gone to the General. Someone else could have taken the jewel to him. She should just have gone home.

She steeled herself and pushed hard against his consciousness, letting him know that she was there. If she were going to break free from his grip, she needed to distract him and force him to turn his attention elsewhere.

The General jolted and looked at her in shock. "What…?"

"Knock knock."

His mouth formed a *what* shape and opened and closed like a fish's. Reg did her best to disrupt him, striking out against random memories and processes. The General's hands opened and closed, grasping at something in front of him, maybe trying to stabilize himself somehow.

"Stop!"

Reg didn't. But she shuffled her feet and stepped backward, finding herself free from his hold. She struck out again, stirring up dark memories, triggering a fear response. She could feel it not just in his mind, but pouring off of him in waves, his aura darkening. She backed away from him more quickly, scrabbling behind her for the doorknob. Finding it, she twisted it and pulled the door open.

The General started to bellow. Reg didn't know whether it was gibberish or his native tongue. To her, it just sounded like incoherent shouts. The soldier who had let her in looked up from his post, his eyes wide.

"You'd better get in there," Reg prompted.

He hesitated for a moment, trying to decide whether to detain and question her or to go to his boss, then made the decision to go to the General. Of course he knew that there was no way Reg could find her way out of the compound without help; she would have to get past numerous guards to do so.

Reg hurried to the next door, which opened into a corridor. She lifted her skirt and sprinted down the hall to the next, then hesitated which way to go. She had tried to keep track of the twists and turns, but hadn't been able to hold them all in her head.

A hand grabbed hers. Not the big, iron hand of a guard detaining her, but a small one like a child's. Reg looked down, but didn't see anything but a faint shadow.

"This way!"

She followed the tug on her hand, and they worked their way through the corridors of the place. Reg was sure they weren't going out the same way she had come in, and there were not nearly as many guards to avoid as she had expected. Whenever she slowed, the hand pulled on her hand harder, making her work hard to keep up. She was puffing like a train engine, but at least there was no one around to hear her.

They went through a long underground tunnel—Reg had definitely not gone through any underground tunnels when she had arrived—and when they reached the end of it, climbed the rungs of a ladder into a cave, then followed the dim light and smell of fresh air until they reached the outside, somewhere in the jungle, the compound nowhere in sight.

CHAPTER FORTY-FOUR

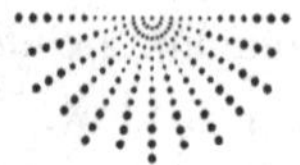

Reg collapsed, sitting down on a log and trying to catch her breath. She wiped tears of exertion from her cheeks. "Well. That was fun."

Ruan appeared beside her. "We should not stop here."

"I'll go on in a moment. Please."

He nodded and waited for her to catch her breath. Reg definitely needed to get into better shape. Especially if she were going to be running away from bad guys very often.

"How did you know the way out?" Reg asked. She didn't need to ask how he had gotten in. Clearly, he had followed her while invisible. She wasn't sure how he had gotten through the magical barrier at the gate. Maybe he had been touching her when the guard escorted her through, the three of them entering in a chain. The same way Corvin had been able to get past Reg's gate.

Ruan considered his answer. "By smell. And by memory."

Smell, Reg could understand. His senses were much more sensitive than hers. He could probably smell the guards a mile away. And even Reg had been able to smell the fresh air that led out of the cave.

"By memory? You've been here before?"

"No. But the underground tunnels are more ancient than the buildings. They are in piskies' memories."

Reg frowned. She rubbed more tears away from the corners of her eyes. At least they were slowing now so she didn't look like she was a damsel in distress. "You remember them? How old are you?"

"Not *my* memories." Ruan looked at her intently to see whether she discerned his meaning. He shook his head. "It is a wonder humans live as long as they do. Reg Rawlins has *no* ancestral memories?"

"Uh… no. I mean, I've heard of things… instinct, and genetic memory, and stuff like that. But science can't really tell us anything about how they work. And they aren't memories like the memories that I have from my life."

"Such big brains for so few memories," he said in a tone of awe.

Reg put her fingers to her temples. Her brain was, at the moment, feeling way overtaxed. The struggle with the General, though only brief, had been difficult. And running with Ruan had tired her body. It was still early in the morning, and she wasn't used to getting out of bed early, let alone trekking to a military compound, doing mental battle with a warlock of some sort, and then making her escape.

The ruby had better be worth it.

"We go on now," Ruan suggested. "You are breathing again."

"Yes, okay." Reg pushed herself up from the log. "Lead the way."

He did so and, in a few minutes, they were joined by Calliopia, who rolled her eyes like a bored teenager.

"You take a long time."

"Sorry. I had a job to do. And then there was the escape…"

She shook her head, expressing her irritation. "Now we go home?"

"I was planning to go back to the village first…"

"Why?"

They both looked at her expectantly. Reg thought about it.

"Well… I was going to pass the message along that I have given the diamond to the General, like Benji asked. And… to say good-bye. They didn't have much, but they did show us hospitality. I should tell Joseph—"

"The diggers will not be back until the evening. And the village will know that the fat man has the diamond." Ruan shrugged. "Everyone will know that he has the diamond."

"How? Because he'll be looking for a buyer?"

"I do not think he will sell."

"You think he'll use it then, its powers?"

Ruan nodded. Reg felt anxiety land in her stomach again. "Why would Benji ask me to give it to him if he is going to use its powers for his own purposes? Won't that make things worse for him and his people?"

Neither of the others answered immediately, and Reg was afraid she was right. Now, not only did the warlord have a choke hold on the villages in the area, stealing their children for slave labor, soldiers, and wives, but now he had a stone of power that would extend his reach and his abilities. How could that be a good thing?

"The stone is cursed," Calliopia pointed out eventually. "The more he uses it, the more it will enslave him."

"How will it affect him? The cursed stones didn't really affect me."

Calliopia looked at Reg speculatively. She licked her lips. "You did not *use* the stones. You only held them. They like you."

"They like me?" It was the most blatant personification of the gems yet. Reg shook her head and laughed. It was true that she had not used the stones for their power. And she had not tried to acquire more. She had only hidden them away, and then when she had the need, tried to trade them in for money. Apparently, that had kept the gemstones happy.

But she was sure from other stories she'd heard about cursed treasure that the treasure was still cursed and made the owner unlucky even if she didn't know anything about the curse and had come by the stones honestly. Unwitting owners and their family members died because of the curses on them.

"They like you," Calliopia repeated. She looked at Ruan, who nodded his agreement.

"They are... at rest," Ruan said, trying to explain it further. "Not active."

"So I'm safe? I don't have to worry about finding the rightful owners of all the rest?" Reg dreaded having to travel to dispose of each little bag of gems. That was a lot of work. And a lot of danger, if this first trip were any indication.

Maybe just the one quest would be enough. The gemstones would see that she was willing to return them to their original countries, to the people who should have held them, and...

"They will not stay at rest," Ruan explained. "Maybe for a short time. But not forever. They will one day activate."

It sounded like Reg was still in the honeymoon period with her stones. Sooner or later, they would begin to test her. It would be better if she could return them to their people before that happened. She didn't really want to find out just how dangerous the curse of the stones could be.

"Okay. Well, great. Maybe you can help me with the rest?"

Ruan didn't jump at the chance. And why would he? It didn't benefit him if she returned all the gems to their rightful places. He had his own life with Calliopia. They didn't have to answer to anyone and could come and go as they pleased.

"Do we go home now?" Calliopia asked plaintively.

"Yes. Yes, let's go home," Reg agreed.

She reached for both of their hands and thought about home.

CHAPTER FORTY-FIVE

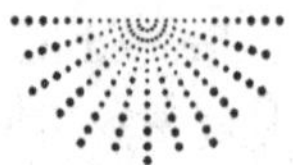

The landings were getting a little smoother. Reg found herself sitting on her couch, with Calliopia and Ruan standing holding her hands. They let go immediately and looked around. Reg gave a long sigh of relief. She was so glad to be back home, like Dorothy at the end of *The Wizard of Oz*.

Starlight jumped up on the kitchen island, where he really wasn't supposed to go, and gave a long, low yowl of disapproval. Calliopia made claw hands and hissed at him. Ruan just looked and said nothing.

"Yes, I'm sorry," Reg apologized. "I know I left you all alone here without any planning. But I'm sure you had enough food in your dish, and Sarah probably gave you more anyway." Reg stood up and went over to him, but he rebuffed her, turning his back to her to jump down from the island and then marching over to his empty bowl.

"I said I'm sorry. But it was only one night. You didn't starve."

Reg turned on the kitchen light. It was dark outside, and the interior was lit by a single lamp in the living room. She opened the fridge and found something that looked like stew. It smelled meaty, so she put a few spoonfuls into Starlight's bowl and set it down on the floor. "There. Okay?"

"We have not eaten," Calliopia pointed out.

Much like a cat.

Reg opened the fridge again and looked for anything that might be suitable for a fairy. She didn't buy milk, but she did get cream for the coffee and tea. And there were a few raw fruits and vegetables, though they were a little more wilted than "crisper drawer" would have one believe. Reg put some cream into a cup and arranged the produce on a plate and took them over to Calliopia. She wrinkled her nose when she looked at them, but she sat down and put them on the coffee table and started to eat.

"What about you?" Reg asked Ruan.

"I am prepared. I saved food from last night." Ruan pulled a few wieners out of his pocket. Reg tried not to roll her eyes or gag. That was just one less body she didn't have to feed. And she herself wasn't ready to eat yet, so she could sit down and relax for a few minutes while Calliopia ate, and then see the couple off. She wasn't sure what she would do then. Maybe watch some TV or lie down for a nap. She was tired and sore after her encounter with the General.

There was the sound of a key in the lock, and Sarah entered. She looked in consternation at the pixie and fairy for a moment, then saw Reg.

"I saw the light. So, you're back."

"Yes. Sorry to disappear without any warning. We had… something that had to be taken care of."

"I tried to call you. But I couldn't get your cell. It said you were out of range."

"Yeah. I guess I was. Sorry about that. But we weren't gone for very long, and I'm back now. Thank you for seeing to Starlight while I was gone."

"A cat doesn't require much care. Though I think he missed you. He was not very happy."

Sarah didn't look very happy herself as she looked at the kitchen table, still occupied with the bags of gems that Reg had sorted earlier.

"You really shouldn't leave these out. I told you before to get a safety deposit box. Leaving them here like this, out in the open. Someone could see or sense them."

"But there are already wards protecting the house and the garden. Who would be able to get in?"

"Someone with more powerful magic. Just because I have woven a spell, that doesn't mean it cannot be defeated or broken. You should know by now that you can't rely upon such things. You still need to beware that someone else's spell could be stronger or there could be a way around it. A spell is only as strong as the person who wove it and the time they put into it."

"Well… okay. I'm sorry about that. I'll take care of them. It won't be a problem."

Sarah glanced at Ruan and Calliopia and didn't say anything, but her mouth was a stern, straight line, a change from her usual demeanor.

"Are you finished your meal, Calliopia?" Reg prompted. "The two of you will be wanting to get on your way."

Calliopia took a deep drink of the cream. When she put the cup down, she was sporting a white mustache. Reg wondered if it were deliberate defiance or if she were just unconcerned with appearances. "I will take the fruit with me?"

"Yes, go ahead," Reg agreed impatiently. Why not? Reg wasn't going to eat it herself.

Calliopia picked up what remained of her meal. She nodded to Ruan, and the two of them left the cottage, Ruan giving Reg a brief nod as he left.

Sarah waited until the door was shut, but the pixie and fairy were probably not out of earshot, considering how sensitive their ears were. "You really should not have folk like that in the house."

"I needed Ruan's help."

Sarah looked at the gems on the table. "With your stones? You couldn't find a human who could help you?"

"Well, no. Since it's apparently bad manners for humans to discuss cursed stones. You didn't have any suggestions. Corvin was going to look some stuff up, but it sounded like that might take forever and a day. So I talked to Ruan, and he helped me."

"Helped himself to the stones, more likely. How many did he take with him?"

"None."

"You'd better make a thorough search of the house to make sure that he hasn't left something behind. If he did, he can come back later when there is no one here, and he will make off with all of them."

"I'll look. But I kept a pretty close eye on them. Besides, he knows they are cursed, so why would he bother to steal them?"

"Pixies are not like us. Don't judge what one of them would do based on what a human would do. They believe that all gems belong to them."

"I know. But I really don't think he's going to try to steal my gems."

Sarah just raised an eyebrow.

"I'll look," Reg promised again. "I will."

Sarah looked around one last time, but apparently couldn't think of anything else to warn or criticize Reg about, and left it at that.

"Well, you can feed the cat now, so I'll leave you to it. I'm glad you're back safe and sound from… wherever you were."

* * *

Reg gathered together the bags of gems, putting them one at a time into the small wooden chest. She had the ruby she had gotten back from the holy man, together with the gems that she and Ruan had both sensed were not cursed. When she was up to it, she could go back to Dreame or The Sapphire Exchange and sell one or two of them to get her bank account balance up to a level that made her comfortable so that she could buy groceries and kitty litter.

She wouldn't sell the ruby, which she sensed she was supposed to hang on to. Maybe she could learn about its powers or the powers of hers that it could magnify. But there were also multiple bags of gems from other locations around the globe. They weren't active yet, so she could afford to take a little while, maybe just take one trip every few weeks to repatriate a bag of gems to its rightful owners. And sooner or later, she would be done and wouldn't have the threat of gems possibly becoming angry and making her or someone in her circle of friends sick.

As Reg packed the last couple of bags into the chest, she realized she was not alone. She whirled around, immediately thinking of Sarah's warning that someone who was more powerful than she was might be able to break through the protective wards to steal the gems. It wasn't so much that she was afraid they would be stolen, as what else a powerful witch or warlock might do to her. If someone stole cursed gems… he would get what he had coming to him.

But there was no burglar behind her. Instead, Harrison sat watching her, his long legs stretched out with his feet resting on the coffee table. He was wearing a pink silk shirt with something printed on it and flowing black pantaloons. Reg took a step or two closer, squinting at the shirt. It looked suspiciously like the patterned print was of black cats. Maybe tuxedo cats like Starlight. Or were they pure black cats like the kattakyns?

"Get your feet off the table," she told Harrison firmly.

He looked at her for a moment, then pulled them off and bent his knees to put his feet on the floor where they belonged.

"Why are feet not allowed on the table?" he asked seriously, as if it were an important question he had about the universe.

"Because feet are dirty. It is rude to put them on the table, where people eat."

"But my feet are not dirty. And this is not an eating table."

"It's still rude."

He raised his brows, but didn't argue about it.

"I didn't call you," Reg said. "Are you here for a reason?"

"There is always a reason."

Reg waited for more, but Harrison did not explain. "I suppose there is," Reg conceded. "Are you here to talk?"

"I am talking."

"Why did you come?" Reg demanded, frustrated.

"I came to see my goddaughter. And her cat." Harrison looked around, but Starlight had not come out at Harrison's appearance, as he normally did.

"He's pouting. He's upset with me for leaving."

"Perhaps you should not have left."

Was that a warning? That she had done something she shouldn't or that she would run into problems if she continued to try to repatriate all the cursed gems? Or was it just an inane comment by an immortal who didn't understand the ways of humans?

"Starlight?" Reg called. "Aren't you going to come out to see Harrison? Harrison didn't do anything to bother you."

He didn't come out. Reg frowned, starting to feel anxious about Starlight's reluctance to come out. He always loved it when Harrison visited.

"Perhaps he has gone somewhere else," Harrison suggested. "Maybe to go see one of the kittens."

Reg shot him a look. "How could he go see one of the kittens? He doesn't have any way to get out of this house without me seeing him. And how would he travel all around the world on his own?"

"The same way you did."

"But I… he's a cat. He doesn't have the same powers."

Reg hurried to the bedroom to reassure herself that Starlight was there and hadn't magically disappeared to visit one of the kattakyns or someone else. She knew he was upset with her for leaving, but it wouldn't have prompted him to leave, would it?

Reg pushed the bedroom door open the rest of the way, holding her breath, worried she would find the room empty.

Starlight was sitting on the windowsill where he often did, watching out the window.

"What are you looking at?" Reg asked, relieved. "Didn't you hear me? Harrison is here. Don't you want to see him?"

Starlight licked his white tuxedo bib, then jumped down from the windowsill, taking his own sweet time about it. He followed her out to the living room and approached Harrison, not even looking at Reg.

"So, you can come here when you want to visit a cat," Reg suggested. "You don't need to go where the kattakyns are."

"The kattakyns?" Harrison asked innocently.

"Destine's kattakyns. You know you need to stay away from them, right?"

"Do I?"

"Yes. You do. We can't risk doing anything that might allow him to re-form as the Witch Doctor. It's too dangerous."

Harrison shrugged. "Perhaps he could take another form," he suggested. He picked Starlight up and held him in front of his face in an undignified pose. "As a cat!" he suggested.

"No. We don't want that. We don't want him to re-form at all. He needs to stay bound."

"An immortal cannot be bound forever."

Francesca had said that the binding might give way in a thousand years. By that time, Reg expected to be dead and gone and forgotten. She wouldn't have to worry about the Witch Doctor and his powers then. She wasn't keen on anything that might reduce the Witch Doctor's term of imprisonment to a year or two.

"Maybe not, but he can be bound for a thousand years. And that's the way we want him to stay. Got it?"

Harrison lowered Starlight to his lap. "Got it?" he echoed.

"No. You say 'got it,'" Reg told him.

"I did."

"No, you didn't. You said it as a question. I want you to say it as a statement. As an agreement that you won't do anything to allow the spell to unravel before that. You won't go visit the kattakyns, and you won't move them to other places, and you won't unbind them so that they can find each other and re-form the Witch Doctor. Or any other form."

Harrison gazed at her, looking perplexed. He petted Starlight in long, even strokes.

"Tell me you got it," Reg encouraged. "You won't do anything to change that."

He didn't answer. Reg closed her eyes, shaking her head. She opened them again, drawing in her breath to give him clear instructions, but he was gone.

Starlight lay on the couch by himself, his tail whipping back and forth.

Did you enjoy this book? Reviews and recommendations are vital to making a book successful.

Please leave a review at your favorite book store or review site and share it with your friends.

Don't miss the following bonus material:
Sign up for mailing list to get a free ebook
Read a sneak preview chapter
Other books by P.D. Workman
Learn more about the author

Sign up for my mailing list at pdworkman.com and get
Gluten-Free Murder for free!

Join my mailing list and

Download a sweet mystery for free

pdworkman.com

PREVIEW OF TIME TO
YOUR ELF

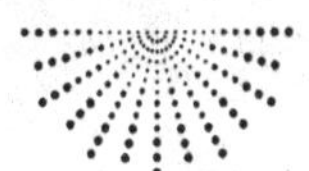

CHAPTER 1

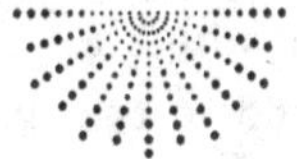

The sun was down and Reg was feeling energized as she looked through the appointment book on her kitchen island. It felt good to have some business coming in again. Her bank account had almost dwindled away to nothing and she had been feeling the pinch.

But she had come back from her most recent adventure determined to get things running again, and her efforts were definitely paying off. There was at least one appointment scheduled every night for the next couple of weeks, and in some cases a couple of readings and a seance.

She had been worried that she wouldn't be able to get any work. There had been quite a reaction in the paranormal community when they discovered that her mother was a siren, and the backlash had not been pleasant. But her landlord, Sarah, had been correct when she had said that it would settle down and people would forget all about it in a few weeks when it was no longer big news. The work was coming back in, and Sarah's wards and charms kept the more militant witches away from the yard and cottage so that they didn't have to keep cleaning raw egg off Reg's front door and the remnants of spells and curses that had been left behind in the yard. All in all, things had been pretty peaceful the last couple of weeks, letting Reg get back into the swing of things.

There was a tap on the door and Sarah let herself in. The older woman was dressed for a night out. A green sequined dress clung to her curves, and despite her more mature figure and a bit of extra padding around the middle, she looked very fetching. Reg was sure that she would have a fun night with whatever group of friends she was hanging out with.

"Just thought I would check in before we go," Sarah announced, smiling. Starlight came running in from the bedroom and jumped up on the island counter, yowling at Sarah in a pleading, plaintive voice that clearly announced that Reg had been neglecting him and no one ever fed him when Sarah was not around.

"Don't believe him!" Reg warned.

"Oh, I know he exaggerates," Sarah agreed. She petted Starlight. "But I don't think it would hurt for me to give him a little treat, do you?"

"For a beast who is starving, he's getting pretty fat," Reg observed. "You'd better not give him too much. I'm going to have to start giving him that special food for overweight cats." She looked Starlight in the eyes, one of them blue and one of them green. "That low calorie, high fiber kibble."

Starlight made a cross meow and turned to look at Sarah and to rub lovingly against her hand.

"You're all ready for your readings tonight." Sarah looked Reg over and gave an approving nod.

Reg didn't know how Sarah could get up so early in the morning when she stayed out half the night with her friends. Weren't old people supposed to need more sleep than younger folks? Even if Sarah only looked to be in her sixties, Reg knew—or at least had been told—that she was actually centuries old. So she should need a lot of sleep, shouldn't she?

But Sarah was always up before Reg was and tsked and shook

her head over the fact that Reg didn't usually manage to get dressed for the day before noon. Young people these days.

"Good to go," Reg agreed. "I'm just going to grab a bite to eat before my first appointment arrives. She looked down at the book. "Eugene Franklin."

"Eugenia," Sarah corrected. "You'd best get that right!"

"Oh." Reg looked at it again. The letters were carefully printed, but Reg had only glanced at the first few letters and assumed the rest. She was not the best reader and used a lot of shortcuts. Sometimes that worked and sometimes it didn't. "So... Eugenia. That must be a woman."

"Yes."

"Got it."

There was another tap on the door, and Reg looked over to see Letticia, the older witch who led Sarah's coven. While Letticia's lined face always looked serious and foreboding, Reg had learned not to make assumptions from her looks. Letticia had helped Reg out in the past and was not quick to prejudge her as others had. She was a lot more compassionate than she looked.

"Are we ready?"

"Just one moment. I need to get the cat something to eat."

Reg rolled her eyes.

Letticia tilted her head and looked amused. "I don't think that cat is going to starve. For someone who claims not to like the creatures, you do tend to put a lot of time into this one."

"Well, somebody should keep an eye on things."

Letticia shook her head slightly, but didn't point out that Reg was standing right there and the cat was clearly not starving to death as he claimed. She waited patiently while Sarah found some tuna and put a spoonful in Starlight's dish. Starlight jumped down from the counter and started to wolf it down.

"What are you guys doing tonight?" Reg asked.

It was probably not a coven night, since Sarah usually dressed in formal black for those. But Reg supposed some of the witches from the coven might go out together for a social activity. It wasn't all chants and spells.

"There is a new club in the city that we are going to check out."

Letticia was not dressed in a slinky, sequined dress like Sarah, which Reg was glad of. Letticia didn't have Sarah's curves and wouldn't look comfortable in something like that. She wore black slacks and a satiny blouse that came up high on her neck. She wouldn't have looked out of place in church or a courtroom, but Reg wondered what kind of club Letticia would feel at home in. Maybe they had a seniors' night.

"Well, you girls have fun and don't stay out too late," Reg told them with a smile.

Sarah gave Starlight one final pet and nodded. "I hope your evening goes well. You really should come out with us one night and relax. Too much work will just burn you out. You need to regenerate too."

"Yeah. Maybe some night," Reg agreed, though she had no intention of going out partying with the older ladies.

"Marian is coming too," Letticia said. "It isn't all witches."

Marian was a psychic like Reg. Her competition. In the beginning, Reg hadn't gotten along with her. Marian had been adversarial toward Reg. Jealous of the work that she was picking up, maybe, or the reputation she was getting for being one of the better psychics in town. In Black Sands, there was no lack of psychics and other practitioners to compete with.

But they had reached a tentative truce. Marian had even sent a couple of referrals over to Reg recently and Reg was watching for the opportunity to send some business back Marian's way. It was better if they cooperated, or at least didn't openly compete with each other.

The two older witches were soon on their way, and Reg looked in the fridge for something that would be good for a quick bite to eat before Eugene showed up.

CHAPTER 2

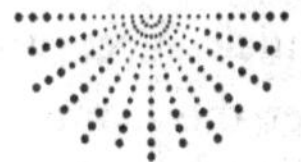

*E*ven after meeting the thin blonde, Reg kept thinking of her as Eugene, which didn't help the reading go particularly well. She tried not to be distracted by the woman's unusual name, but she kept worrying that she would slip out with "Eugene" during the reading.

Despite her distraction, Reg was able to give the woman a few tidbits that she thought were worth her money, so Eugenia went away satisfied with the session. At least, as far as Reg could tell. Maybe the woman thought she was just an idiot or a charlatan, but if she did, she didn't announce the fact or think it obviously enough for Reg to read. Hopefully, she would tell her friends that Reg was the real thing and get them to sign up. Reg had started to offer referral discounts so that if Eugenia got her friends to sign up for sessions, Eugenia could get a lower rate at her next reading. That encouraged repeat business and referrals, both of which were helpful to Reg in rebuilding her business.

Her next appointment was a seance for a group of friends, one of whom had received the session as a birthday gift. Oddly enough, seances were an increasingly popular birthday gift, at least around Black Sands. Reg was happy to take advantage of the trend. She enjoyed doing seances. The energy of the group was a boost, and in the odd event that there were not enough spirits around to provide commentary—and Reg rarely lacked for extra voices in her head—it was easy to ad lib and keep the clients happy.

"This is Sharon," one of the women pointed to a dark-haired Latino girl. "She turns thirty today! At midnight! And this is Rachel, Sunny, Deb, and I'm April."

Reg blinked at the quick succession of names. "You might need to remind me if I get the names wrong," she apologized in advance. It might be a good idea for her to start supplying groups with stick-on name tags so that she didn't have to remember them all. It just wasn't a good idea to call people by the wrong name in the middle of a seance. It could be brushed off as the mistake of a confused spirit or perhaps the name from a past life, but it was always best to get them right in the first place.

"We'll let you know!" April laughed. "We're always confusing people. Should we sit down here?" She gestured to the dining room table, eager to get right to it.

"Sure," Reg agreed. "Make yourselves comfortable. Does anyone want tea? Drinks?"

"Drinks!" one of the women, perhaps Deb, echoed excitedly.

"You've already had enough margaritas," Sharon told her. "If you keep it up, you won't remember anything about tonight. How about tea?"

"No, drinks," the others protested as a group.

Sharon shook her head at Reg and rolled her eyes. "I guess it's drinks," she sighed.

"Shall I make you a tea? I can..."

"No, no point in going to the extra work. I'll have the same as everyone else."

Beverages were arranged and, in a few minutes, everyone was sitting at the table, drinks in hand, giggling nervously about the upcoming seance. With them so well-lubricated, Reg didn't foresee any problems. They would all be very suggestible. The only question would be whether they would remember it in the morning. If they didn't remember the seance, they couldn't exactly recommend her to others.

"Okay, if you are all ready, we'll get started. Is there someone in particular that you are trying to reach? Or a question that you would like answered?"

They all looked at each other, reluctant to speak up first.

"Birthday girl?" Reg suggested, looking at Sharon.

Sharon shrugged, blushing. "I don't know. I've never done anything like this before. It's just kind of... a gag."

Reg nodded, smiling, so that Sharon would know that she wasn't offended. "A lot of people come just on a whim, to see what they get out of it. That's okay. Nothing then? Nothing special?"

Sharon shrugged and shook her head. "No... just, whatever. I guess. Will you do that thing where you say there is a spirit whose name starts with G and does anyone know someone who died whose name started with the letter G?"

"No. I don't do that. I can see who a spirit is attached to, if they are attached to someone. And sometimes, it's just one of the spirits that I'm familiar with, who might have a message or insight to be passed on. It just depends on who speaks to me."

"Does someone always speak do you?"

Reg shrugged. "That's what I'm here for."

"So you're a real medium? This is real?"

Reg pointed to the placard on the table. For entertainment purposes only. That little disclaimer that kept her from getting charged for fraud by people who decided they didn't like what she had to say or thought that she wasn't a real medium. She preferred to keep the police out of her life, if she could.

"Oh." Sharon nodded, looking disappointed.

"Let's join hands," Reg suggested. She sat down in her seat at the end of the table and held out a hand to each of the women sitting next to her. The girls quieted immediately, and everybody put down their drinks for the moment and grasped each other's hands.

Reg rolled her eyes upward and listened to the voices, waiting for one of them to come to the forefront.

"We reach out to the spirit world," she announced, "on behalf of this group of friends. Do any of the spirits have messages to be passed on?"

There were plenty of voices. A lot of them fought and bickered with each other like old married couples, they had been with her for so long.

"Perhaps someone here has recently lost a loved one?" Reg suggested. "Or maybe someone looking for love?"

There was a ripple of laughter around the circle, which seemed to be directed at April. Reg felt a surge in the energy level, and watched a rosy aura develop around April. A seeker. Reg could find one in most groups. The one person who was most likely to believe what they saw and heard. Not a dupe, exactly, but the one who really wanted to receive a message.

"April," Reg intoned. She listened to the voices whispering around her. She closed her eyes most of the way but could still see the faux candles flickering in their jars around the room. Little twinkle lights, because it was too dangerous for her to have real candles in the house without an experienced fire caster around to make sure that Reg didn't accidentally burn the whole house down around her. That would not impress Sarah. "April has come looking for love."

I see, a voice whispered in her ear, let me tell you what I see.

"Do you have a message for April?" Reg asked, wanting to make sure that she didn't give a message to the wrong person. It would be just like some impatient spirit to speak up and pass along a message intended for someone else. They needed a bit of managing.

Yes. A message for April, the spirit insisted.

"What message do you have?"

A stranger he is, but soon they will meet.

Reg spoke the words in her own voice and gave herself over to the spirit to give the rest of the message.

Handsome but dangerous. The man in black. He will come soon.

Handsome but dangerous. Reg gave a little shiver at the words, thinking of Corvin. She couldn't think of who fit the description better. The warlock was one of the most attractive men Reg had ever seen. Maybe the most handsome she had ever met in person. And his magical charms made him even more desirable. And for an unsuspecting woman who didn't know that he could steal magical gifts, he was very dangerous. He was very clever at getting his own way. Reg could not recall the morning she had woken up to silence in her head without a shudder and a sense of deep loneliness and loss. He had given her powers back to her, something that was never, ever done, but the circumstances had been unusual.

Reg never wanted to feel that emptiness again.

And she never wanted anyone else to experience it either.

"Be careful," she warned April, opening her eyes and being sure to meet the other woman's gaze. "Please beware."

April nodded. But her eyes were shining with excitement. She wouldn't be careful. She would be looking for this handsome stranger wherever she went now, eager to meet him and fulfill the prophesy.

Reg opened her mouth to inquire whether there were more messages for the group or whether there were other questions that the women hoped to have answered.

But something strange was happening in the living room. Reg blinked her eyes a few times and tried to focus on the dancing lights that had suddenly materialized. They swirled around like fireflies, or like moths around a light, but Reg couldn't tell where the light originated.

The women started to ask questions. Most just wanted to know what Reg had seen, why she was so distracted. Or wondering whether it was some kind of show she was putting on. But April gasped, her eyes focused on the swirling lights.

"What is that? How are you doing that?"

"It's not me," Reg told her.

They both watched the space, mesmerized.

* * *

Time to Your Elf, Book #14 of the *Reg Rawlins, Psychic Investigator series* by P.D. Workman can be ordered at pdworkman.com

ABOUT THE AUTHOR

Award-winning and USA Today bestselling author P.D. (Pamela) Workman writes riveting mystery/suspense and young adult books dealing with mental illness, addiction, abuse, and other real-life issues. For as long as she can remember, the blank page has held an incredible allure and from a very young age she was trying to write her own books.

Workman wrote her first complete novel at the age of twelve and continued to write as a hobby for many years. She started publishing in 2013. She has won several literary awards from Library Services for Youth in Custody for her young adult fiction. She currently has over 70 published titles and can be found at pdworkman.com.

Born and raised in Alberta, Workman has been married for over 25 years and has one son.

* * *

Please visit P.D. Workman at pdworkman.com to see what else she is working on, to join her mailing list, and to link to her social networks.

* * *

If you enjoyed this book, please take the time to recommend it to other purchasers with a review or star rating and share it with your friends!

facebook.com/pdworkmanauthor

twitter.com/pdworkmanauthor

instagram.com/pdworkmanauthor

amazon.com/author/pdworkman

bookbub.com/authors/p-d-workman

goodreads.com/pdworkman

linkedin.com/in/pdworkman

pinterest.com/pdworkmanauthor

youtube.com/pdworkman

www.ingramcontent.com/pod-product-compliance
Lightning Source LLC
Chambersburg PA
CBHW011149190726
48288CB00010B/3248